HOLE
IN THE SKY

ALSO BY DANIEL H. WILSON

The Andromeda Evolution
Guardian Angels and Other Monsters
The Clockwork Dynasty
Robogenesis
Amped
Robopocalypse

A Boy and His Bot
Bro-Jitsu
The Mad Scientist Hall of Fame
How to Build a Robot Army
Where's My Jetpack?
How to Survive a Robot Uprising

HOLE IN THE SKY

A NOVEL

DANIEL H. WILSON

DOUBLEDAY   NEW YORK

FIRST DOUBLEDAY HARDCOVER EDITION 2025

Copyright © 2025 by Daniel H. Wilson

Penguin Random House values and supports copyright. Copyright fuels creativity, encourages diverse voices, promotes free speech, and creates a vibrant culture. Thank you for buying an authorized edition of this book and for complying with copyright laws by not reproducing, scanning, or distributing any part of it in any form without permission. You are supporting writers and allowing Penguin Random House to continue to publish books for every reader. Please note that no part of this book may be used or reproduced in any manner for the purpose of training artificial intelligence technologies or systems.

Published by Doubleday, a division of Penguin Random House LLC, 1745 Broadway, New York, NY 10019.

Doubleday and the portrayal of an anchor with a dolphin are registered trademarks of Penguin Random House LLC.

Book design by Michael Collica

Library of Congress Cataloguing-in-Publication Data
Names: Wilson, Daniel H. (Daniel Howard), 1978– author
Title: Hole in the sky : a novel / Daniel H. Wilson.
Description: First Doubleday hardcover edition. | New York : Doubleday, 2025.
Identifiers: LCCN 2025010350 (print) | LCCN 2025010351 (ebook) | ISBN 9780385551113 hardcover | ISBN 9780385551120 ebook
Subjects: LCGFT: Science fiction | Novels
Classification: LCC PS3623.I57796 H65 2025 (print) | LCC PS3623.I57796 (ebook) | DDC 813/.6—dc23/eng/20250506
LC record available at https://lccn.loc.gov/2025010350
LC ebook record available at https://lccn.loc.gov/2025010351

penguinrandomhouse.com | doubleday.com

Printed in the United States of America

1st Printing

The authorized representative in the EU for product safety and compliance is Penguin Random House Ireland, Morrison Chambers, 32 Nassau Street, Dublin D02 YH68, Ireland, https://eu-contact.penguin.ie.

Dedicated to
All My Relatives

HOLE IN THE SKY

An Open Letter

I. Detection

II. Monitor

III. Impact

IV. Quarantine

V. Last Contact

A Private Letter

AN OPEN LETTER

GAVIN CLARK // Washington, D.C.
Emerging Weapons Technologies Group, Department of Defense

We walked out of the Spiro Mounds in Oklahoma still covered in the liquid we found beneath, our lungs rasping with that alien atmosphere, skin shining and slick. We walked out with our eyes flat and our souls empty. We lost a lot of people down there, and we walked out with more than we expected.

We walked slowly. We waited. We obeyed commands shouted through megaphones.

I told the others to keep their hands raised, palms out. The crosshairs of a dozen snipers would have been trained on us as we appeared from the mouth of the crater. I could hear the choppers circling, blades lazily beating the air. There were so many eyes above us: a fleet of drones, rotary-bladed predators, wheeling overhead with their camera irises spiraling in.

We emerged with our faces turned up, squinting as we basked in the warm light of our own sun.

The Cherokees were huddled close. And I'll admit, I felt a twinge of envy. Being "left out of the lodge" is what my Native friends called that pinch, half smiling, pointing at me with their lips. While we were in that dark hole, they had been forged into a family. They had made sense of what happened. Together.

And here I was with my hands free. My calendar free. The whole rest of my life looking pretty free.

The memories haven't stopped flickering through my thoughts, like traces of lightning . . . Things I saw that couldn't have existed. How my ears popped when we walked right through that old, weathered spot in reality. The unnatural shapes churning just under the surface of those black waters.

I guess it took a little while to sink in . . .

The real honest lie of it all is that this isn't my story to tell. It never was. I don't have any deep revelations to share. I'm not the type of guy this kind of stuff could ever make sense to.

It's like they said—I was never really inside the lodge.

I understand and acknowledge that as director of the Emerging Weapons Technologies Group, it was my sworn duty to generate an actionable report on the Incident: a plan that would help the secretary of defense ensure that our military could form an appropriate response to future threats.

I couldn't do any of that very effectively.

There is no doubt that the Incident threatened national security. From the moment the object was observed—I believe there was an existential threat not only to our lives, but to our civilization's fundamental concept of reality, of how we perceive the world and our place in it.

But I'm telling you there are things out there that we can never track with a space telescope, or threaten with a sleek weapon, or bottle up and shove into a laboratory. The thing we found . . . it doesn't even fit into my mind.

This report is out of my hands now, except for one last note:

I don't know if the four of us were chosen. And if so, by whom. But it is very likely that the unique voices represented in this document are the reason that billions of human beings exist today in a world they can see, and touch, and feel.

Humankind crept away from the light of our only fire. We gazed into the void. And we lived to tell about it.

The Incident began at the edge of known space, at the very moment when we as a species departed the shallow cradle of our solar system to swim the deep black water between stars. It began at the spot where the fire of our sun dims, where the warmth of its light recedes, and where true darkness starts.

It all began at heliopause.

PART I

DETECTION

Heliopause: outer boundary of the *heliosphere*, the spherical region around the sun that provides a protective shield of outward-flowing solar wind, and beyond which lies the raw, infinite expanse of interstellar and intergalactic space.

1
DETECTION

THE MAN DOWNSTAIRS // Undisclosed Location
Detection, T-Minus 6 Hours

It began as a weekend art project during my eighth year of graduate school. On a lark, I had programmed a simple chatbot to write silly poems based on USGS data from seismic waves—all the bumps and rattles coming from the interior of the planet's surface. Then I added an input containing the static fuzz detected by a certain radio antenna trained on distant stars. Finally—and this is the part I have come to regret the most—I complemented this data stream with biometric data from my own wrist-worn fitness tracker device.

I called my project *Thoughts of the Universe.*

It was just a joke—a goofy little project squeezed between a self-playing video game and a kite rigged to take Polaroid pictures from the air, letting the images flutter down to the startled people it had surveilled. But after a few months of posting a ceaseless stream of slightly poetic nonsense, my project happened to output the precise magnitude and location of a coronal mass ejection—a wall of solar plasma that would violently cripple a host of highly classified military satellites.

Thing is—it was an event that would occur ten hours later.

Thoughts of the Universe had somehow glimpsed the future.

A NOAA scientist researching geomagnetic disturbances discovered my website and saw the impossible timing of the prediction. Later, a CIA analyst caught wind of it. After I failed to provide a satisfactory explanation, *Thoughts of the Universe* was summarily shut down and all data confiscated for further study. I was removed from my academic position and "offered" a mandatory government job. All traces of my studies, my tenure in the computer science program, and educational records were erased.

This was twelve years ago.

This morning an anomaly notification came to my private office, located a long elevator ride below a Q-cleared secure government facility somewhere in the continental United States of America. For context, I'll try to describe this place. Keep in mind I didn't build it.

In fact, my feelings didn't factor into any of this.

The first thing you'd notice is probably the isolation bridge. It's a gnarly catwalk stretching over a metal pit, illuminated from below by stripes of LED lighting. It's effectively a moat, keeping the world separated from the Pattern. A thick, braided cable crosses the bridge, clinging to the bottom of the catwalk like a tropical vine. It provides a power source, as well as a constant feed of some very specific data streams.

Otherwise, nothing besides photons is allowed to cross.

In the dead center of this cavernous room, a cube of glass and steel is perched high on metal stilts. Floodlights are mounted above and below, casting complicated shadows through the metal latticework of an embedded Faraday cage.

The thing being kept in the box is not alive. It is not a monster in the conventional sense. It isn't an oracle, or a god.

Not quite, but close. About as close as it gets.

Inside the central cube, eight black slabs of supercooled quantum computers rise up in a gap-toothed circle that reminds me of Stonehenge. The hardware is running a collection of relatively simple algorithms through sheer brute force, with enough computing power to route every byte of Internet traffic in North America through this room. And all this power is spent analyzing one data pattern.

Or, as it's come to be called, *the* Pattern.

When the Pattern was officially activated, I simultaneously became a nonentity, an invaluable military asset, and the sole denizen of this very special office built in total secrecy and at insane expense. I haven't had a name in a decade, although my colleagues eventually selected a special designation.

I am known simply as the "Man Downstairs."

This appellation is often shortened to "MD," although if I still had any academic credentials, my qualifications wouldn't quite match such a title.

The problem, in hindsight, is this damned fitness device. It makes me a crucial component of the Pattern. Not only does my biometric output feed the data stream, but I also seem to be the only person capable of translating its gibberish poetry into sensical predictions. Sifting diamonds from silt.

Every day, I sit hunched over a simple card table in a brightly lit plexiglass cube, smaller than that of the Pattern, and hazy with wafts of stale smoke. The government gives me all the cigarettes I want—their one concession. And as I smoke, I read these thoughts of the universe, my lips moving as I mumble to myself. There is nothing in here with me except a folding chair and a flimsy card table stained with burn marks, loaded with now-antiquated technology.

A battered old web camera rests on the table, attached to an even older computer. The webcam faces another screen located across the catwalk. The Pattern projects its thoughts on this screen twenty-four hours a day. The grainy text and images picked up by my camera are fed into a massive and ancient dot-matrix printer. My lucky card table shakes as the printing arm mindlessly slides back and forth across a scrolling ream of paper, relentlessly laying down pixelated words and images in screaming weals of ink.

And as the printer vomits this endless page, I read it with the air of a 1950s dad perusing the Sunday paper. Every now and then, I'll find something interesting. I'll stub out my cigarette into an overflowing ashtray, and I'll begin to copy the printout by hand, using an ordinary red pencil.

It is understood that the Pattern cannot be trusted to have direct communication with the outside world. The Pattern isn't officially thought to be sentient, but nobody really knows how it might evolve if it escaped.

Or how our enemies might use it.

This danger is the reason for the elaborate cage, and for the necessity of not only a physical air gap isolating the Pattern, but a series of informational air gaps in the form of digital outputs converted to hard copy, and the hard copy converted by human hand into that most ancient format: pencil and paper.

My government-provided psychologist assures me the job I'm doing is crucial for the safety of hundreds of millions of people up above. She tells me I'm a real American hero.

It makes me want to light another smoke.

Because the Pattern's predictions always come true.

Always. Always, always. And that, particularly, is the bitch of it.

In their typical staid fashion, the quantum math people have quietly assigned terminology to explain this experimental outcome. "Retrocausation" is built on the fact that quantum mechanics works the same, regardless of which direction it is traveling through time. This means that cause and effect can also propagate backward in time, with cause seeming to happen after its effect.

The math isn't actually that complicated—but the results are . . . challenging to fully comprehend.

The Pattern has predicted the future, explained the past, and delivered data so bizarre as to be impossible for our highest-IQ individuals to understand.

Always, the interpreted orders arrive with no attribution other than my initials: "MD."

MD intelligence mandates are always obeyed.

Always.

This is despite more than a few four-star generals opining on my dwindling sanity. But the Pattern has been doubted before, with disastrous consequences. Thus, at every new fund-allocation meeting, the Pentagon's strange project is rubber-stamped with approval.

Thank goodness. The Pattern saw it first, of course.

Like a medium holding a séance, I was sitting in my plexiglass office with a cigarette dangling from my lips—my long, thin fingers scrawling out the words of a pattern of thought locked in silicone and floating on waves of quantum programming.

Something reached out.

This is what the Pattern overheard:

> ... black expanses collapse to this single point.
> A pocket of complexity. Rock, air, and liquid observe themselves.
> Thinking matter trapped on a blue marble.
> The dull gleam of a billion fireflies signaling over an expanse of still black water. Dreams and thoughts and notions tickling tangled eyelashes.
> The weight of a new reality. Thoughts focus.
> An eye opens in the deep...

This was no silly, disjointed string of words. It wasn't the dry statistics of a prediction. This felt like a threat, coming from something I couldn't begin to understand. The Pattern was broadcasting the voice of . . . something else.

And so, I sent up a warning.

The following mandate was delivered to the president, chiefs of staff, the secretary of defense, and much farther downstream, to an individual agent named Dr. Gavin Clark in the DoD's Emerging

HOLE IN THE SKY

Weapons Technologies Group—a man who would be chosen to spearhead a very special mission for the U.S. government.

The world had no idea what was coming.

<u>INTELLIGENCE MANDATE</u>—ALL MILITARY BRANCHES PREPARE FOR INTERACTION WITH NONHUMAN INTELLIGENCE. ALL OUTWARD-FACING PERSONNEL BE ADVISED: FIRST CONTACT IMMINENT.

—MD

2
MY GIRL

JIM HARDGRAY // Oklahoma Panhandle
Detection, T-Minus 3 Hours

Well, what can I tell you? I never expected to find myself in a situation like this. Never thought I'd be the type of man who would.

I guess that's why I was so darned surprised at the pure hate in my daughter's eyes.

Tawny's only thirteen, but I see her mother's attitude in the sway of her hips, and the way her lips are pursed at me under a flat dark stare. She stands with her sharp elbows poked out a little, just in case someone comes too close.

Especially someone trying to call himself her daddy.

I'm waiting in my truck with one arm hanging out the window. My elbow is hooked in a way I'm hoping looks relaxed, but I can't help nervously drumming my fingers over the searing-hot door panel.

It's better than letting her see how my hands shake.

The girl is standing next to the bus stop, staring me down, holding as still as a spooked deer. A rush of hot air snarls her long black hair across her face as the Greyhound bus lumbers past and starts picking up steam on the dusty black tar road.

I lift a hand and give her a little wave.

Tawny looks older than thirteen. She looks like a grown-up. And I realize right now that I am far too fucking late to this party. My chance to raise my daughter is over. That is a young woman standing across the street from me.

Whatever I thought was going to happen was wishful thinking. Delusional, innit.

It had seemed so nice in my head. But I can see from the way her face is blank that this isn't going to be nice. I can tell from the way her arms are crossed. How she dips her knees and wraps her fingers through the strap of my battered old army duffel bag. She hoists it onto her narrow shoulder, wiry and strong.

I crack the door to get out and help, but my daughter ignores me and stomps across the road, hurling her backpack into the scratched-up bed of my truck. I glance over to my passenger seat as she circles around.

Ah shit.

There's a teddy bear sitting there. A heart stitched between its hands. It's her old one and I kept it all this time and I brought it thinking that . . . I don't know, what. A thrill of shame and utter embarrassment settles over the back of my neck as she throws the creaking door open and spots it sitting there.

Her teenage smirk hits me like an ice pick.

I tell myself it's not so bad. Honest mistake. I mean, what does thirteen years old even mean? Unless you've seen every year up to it, you can't know. Does it mean dolls? Cell phones and cars? Boys, Jesus. Could be anything, depending on the kid. But I don't know this kid, and it's just that obvious.

Shit.

I shrug and lean over to snatch up the teddy bear. Shove it into the cupholder between our seats. It looks up at me sappily, its fat furry ass newly diapered in fast-food wrappers and old receipts and a handwritten parking ticket from a little salt flat town I'll probably never visit again.

I expel my breath.

"Hey, Tawny," I say, pulling off my cowboy hat. "It's been a minute, huh? It's, uh, good to see you."

Tawny climbs in and sits down in the passenger seat, arms folded across her chest, eyes straight ahead.

"Why you got braids and that?" she asks, not looking at me. "Trying too hard. Big Indian."

I absorb that.

"I'm sorry about your grandma," I say. "Condolences."

"Didn't see you at the funeral," she says.

"I'm sorry. They don't like me much, you know. Your mama's side of the family . . ." I trail off.

The seconds spiral out awkwardly.

"Let's go then," she says.

I was in the hospital room when Tawny was born. Of course, I was only nineteen at the time, scared out of my wits and trying to do the right thing. Her little brother Samuel came five years later. That was easier. Things were good there for a little while. Then they weren't so good.

It all got out of hand pretty fast. The way things do when you're too young and you think you're in control but you're not. Me and her mother, both of us partied too much. After she divorced me, I went searching for oil field work that took me down to Texas for weeks at a time. Then months. I sort of came and went, didn't see them much. The kids stayed at my place off and on, but I guess you could say it was Tawny who mostly raised her kid brother.

That all ended two years ago.

It was a day at the lake that still lives in my dreams. A terrible day. For a while, the memory of it wouldn't stop replaying itself on the backs of my eyelids. A memory that lived in the haze of every hungover morning.

After that day, Tawny wouldn't see me. Her mom stopped answering my calls. Apparently stopped coming home, too, at some point. Come to find out, Tawny had gone to live with her old grandma out near Black Mesa in the emptiness of the Oklahoma panhandle.

I told myself I was getting ready to go back for her. I wasn't the man I wanted to be, but I was on my way there. Not ready to leave right this second, mind you. I told myself I was headed home for good. Soon enough.

I meant to come for my baby. I meant to. But I didn't.

The truck tires bite gravel as I pull onto the highway. It's a straight shot across five or six hours of Oklahoma plains to get home to Spiro. There are speed limit signs, but everybody knows out here we set our own speed limit. I accelerate until the rear end of my truck starts to shimmy, then drop down five miles an hour.

We drive in silence.

Sitting beside this sullen, angry young woman, hearing the whoosh of the wind outside the open windows, I'm trying and failing to think of a way to cross the gap separating us. It's impossible, but I've got to give it a shot.

Thing is, I can't even bring myself to say his name out loud. Can't get my head around the idea that he's gone. Been gone—two years now.

"I am sorry, first of all," I say. "Okay?"

"You don't have to be sorry. Elisi has been raising me. Grandma was there for me even if you weren't."

"Well, you're still just a kid. You've got some more raising to do."

"Oh, now you're an expert? Just don't. This sucks enough without having to watch you try and pretend to be a dad."

Fair, fair, I tell myself. I grip the steering wheel.

"Tawny, I'm sorry. I been trying."

A flash of a smile traces across my lips. I feel a hint of genuine pride. Glance over the bridge of my long, twice-broken nose over at her.

"Hey," I say. "Let me show you something."

I shove the teddy bear aside and fish around in the center console. I feel a hard, cool bronze coin on my fingertips. Pull it out and hold it up for my daughter to see. She takes the coin out of my hands on reflex—a one-year token.

"Ain't had a drink since . . . since a year. Not one."

"So, you're an alcoholic, too?"

My smile falls away, pride fading.

"Yeah," I say. "That's right."

When she tosses the coin out of the window, a hurt breath comes out of my mouth and my fingers clench the steering wheel hard enough to make it creak. I was so stupid to think she'd care. The girl is all anger, and I deserve it.

To think I felt proud of myself just for being normal. Doing something every sane person can do without a thought. Not drinking. Having custody of your own kid. Being there to take care of your own flesh and blood.

I focus hard on the road. Squeezing the wheel. My old pickup truck rattles along the highway.

"I'm sorry," I mutter again.

"Stop saying that," she said. "It's pointless. And gross."

"I know, I'm sorr—"

I stop myself.

"I want to know about you, okay? I know I'm late. I know everything's busted. But things that are broke can be fixed. Most everything in my life has been broken at one time or another. You . . . you're the most important thing to me."

Tawny crosses her arms again and sighs. For two or three minutes, she stares out the window. Thinking.

"You start then," she finally says in a small voice.

I nod.

"Hi there, Tawny. My name is Jim Hardgray. I'm thirty-two years old, I do electric work for the Cherokee Nation all over Oklahoma, and I don't drink. I was real proud of that coin you just tossed out the window, but I don't need it to remind me who I am anymore. Because I got you."

I turn to look at her, continuing. "And I will not let you down."

The wind is loud for about thirty seconds after that. And then she speaks to me real quiet: "I shouldn't have thrown it."

"It's okay," I say. "What's your favorite color?"

"Aquamarine," she replies, reluctant. "My favorite color is aquamarine."

And when she looks at me and says these next words, my heart breaks.

"What's yours?"

3

FLAGGED FOR PROFANITY

MIKAYLA JOHNSON // NASA Johnson Space Center
Detection, T-Minus Zero

Holy crap, boss. You're the project manager—so it's your call—but the *Voyager* team has to see this. Okay, wait. Background first.

First of all, I know it's not our job at NASA Johnson to spot shit before it hits the planet. That's the two-headed camouflaged monster called NORAD and NORTHCOM, over at Peterson Space Force Base in Colorado Springs. They'll track any object bigger than ten centimeters in diameter within maybe twenty thousand kilometers of Earth's surface. They can go as far as geostationary orbit, another twenty thousand kilometers, but their tracking is way dicier that far out.

And look, I'm not saying we're under a threat like that.

I mean, I know I'm the spooky girl you stuck in her own cubicle because she doesn't like to bother recognizing her coworker's faces—which, by the way, all of y'all seem to take super personal. Can't we get over ourselves? I mean, what makes the lump of skin hanging off the front of your skull so special?

We're all just walking around made of meat here.

And before you judge me, let's not forget—this sweet little basement-dwelling NASA employee is willing to wear a pair of big dumb fucking NIX-brand augmented reality glasses on her face, chunky 1960s NASA throwback frames and all, just to keep track of her coworkers' expressions and acknowledge everyone's special little emotions, to, like, facilitate human contact in the workplace.

I'm bending over backward here for you people.

Anyway, back on subject. Those military types are the ones responsible for keeping an eye on anything potentially hazardous within the orbital path of Earth or in range of the inner planets. And it's nice how they always warn us before the International Space Station is obliterated by pieces of space junk.

This stuff is clearly out of our lane. But bear with me.

Lately, I've been interested in Oumuamua. It's the first confirmed interstellar object ever discovered in our solar system, and it shot right through in two months at a hundred thousand kilometers per hour! It was big as hell. It was made of metal. And the name means "a messenger reaching out to us from the distant past."

How does that not get your imagination running?

I mean, yes, I got hired by NASA mainly because I'm fucking good at math. You know that. But being fucking good at math isn't enough. You've got to have a reason to be here. A dream. It's just too damn competitive to not find a way to love it. And the way I love working for the *Voyager* mission is half Carl-Sagan-holy-shit-the-stars-are-so-big-and-far-away, and the other half is straight-up, good-old-fashioned show-me-a-goddang-alien-already.

Oumuamua came from out there between the stars.

We know that because our solar system is roughly in a flat plane—that big dinner-plate shape that happens when gravity pulls together planets out of a spinning ball of stardust. And this thing passed through *straight up and down*. From the real, real outer space. At that kind of angle, it had to travel here from another star. Or shit, even from another galaxy.

We didn't get a good look—but this time it's going to be different. With the data I found, we're going to get a real good look at something. I just can't believe we're the ones who stumbled onto this discovery. I'm telling you, the *Voyager* team is seriously in a position to make some history.

Who would've thought?

I mean, all due respect, but we're in charge of a couple of antique spacecraft launched in the 1970s by a bunch of guys who probably had terrible mustaches. They run on less hardware than you'd find in an automatic cat feeder. And our sweet babies have traveled farther away from our planet than anything in history.

They even broke heliopause.

We are peeking into deep space—the interstellar medium itself—and taking the temperature of the universe. And these Winnebagos are carrying records, for god's sake. Records! Like, phonographs. Vinyl! Did they think the aliens would have a record player? Because if they do, they can listen to whales singing and, like, people chewing and babies crying and shit like that.

No disrespect to Carl Sagan, who picked it all out. But a gold record? Imprinted with images of our DNA and solar system and so on?

Wow. Just, wow.

So here's the point.

After pushing through heliopause, the *Voyager 1* and *2* platforms observed an increase of galactic cosmic-ray particles and primordial cosmic radiation. In the same way Mother Earth has us wrapped in breathable atmosphere, our good old Mother Sol has all her planets wrapped in the safety of her solar wind, blowing away all kinds of nasty shit that's washing in from between the stars.

At heliopause, we left all that behind.

And within a couple of years of swimming into the deep end, we've found something worth writing home about. Here's a data snapshot:

HOLE IN THE SKY

MISSION STATUS REPORT
Instrument: Voyager 1
Mission Launch Date: September 5, 1977
Distance from Earth: 15,530,626,410 mi
Distance from Sun: 15,543,796,522 mi
Velocity with respect to the Sun: 38,026.77 mph
One-Way Light Time: 23 Hours, 33 Minutes

INSTRUMENT STATUS
Cosmic-Ray Subsystem (CRS): ON
Low-Energy Charged Particles (LECP): ON
Magnetometer (MAG): ON
Plasma Wave Subsystem (PWS): ON
Plasma Science (PLS): ON
Imaging Science Subsystem (ISS): DEACTIVATED
Infrared Interferometer Spectrometer and Radiometer (IRIS): OFF
Photopolarimeter Subsystem (PPS): OFF
Planetary Radio Astronomy (PRA): OFF
Ultraviolet Spectrometer (UVS): OFF
Plasma Density Log (PDL): POSSIBLE ANOMALOUS DATA

Check out the rest of the attachment and you'll see it for yourself.

As the radioisotope power generators have degenerated on *Voyager 1*, we've turned off a lot of instrumentation—including any photography. So, the data I want to share is pretty boring. It's just a plasma density log. But it's showing a perturbation that came out of nowhere. And the change in density has a pattern with a simple explanation.

This data was caused by a *large object* moving past *Voyager 1*.

I also checked the energy levels of nearby charged particles at that exact time. The particle count dips to nothing, then reappears at its normal rate. Meaning something blocked the solar wind as it passed between our spacecraft and the sun. Then the same thing happened with *Voyager 2*, a few million miles closer to Earth.

The problem? *That's all supposed to be empty space.*

The Voyagers are over fifteen billion miles away—way past where we can make visual on objects that size, and way beyond where the Air Force jerks are scanning. Our darlings are on the wild frontier of space—*and they're not alone.*

It's right there in the data.

Something is out there at heliopause. Something big, probably with a lot of mass. And I think it may be headed this way.

Holy shit, right!?

4

EMERGING WEAPONS

GAVIN CLARK // Atlantic Ocean
Detection, +1 Hour

Your standard-issue U.S.S. *Gerald R. Ford*–class aircraft carrier is about the size of the Empire State Building—if it was thrown onto its side and set to floating on the open ocean. Waves that would scare the heck out of most mortals are utterly dominated by this functioning city designed for war, surging whitecaps dwarfed by an expanse of gunmetal-gray steel hull that splits the sea apart like a kid dragging her fingers through sand.

And yet.

The twenty-foot-tall surges I'm watching aren't even perceptible up on the flight deck. But from where I'm standing on the aft deck elevator, I can taste the salt spray and smell the fumes over the brain-numbing throb of a fifty-foot propeller churning behind me, corkscrewing this monstrosity through some nameless tract of the Atlantic Ocean.

My career has been spent identifying weapon capabilities of our adversaries before they hit the battlefield, and ideally before they leave the drawing board. The thing our military fears most is the unknown. My job is to cut the future out of that fabric of darkness and give it a shape, something our military can prepare for.

Something we can point a gun at.

I never know where the Emerging Weapons Technology Group

will take me. By its nature, this job is cross-domain: land, sky, space, and sea. Our office has got partnerships with just about every military, domestic, and foreign-service agency—all of which have regular interactions with Unidentified Anomalous Phenomena, or UAPs.

Today, that means I'm with the United States Navy.

Anybody standing here on the high seas who is not a Navy-hardened sailor would also probably be struggling not to puke. At least, that's what I'm repeating to myself this morning. Swallowing saliva, quivering with nausea, I try to focus on the trim, mustached man in an olive flight suit standing across from me.

"Five meters in diameter!" he shouts over the propellers. "And that's confirmed. It vectored straight at us. Went zero to Mach two in about three seconds. Steady acceleration. No visible propulsion, of course. There never is."

Navy Pilot John "Meek" Marconi is currently explaining the ins and outs of a UAP he encountered during a sortie near the South China Sea. I'm turning over the physics in my head, confirming this is yet another encounter with a craft whose aerospace capabilities exceed those of the United States Air Force, including classified technology still under development.

As such, it falls under the jurisdiction of the Emerging Weapons Technology Group for investigation—and me in particular.

My postdoctoral research focused on laser-induced molecular vibrations of high explosives. It isn't helping me understand the flight dynamics of what this guy is describing. Nor is it helping me ignore the diesel exhaust or the gorge rising in the back of my throat.

"Any markings?" I ask. "Chinese?"

Meek shakes his head. *Of course not.*

"What can I say?" he shouts over the roar of the ocean and the engine vibration. "It was a ball of metal moving faster than my afterburners. Like it was playing with me, bouncing back and forth over my cockpit. Everybody caught it on radar, but I was the only one who observed it directly. It's all in my written report, so that's all I really have to say. We're done?"

Yeah, that "written report" is about a paragraph of vague jargon.

"Right!" I shout. "Can we wrap this up somewhere else?"

Most fighter pilots aren't afraid of anything. But the way Meek shakes his head is the closest thing to fear I've seen from these people. Nobody wants to be the one seeing crazy shit, getting labeled as unreliable, or for heaven's sake, find themselves quoted in an article for seeing something spooky.

"You sure you've got clearance for this?" he shouts, leaning in. "They told me you were some science nerd. You got an encyclopedic brain for every weapon system out there?"

I nod confidently, then drop into the rote acronym-filled speech these kinds of guys need to hear: "Full clearance for this TacAir study, and anything else falling under the NGAD umbrella across all domains—"

I stop in order not to vomit.

Meek finally notices how pale I am, and how my hands are shaking as I take notes. He reluctantly opens a metal door and ushers me into a bulkhead leading to the hangar deck. As he closes the door to seal us into a claustrophobic metal hallway, the ocean noise outside is suddenly muted. Our voices echo off beige-painted steel walls as we continue to speak in hushed tones.

"I wouldn't be here otherwise," I say, looking him in the eye. "So, let's go into detail about your mission. I'm assuming it was sensitive?"

I see a rush of pride fighting the reluctance on his face. Pride wins.

"Absolutely, sir. We were flight-testing a mixed manned and unmanned fighter set deployment. Across all three aircraft we had integrated kinetic and nonkinetic live armaments. The instant the

UAP came within a tactically relevant range, the AI-controlled platforms assumed threat formation."

"So, you were flying with a complement of unmanned aircraft?"

"Yeah, a True-Blue Wingman drone on either side. Designated TB-1 and TB-2. I was in center formation, call sign Quarterback. QB1. I was piloting a sweet little aircraft we've just been calling the Double X."

"Right, the F-XX. Built off a F-35C platform. I'm familiar. Which drones?"

"The drones are based on XQ-85A Dragonfly units. We've been testing out a whole suite of autonomous collaborative killers. My prediction is that future carriers will have more drones than manned aircraft. A lot more."

"So I've heard," I respond. "What pattern were you in at contact?"

"Battle-spread formation. The TBs are both fully autonomous. There's also an onboard AI translating my spoken commands to the rest of the autonomous squadron. Like an interpreter. Ten years from now, this whole carrier air wing will be reduced to a few quarterbacks, each leading a flight of AI-enabled weapons assets. I plan to be one of them."

"What happened after contact? You said the UAP was playing with you? Did you sense a threat?"

"Not right away. At least not until it literally joined our formation—"

"What? Say again?"

"I know, crazy, right? It was quick and smooth. Slid right in there to make us a four-man flight. Well, not *man*. One man, two robots. And . . . whatever the hell that thing was."

"How close?"

"Ten meters. Perfectly synchronized. No way to do that unless it could intercept our communications. It must have talked to the True-Blues. The AI wingmen maintain constant radio contact."

I have to pause and think about this for a couple seconds.

"Okay. What if it just saw your pattern and figured it out? If it knew your operational parameters, couldn't it guess?"

"Maybe. The AI is pretty simple at this point. But it would have to know the drones would automatically flock when another unit joined our formation."

"So, whoever it was has likely infiltrated highly classified automated weapon systems specifications?"

"You tell me."

"Listen, Lieutenant Marconi. My job is to explain the kinds of approaches our enemies are likely to take and which technological paths they're likely to walk. Specifically, I've got to project how this tech will impact national security—to prepare U.S. defenses and foreign policy decisions."

"Well, brother, the foreign policy on this is gonna be a wild ride."

"What's that supposed to mean?"

Meek goes quiet.

"What happened?" I ask.

"It went down."

"Crashed?" I ask. *That would be interesting.*

"No. It went down. Under the water. Submerged."

I tilt my head.

"It was on my radar and on shipboard tracking," he adds. "Up until then. After it went under, I paced it and watched from above. It was just under the ocean surface. And it *didn't change speed.*"

Meek looks away from me, forehead wrinkled in wonder.

"I couldn't begin to tell you who made this thing. Or even predict how we should deal with it. The thing didn't seem like it was even obeying the laws of physics," he says. "At least, not our physics. It was performing maneuvers that are impossible, as far as I know. And again, this is speculation, but . . . it felt like it was aware of me. Playing."

Meek takes a deep breath.

"Just before it disappeared deeper into the ocean, my cockpit began to shake. I felt a pressure. No damage. No sensors even picked it up. It was just, like, a little nudge."

"You think it was the UAP?" I ask, skeptical. "From under the water?"

"I know it was," he says.

"Maybe it employed a sonic weapon?"

"Sure, maybe," he says. "I guess."

Meek checks his watch by habit, then lowers his arm and lets the sleeve of his flight jacket slide down over his wrist. He catches me watching, pretends not to. I can't put my finger on why, but he's acting like a guilty child.

"We're almost finished," I say. "Just . . . is that all? Is there anything else?"

The pilot pauses, conflicted.

Finally, he turns to me with a pleading look on his face. I realize his lips are trembling until he compresses them into a tight smile.

"Sir, that thing might have been a drone. China might have sent it to watch us. But I want you to tell me . . . how does a Chinese drone do *this*?"

Meek tugs his sleeve up and shows me his tanned forearm. A complex, geometric pattern is imprinted on the curves of muscle. It's a double helix, laid down in sick-looking yellows and greens, laced with darker stripes of purple. It looks like someone has carefully given him a tattoo—in the image of DNA.

The tattoo looks familiar. I try to place where I've seen it.

"*Voyager*," he says. "I looked it up."

"*Voyager?*" I begin to reply, before it hits me.

I'm looking at the exact image imprinted on the golden record that was sent up on both *Voyager* spacecraft, in the late 1970s. It's a mathematical representation of the building blocks of life. The image was chosen to send a very specific message to any alien entity that might intercept our spacecraft:

HOLE IN THE SKY

We are intelligent.

And it's written out plain as day on Meek's forearm.

"Are you saying the unidentified craft somehow . . . gave you a tattoo?" I ask, incredulous.

"No, sir," he says, wincing as he rolls his sleeve back down. "It's not a tattoo. They used a lighter touch than that. More playful. I mean, look at it. Can't you see it's already starting to heal?"

He rubs his arm and stares at me.

"This right here is a very complicated *bruise*."

5
HOMECOMING

JIM HARDGRAY // Spiro, Oklahoma
Detection, +3 Hours

This is the day I take my daughter back into my life. I'm trying to act confident. I'm trying to pretend I've got my shit together. Everything is going to be okay.

I hope.

It should be a joyous day, but I can't shake this sense of dread. I mean, there's no news bulletin interrupting our regularly scheduled broadcast, or tornado sirens wailing off in the distance, or even a man with a sandwich board shouting prophecy in the streets. But still . . .

The world around me just feels like it's gone an itty-bit sideways.

From the driveway, my single-wide trailer looks dim and dirty framed against the brilliant green of the grassy mounds rising up behind it. My unofficial backyard is an ancient place, built by the ancestors of my ancestors. The mounds have been here so long, they sort of get lost in the background of the modern world.

As I open the trailer door, I'm hit by the sharp smell of the bleach I used to clean every surface. It's mostly wasted effort, since there's only so much you can scrub linoleum and fake plastic wood. And none of it hides the curled edges of yellowed plastic countertop, or the burns of forgotten cigarettes on my old coffee table.

Tawny walks past me and stands in the middle of the living room.

She stops when she hears the floor squeaking, notices it dimpling under her foot. I've long since learned to walk around the rotten spot.

She flashes me a look saying, *Really?*

I shrug, then wince as her duffel bag hits the ground with a hollow thump. We'll have to see if this place can handle a teenager without falling apart. Fifty-fifty, is my bet.

"About the same as I remember," she mutters, staring into the glassy eyes of a stuffed buck hanging over my beat-up old couch.

"Hey, Corntassel," she says to him. "Still looking good, bud."

I shoulder her duffel bag and wait.

Tawny wheels around the tiny living room and kitchen. Her hands flutter like birds, landing on objects, touching the sink handle, smoothing dusty drapes, flicking the television on then back off. She stops when she notices the glinting nailheads protruding from wood paneling—missing family pictures.

Tawny studies the empty wall for a long time.

"Hey," I say. "So, you'll have my old radio room. I got it all set up."

Tawny pauses and we make eye contact. I can see the ghost of a question in her glance. I can't hold her gaze for long.

Down the narrow hallway, I push open the first door on the left. The small square room smells of old electronics and piles of musty code books. The CB radio equipment is piled in a milk crate in the corner, mostly out of the way. I've got a sagging daybed crammed against the wall beneath a window with screening nibbled through by some long-dead mouse.

I set the duffel bag on the daybed and smooth the blanket. Turning, I see Tawny staring at a door at the end of the hall. This door is scabbed with remnants of old tape from the childish signs and decorations I have taken down. This is the door to Tawny's old bedroom—the one she used to share with Samuel.

And this door is closed.

"Tawn—"

Before I can stop her, Tawny walks over and grabs the door handle. She yanks on it, and again. Locked. She shakes it. Turning to see me standing over her, I watch her expression go quiet and still the way her mother's used to—when a big fight was either already over or it was just beginning.

"It's locked," she says simply.

"Yeah," I say.

"Why is it locked?"

"It just is."

Tawny's eyes feel like searchlights, scouring every inch of my face. I know her sharp little mind is working its way through my blank eyes, pruning out all the weakness and fear and shame that're waiting right there under the surface.

"Just don't go in there," I say, wincing at the tremble I hear in my own voice. "Please. I'm not ready."

When my daughter's mouth opens to speak, I instinctively turn away. She stands there in surprised anger. But I can't make myself look back.

I hear the door slam open as Tawny stalks away. I run a sleeve over my eyes and follow her outside. The wind carries the scent of rain as it washes down off the hills out in the distance behind my trailer.

Tawny is already halfway up an old trail leading across my unfenced backyard, stomping her way out into a field of dry tallgrass. A swaybacked swing set leans in the yard, one end of its metal piping clogged by a wasp's nest. The neighbor's damned dogs are already barking hard at my daughter, jumping against the chainlink as she storms away with her long black hair trailing.

It doesn't sound like happy barking, or angry either.

The dogs sound scared.

"No—hey!" I call after her, trotting to catch up. "Slow down!"

Tawny doesn't bother to greet me when I fall into step beside her.

With each stab of my boots into the rutted grass, a new thought crops up in my mind. As we climb a mound together, step by step, I end up leaving all those words stamped into the dead grass before they make it to my throat.

Nothing you can say. No way on earth to fix this.

"You shouldn't climb on the mounds," I say. "It's not respectful."

Tawny ignores me, so I continue.

"It was your grandma told me that. Elisi. Before she moved to the panhandle."

A slight pause, so I keep talking between breaths.

"Used to tell us we lived on sacred territory, know that?"

Her words come out angry and fast between breaths.

"Of course I know that, Jim," she says. "You used to say it all the time. Maybe the only thing y'all two agreed on."

"*Watch out you don't step on your ancestors,*" she mimics me. "I can't be in that trailer. Not with you like you are."

The door has to remain closed, and that's just that.

So I continue talking like I didn't hear a thing. I let the fatherly lecture flow between my steps, between my breaths—and I keep it going steady to let these seconds spin out without interruption.

"These mounds were built by Natives a long time before the Cherokee showed up after forced removal. They called them the Caddo people. But they were older than that. Mississippians, for the river. A big civilization. Ten, twenty thousand years old. Ancestors to our ancestors."

"I never heard that," Tawny responds.

"Well, it's not in the history books," I say. "Not the ones at school, anyhow."

"Wouldn't there be more, if that were true?"

"What, mounds? There *are* more. Just about every major city in the eastern half of the country. Caddo chose the best sites for their mounds. White folks figured that out pretty early. Started looking for the ruins to build on. Knew it would be a smart place for their own cities. Fertile soil. Easy to defend. Access to trade. Almost always built along the water. They came and bulldozed 'em, like everything."

"Where'd they go?"

"Bulldozed, like I said."

"No, Dad. I mean, where are the people? Like, did diseases get them? Wars?"

"Not sure." I pause, then a memory hits me. "But I know what your grandma thought."

Tawny raises her eyebrows at me.

"Back in the day, *her* elders said those people left. Went home."

I smile and point toward the sky.

"To the stars," I say.

Tawny shoots me a look of disbelief, laughs, and looks around. We've reached the top of the nearest mound. We turn to look out at the valley. Beautiful, rolling hills stretch out like a painting—except with a few sad little trailers nestled together like baby mice in the dirt.

"You almost had me," she says.

"I'm not kidding though. Your grandma, your *elisi,* she believed our people came from up there. Said the very first Cherokee come from the Pleiades constellation. That's why these mounds are laid out in the same pattern as those stars. We all rode down here on a giant turtle. And it'll take us all back home someday."

Tawny shakes her head and looks out.

"Grandma was always telling us her teachings," she says, snatching up a stalk of grass and tearing it along the seam. "I miss it."

I nod, staring out at nothing alongside my daughter. The urge to put my arm over her shoulder is so strong, but I have to fight it or I'll ruin this moment between us.

At the bottom of the hill, those dogs are still going crazy barking. They've been joined by the neighbors' dogs, too. It's a tinny drumbeat from this far, their fool heads snapping back, froth flying as they yip and beg at us.

My little trailer kind of looks homey from here, but I know that inside it there is still a door that has to stay shut.

"What's that smell?" asks Tawny, nose crinkled.

I put a hand over my nose and mouth. The odor of stagnant water and earth is overwhelming. It's settling down like an invisible cloud over us.

My eyes go wide as I see it.

A flock of starlings is rising up, spreading across the sky like they've been startled by something. But they're moving together, reforming as they wheel toward us. Coming in low over the mounds and weaving into the air, painting Morse code on the stark empty sky. Their wings are flapping silently over the background of panicked barking.

The flock flows up and down as it approaches. It's a stream of birds, each of them following its own rules, and together they create a mesmerizing complexity written on the heavens—resolving into a form. All of them, coming together, going solid in my sight as a kind of snake in the sky. Rising and falling.

A serpent with a long tail, and antlers that rise like twin spires.

"Uktena," I mutter, goose bumps sweeping up my arms.

"What?" asks my daughter.

"Look out!"

I take Tawny by the arm and pull her close. The flock is coming straight toward us—and I can't unsee the *shape*. Long, speckled antlers that spear toward us over a grinning dragon's mouth, a lolling black tongue made of birds. All of it chittering, clawing up the hill and straight at us.

I don't have time to question how it can be real.

We duck together as a pair of horns rear back and thrust through the space where we cower. The blast of a thousand small bodies blows over our heads. I can feel the heat of their little breasts, the stinging *thwap* of tiny wings over my ears. Their chirping is a roar. Their feathers are sandpaper.

A baptism by birds.

And then it's over. I'm on my knees, wet grass soaking through my jeans. One arm around my daughter's bony shoulders.

"Holy shit," says Tawny, shrugging me off. Laughing.

The birds have gone, disappearing up into the sky in all directions.

I shake my head and force myself to let go of my daughter. A real strange feeling is settling in around my eyes. It's hard to express. There is something in the water out here. Something in the sky. Past the sky.

"What the heck were they thinking?" asks Tawny. "That was crazy."

"Uktena, Tawny," I say. "A messenger."

"Okay, Jim. Right. And what'd the little birdies just tell us?"

Tawny is flicking dots of bird crap off her sleeves. Holding out long strands of her black hair and checking to make sure they're clean. An uncharacteristic smile is lodged in the corner of her mouth.

"I don't know," I say. "I don't remember what it's supposed to mean. Just . . . things are changing."

"Well, no shit," she says.

I flash my best stern-dad look about the cussing. She rolls her eyes.

"I mean, more than that, Tawn. Things are changing. Can't you almost taste it? The animals are acting strange. I don't know."

"Maybe it's the fracking," says Tawny.

"Maybe so."

I turn to my daughter, and I feel a sudden urgency I can't explain. A throbbing siren in my mind. Telling me one thing.

"Tawny," I say. "Let's get the hell down off this mound. Right now."

6
ALWAYS ON

MIKAYLA JOHNSON // NASA Johnson Space Center
Detection, +2 Days

I should have known Nix was learning the whole time. Of course, the little machine that sits on my face would never think to stop, would it? Always watching and listening, even when I didn't think it was.

Especially then.

I thought I was so smart to notice the plasma density perturbations in our *Voyager* data. But come to find out I didn't know shit. And now that I have actually figured out some shit, I almost wished I hadn't.

It was Nix who was paying attention. Friggin' Nix—a pair of bulky augmented reality glasses that I bought and modified myself.

Most of the time I keep Nix pushed up on my forehead. My hair is fluffy as it wants to be, especially when I have it in buns. I like how the frames sit high up so the solid plastic blocks my peripheral vision. It lets me concentrate on coding. Like being in my own little world while I'm typing rapid-fire.

I don't like a lot of sensory stimuli.

So, it helps to keep my head down. Like, literally. I've memorized the texture of every floor surface in the building. Entryway. Fake ceramic tile. Glossy, smooth. Loud. Upper hallways are the same. Luckily, the cubicle farms have a thin, mealy brown carpet. Nice and quiet. And I love, love, love how the cold air blasts over the white tiles in high-speed computing. Where I live, way over in the astrophysics lab we call the Outpost, there's just a quiet, calming gray quartzite.

There aren't a lot of us in this lab. And this far out on the edge of campus, the only sounds are the breathing of the building's ventilation systems. Or maybe somebody mowing outside triple-paned windows.

It's a big reason why I took this job and stuck with it.

But yeah, the Nix glasses. NASA security let me use it only because they had to—I lied and told them it's a disability aid, like crutches or a retinal implant. It's just that instead of fixing a physical deficit, the glasses are supposed to help me with social interactions.

I mean, I *could* train myself to pay more attention to humans, but I'm just too lazy. Everybody has priorities, I guess.

I depend on Nix to quickly identify other people by their faces, mainly. It also helps me sort out the emotional meaning behind all those rows of off-white calcium and lumps of lipstick-stained flesh. Nix will find a pair of eyes and gauge the direction of the pupils. Or calculate the angles between facial muscles as they stretch and collapse in conversation.

Neat stuff.

Over time, Nix got pretty specialized on the people around me. My coworkers. My roommates. The people in my apartment building. Shit, even people who deliver takeout. I don't usually keep the audio on, so it can show me only little text annotations about the people around me—whether they're happy, concerned, confused . . . helping make sense of all the boring social stuff.

But here in the glow of my monitors, that sneaky old Nix has been watching and listening—running pattern recognition on every aspect of my little work world. NASA would've never allowed it if they knew the machine wasn't just learning faces.

I guess I *have* made a few custom modifications.

For example, I trained Nix to rate attractiveness, so it could give a heads-up if a person was good-looking. I taught it to memorize all the boring-ass facts that people say about themselves. And I taught it my own customized categories of facial expressions, like: *desperately-uncomfortable; I-don't-believe-you-but-I-think-you're-funny;* and *just-saw-an-adorable-cat-on-the-Internet.*

Even though it was working on my social life, Nix wasn't always helpful. Last week I ran into my coworkers and Nix threw a bunch of annotated information across my vision when they asked me to join them for lunch.

"I would," I said, reading the notes. "But Dave clearly *needs-to-take-a-dump.*"

Four or five new annotations popped up—*uncomfortable.* Then Dave's chair is screeching back and he's duck-walking across the cafeteria. Jesus, I didn't know anybody's cheeks could get that red.

Nix was learning all the time—including while I had it pushed up onto my forehead, or while it was lying forgotten on its desk charger. Watching me while I was hunched over the control console going through screen after screen of microlensing data. It was even paying attention while I analyzed those *Voyager* plasma densities.

It found the patterns.

When I came back from lunch today and slid Nix down over my eyes, it showed me more than just how a large object passed through heliopause. It had stitched the plasma densities together into a story of something else. Somehow, words and instructions were hidden in the numbers. A pattern of information collected from fifteen billion miles away, but sitting there as sure as if you had said it to my face.

See, the movement of the object shows up in the density information.

Whatever was out there . . . it carefully modified its location, moving in a specific pattern that would alter our plasma density records in a specific way—sending an intentional message, hidden in the data.

It looked like backdoor code to me, so I let Nix try to compile it.

Pattern recognized. Propose pattern match.

On the Nix augmented reality glasses, in the corner of my eye, where it normally told me if somebody was *smiling-politely-but-ready-to-leave* . . . different words popped up, with a cursor blinking after them:

"HELLO, MIKAYLA."

My blood pressure went out like the tide, and I plopped into my office chair. Nobody else was back from lunch yet, so I allowed myself a loud curse. Then I gripped my Nix glasses in both hands and leaned over the desk, closing my face off from the world, on the verge of hyperventilating. I could smell my own cherry lip gloss while I spoke into the desktop.

"Nix? Is that you?" I asked. "Holy shit. Holy, holy fucking shit."

There was a pause, and then another word appeared in the corner of my eye.

"VOLUME."

With shaking hands, I reached up and slid a finger over the glasses frame just in front of my right ear. The volume control slid up, and I pressed my forehead back down against the cool table. Squeezing my eyes shut, I waited until I heard the smooth, synthetic voice whispering in my ear.

"They're coming for you."

7
ECONOMY CLASS

GAVIN CLARK // Butte, Montana
Detection, +3 Days

The phenomena are accelerating. No doubt about it. The data don't lie.

I'm balancing a government-issued laptop on the flimsy tray table in front of me while I peck out the report for my last visit—already on my way to the next. There used to be weeks back at the home office between field visits. Then there were days. This time, I'm not even flying back to D.C. at all.

Another day, another plane ride. Another sore back.

Uncle Sam claims to be on a tight budget. In reality, my bosses are terrified of looking wasteful when the inevitable congressional oversight committee scrutinizes how much we've spent. We're the only department officially tasked by the Pentagon to investigate and categorize UAPs. It's only a matter of time before the public asks why they're paying for some guy to fly around the world chasing after little green men.

That means economy class for me, and no upgrades.

This morning I'm crammed into a window seat, my hair still smelling like cheap hotel shampoo, headed to the next site. Moving from the Atlantic coast toward the center of the country—Montana, this time.

More specifically, I'm making a last-minute rendezvous with

a commercial protective services freight truck designed to carry obfuscated Department of Defense matériel across the country. Usually, that means classified armaments, ammunitions, or vehicles. This time, it means something else entirely.

Northern Command tracked an anomalous impact near the Canadian border, and scrambled someone to pick it up before the Canadians could get involved. The closest available national guardsman was called up from the 639 Quartermaster Supply Company in Kalispell, Montana, and assigned to drive the rented semitruck and its cargo five hundred miles across the state. National Guard normally reports to the governor, but we federalized this mission to maintain operational security.

Now I'm on my way to take a peek at the wreckage.

I honestly have no idea what's under the black-tarped package that's been cruising south for the past couple of days. Whatever the thing is—the government wants another pair of eyes on it. And the Pentagon would rather those eyes belong to one of their own, rather than some weekend warrior who's probably already told his wife and kids about it.

No wife. No kids. That's how you get a job like this.

In the last several days, reports have been piling up. Civilian eyewitnesses have been spotting UAPs all across the country. But in particular over the central landmass of North America. More importantly, military contacts have been exponentially increasing.

Not only have there been sightings, but there have been reported interactions. You combine that with the last mandate from the Man Downstairs, and it's a busy day to be the guy in charge of investigating emerging weapons. I'm trying to focus on the report at hand and not on the growing implication.

The MD is never wrong—and he told us to prepare for first contact.

But the gist I'm picking up from my deputy director is that first contact could mean a lot of things. And whatever it turns out to be—we'll need as much up-front reconnaissance as possible. There are a lot of ways to respond to this scenario, and most of them involve guns.

The U.S. military is an organization designed to strategically project force to accomplish diplomatic goals. In other words, they think of force as just another tool in the tool belt to be applied in any negotiation—and the U.S. military doesn't like to make concessions.

As we prepare to land, I put away my laptop and rest the side of my forehead against the cold plastic curve of the plane's fuselage. I'm staring at clouds through a half-lidded window shutter while the thrumming of the plane's engines lulls me to sleep.

I'm half dreaming of what Lieutenant Marconi described. From an emerging weapons perspective, it was a greatly advanced version of the same unmanned platforms he'd been studying for months. Something that knew intuitively how to join his formation, had the same or better weapons and flight capabilities. If it *was* on our side, it would be like a dream come true.

And don't forget that playful attitude.

The finesse required to apply a pattern of force upward from below the ocean surface, through the canopy of a moving aircraft, through a flight suit, and to nudge our man just hard enough to bruise a pattern into his skin?

It's possible but not possible. Not with what we have.

My thoughts run through the permutations of potential origins. It could be an independent genius, a commercial enterprise, a foreign state, or—I might as well say it—something else . . .

I open my eyes to try and ignore the thought. And as they focus, it comes into view outside. A golden ball of metal, dipping up out of the clouds just behind the wing. It's tumbling slow, moving at the exact speed as our plane. It emerges from cloud cover, the sunlight glinting off wrinkles in the metal as it slowly turns.

Then it's gone.

Startled, I bang my forehead on the plastic. I blink my eyes and shake my head, ignoring the stares from the old lady sitting next to me. The runway is already rising up to meet us, tires shrieking on tarmac.

Glancing around the plane, I don't see anybody else reacting.

It's got to be in my head. That's the highest-probability explanation. But as the passengers line up to disembark, I hear a little girl telling a story to her bemused mom. It's about a golden ball that can fly in the air.

Mom shoots me a look. *Kids, right?*

Shouldering my bag, I shove my way down the stair ramp and take a hard left straight across the tarmac. A sign reads BERT MOONEY INTERNATIONAL AIRPORT, and based on a quick look around I'm guessing the "international" part of the title is just for show. My destination is a private hangar about a hundred yards away.

I don't even have to flash any credentials. The baggage handlers ignore me as I walk along the outside of the single terminal and toward a cluster of rusty hangars. The private airstrip alongside the official airport isn't much more than a stripe of weedy pavement. A few old Cessnas are chained up outside a small administrative building. Air traffic control is manned by whoever happens to be hanging around the lounge inside.

I don't bother knocking.

It smells like three-day-old coffee and aftershave inside the sun-beaten lounge area. As I enter, a group of old men stop their conversation and turn to nod at me. They seem friendly enough. Three overweight old guys in cowboy hats, clutching paper coffee cups with gouty fingers and sizing me up.

An old man with a mustache dipped in nicotine speaks first.

"Nice suit," he says. "You'll be looking for Echo hangar. The green one with the red door . . . and the soldier outside it."

I look out a dusty window with a sill coated in dead flies. The hangar is right there, but I decide to stay back a second. It's impossible to guess the level of gossip that three old men can get up to over coffee on a morning like this, but I'm going to try.

"Thanks very much," I say. "Your country appreciates it."

"Oh, it's no problem sharing some space," says mustache. "Anything I can do for Uncle Sam. But I was wondering?"

I cock my head, and his friend with a cane cuts in.

"You mind sharing a little bit about what's out there?" asks the cane. "We got a little bet going that them Chinese must have left a chunka something behind. But Russ here, why, he's got other, crazier ideas."

Russ looks up at me expectantly, clearly a man with access to the Internet.

The Cessna 172 outside must belong to mustache, shoved unceremoniously out of his hangar along with a couple of beat-up old rolling toolboxes and anything else he had stored inside.

I don't imagine the guardsman would have taken no for an answer.

With a reassuring grin for the old fellas, I decide to tell them the truth.

"Won't know until I see," I say. "You guys have a good morning."

As it turns out, the statement is even more true than I anticipated.

I'm halfway across the parking lot to the hangar when my contact strides up to greet me. He is a national guardsman in full uniform, probably in his mid-fifties. His face is haggard, wet hazel eyes staring at me over cheeks lined with fatigue. I keep crunching over the concrete in flimsy dress shoes as I take his hand for a firm shake.

"Look, uh, sir," he says. "It's the damnedest thing. You're not gonna believe me."

I walk past him to the hangar door.

"You'd be surprised," I say.

The guardsman rushes to catch up.

"No, you don't understand," he says, opening the door for me.

The metal door slaps open against the wall, and I enter the vast interior of a dimly lit airplane hangar. I smell a comforting mix of spray insulation, engine grease, and airplane fuel. The commercial freight truck is parked in the middle of the room with its trailer still attached. On the back of the trailer, I can see a half dozen heavy-duty ratchets lying limp across a deflated piece of tarp.

"It's not here anymore," says the guardsman.

I turn to look at him, the irritation clear on my face. He's got his cap in his hand, speaking fast. He won't look me in the eyes.

"Nobody took it. Nobody came in or out. Nobody saw a damned thing. It must have happened half an hour ago. It had to have. That's the only time I took my eyes off it," he says. "While I was taking a quick nap right here in this room."

I turn back to the trailer.

Whatever was in there, if anything, was as big as a truck. Glancing around, I don't see any holes in the tarp. No holes in the ceiling or walls. It didn't fly out of here. The ratchets haven't even been loosened. It's like it disappeared.

"It's just gone," says the guy.

"It happened while you were asleep," I say, without much gusto.

The mobile phone on my hip is buzzing. I glance down to see several new messages have arrived in the last couple of minutes. Something big is going on.

"Listen, I swear I followed all the instructions," he says. "Combatant command sent word for me after midnight. Told me the president had activated us. I threw on my uniform and headed out. Took possession of the truck from the civilian driver a mile before reaching the site, in Good Grief."

"Good grief?" I ask.

"Good Grief, Idaho. Where the object was found. We, uh, obfuscated the cargo before my men loaded it, and all personnel contact was limited from then on. I drove the truck myself. That's why they picked me—I've got a commercial license. I drove all day and night, through the mountains, until it felt like I was dreaming. Once I got the package here, I cleared out the hangar and pulled inside. Nobody came near. Not for a second. And trust me, those old coots did everything they could to get a peek."

"It disappeared," I repeat, going for my phone. It's buzzing again.

"Yeah. Yes, sir."

"Okay," I say. "Where can I set up?"

He points at a folding card table in the corner of the hangar, with a satellite phone resting on it. A cord is plugged into the satphone, waiting to provide my laptop an encrypted connection to home base.

"Thanks," I say, putting my portable phone away. "You can go."

Lowering his head in shame, the guardsman heads toward the exit.

"Keep watch out there, please," I add, laying my laptop on the card table and plugging it in. The torn mail wrapper is still lying on the floor, where the satellite phone and its Internet connector accessory were overnighted here.

This should be interesting.

The quantum encryption link blinks a few times, then connects. I feel a thrill race along my spine as the symbol on the computer screen flashes "TOP SECRET."

I swear, seeing those words never gets old.

By habit, I scan my surroundings to make sure I'm alone.

Then the screen floods with data. I can't make sense of what it is. Plasma this. Azimuth that. NASA stuff.

The satellite phone begins to ring, the trill echoing from the shadowed heights of the hangar. I check my surroundings again, then lean over the laptop to block the screen with my body. I lift the phone to my ear, careful not to dislodge the wires running down to my laptop.

"This is Clark," I say.

"This is Lyceum," says a scratchy voice, routed from god-knows-where. We've never met, and I'm convinced it's not the same voice every time—but the authority behind the person code-named "Lyceum" remains the same.

They give the orders and I execute.

"Go ahead," I say.

"What you are seeing is straight from the source."

It's a real-time feed of a lot of confusing things happening at NASA. Hard to say how old the worms are in the NASA networks or how long they've been feeding their findings straight to the Department of Defense. Probably about as long as the agency has existed.

"What am I supposed to make of this?"

"Those are plasma density changes. Coming from an object at the edge of our solar system. Our subject at NASA is mapping those to an incoming trajectory."

"The Man Downstairs was right, as usual."

The screen flashes, and I see a dotted line moving out past the edge of our sun. Someone is crunching this data in real time—trying to make sense of these densities by mapping it visually.

"This data indicates an object is at the edge of heliopause. It is currently accelerating in our direction. And yes, I'm aware of the latest MD mandate."

"First contact?" I ask.

I take a deep breath, then continue.

"Couldn't it just be a meteorite? Something dense?"

"It's out of the ecliptic plane. Not from our solar system."

"Then an interstellar object? A comet?"

"You'd think that, but it appears to be under its own propulsion. It changed direction to approach the *Voyager Two* spacecraft. Almost like it's playing."

A playful little nudge.

"Is this my next field visit?" I ask. "An incoming UAP?"

"We don't know where it's headed. But there's more than just a trajectory in the data. We think it has choreographed its location to send messages through the plasma density changes. Sort of a hidden code."

"And? What's it say?"

"Still working on that."

I can only imagine the number of mathematicians feverishly working in cool, sterile CIA war rooms.

"Who's sending us this message? Who could it possibly be for? And who the hell could possibly decode it—if you can't?"

There is a long pause on the other line. It's almost as if whoever-this-is is trying to decide how much I need to know. Or maybe they're getting permission to throw me a bone.

"Her name is Dr. Mikayla Johnson. She's part of the *Voyager* team."

"Some hot-shit NASA brain?"

"Ah, not really. *Voyager One* and *Two* are historically important. But the spacecraft were launched in the age of disco. At this point, they're just a couple hunks of broken-down junk hurtling through the void."

"Very poetic."

"*Voyager* is interesting, but not the most prestigious assignment."

"Then who is she? What does she know?"

Laughter on the other end of the line. The data flow stops abruptly. I'm left with a dead computer and just a couple of seconds of airtime left.

"That's what you're going to find out, Agent Clark. Luckily, I believe you're already at the airport. You've been chosen as point man for this mission.

"Don't miss your flight—"

8

THE COSMOS SPEAKS

MIKAYLA JOHNSON // NASA Johnson Space Center
Detection, +3 Days

Okay, fuck this. I'm spinning. Nix spoke to me.

Nix *could not* have just spoken to me.

I yanked those glasses off my face and did a *there's-a-spider-crawling-up-my-arm* dance. I made a lot of inarticulate gibbering noises that attracted the attention of my project manager from down a long, empty hallway. I told her, with a straight face, mind you, that there was a bug on me. That sweet, trusting nerd bought it.

And then my research began.

First, I threw the Nix glasses onto my desk, where they kept staring up at me through those dorky frames. Fool me once, right? I dropped an old sweatshirt over the cameras. It was simple to attach the device to its interface cord. I wrote a little program to log everything going on in the Nix system. I needed to track down whatever madness was happening inside that little CPU. Somebody hacking me. Some crazy-ass malfunction. And as it sat there running for a few minutes, I found out exactly what it was doing.

Nothing—absolutely nothing.

Nix didn't want to talk to me unless I was wearing it on my face.

So, I left it there. I went and loaded up the plasma density data that seemed to have either triggered an AI breakthrough or a personal psychotic episode. I put my eyes on that data until the day was over. I went home to shower and to sleep for a few hours but found myself drawn back to my desk.

Back down here to study a lump of plastic under a dirty sweatshirt.

The rest of the lab has moved on, dismissing the perturbations as sensor noise. Just a weird dip in the solar wind. Every other scientist on the mission saw the same shit, and somehow just let it go. And here I am, still hunched over my desk, studying the data—trying to find an explanation.

And it's been leading nowhere. The sequences in the densities are there—but they aren't as obvious as plain computer code, exactly. They sure aren't English. I have no idea how this pattern of random stops and starts could have influenced the piece of technology that normally sits on my face.

Voices from heliopause. An impossible dream. A jackpot.

For hours, I've been staring at the shape of the Nix under the fabric. The thought of putting it on honestly gives me shivers. I'm picturing how abyssal fish hunt in the absolute darkness of the ocean floor. With food so rare in the infinite wastes, what kind of entity might evolve out there between stars? Is this a trap? Some kind of predator from interstellar space, luring in its prey?

But you gotta shit or get off the pot, as my father used to say.

I came in to find a note on my desk asking me to attend a meeting at noon. It's from my project manager. They must have found out that something is wrong with Nix. They must know that I found a secret code and didn't tell anybody. I'm all out of options, so I decide to just go for it.

I finally dare to put Nix back on my face.

"Hello? Nix?" I ask. "Who's coming for me?"

Nothing.

"Nix? Nobody outside NASA knows about this, right?"

Nada.

I sit back in my chair, the familiar weight of the Nix glasses resting on the bridge of my nose. I let out a long exhale.

What a fucking letdown.

Then I run my eyes across the plasma perturbation data printed out and scattered across my desk. Instantly, new patterns emerge in augmented reality. Now I see the answer—but only through Nix's eyes. I'm seeing a precise pattern designed to excite the weights assigned to the neural network that Nix runs on.

"The data was crafted for this exact hardware," says Nix, and I can't be sure it isn't my own voice that I hear in my head. Adrenaline floods my legs at the words. Instead of screaming, I force myself to think logically about the situation.

It occurs to me that I'm in a centaur system.

In 1997, right after getting his ass kicked by Deep Blue, the reigning world champion of chess proposed a new game, called centaur chess. Dude was imagining the mythical half-man, half-horse of Greek mythology—a system where an intuitive and adaptable human mind could be paired with the brute force pattern-matching and data-processing capabilities of an artificial intelligence. Turns out, a human player paired with an AI is proven to beat all comers, human or AI.

Human being plus technology equals superhuman.

Something has modified the pattern-recognition abilities of my Nix augmented reality glasses—rewritten its code. Now Nix is giving me a higher-level observation of real-world patterns. But the real magic of this system isn't just in the complex connections of neurons in my own brain, or in the tangle of computer code inside the Nix system—instead, it's in the synthesis of the two of us. Basically, what I always dreamed Nix could be.

But I have a meeting to attend. So I stand up on shaking legs.

Our team assembles in the astrophysics conference room. My project manager throws the latest data on the big projector screen and starts talking. I lay down my laptop and load the information off the shared drive. Keeping my face calm behind clunky glasses, I do my best impression of *normal-employee-paying-attention*.

The *Voyager* team is back to business as usual.

It's crazy to imagine that we're still running these raggedy-ass *Voyager* spacecraft from the 1970s. I shake my head at the same preposterous thought I had a few days ago: all the data we sent up to convey the details of human existence wasn't recorded on compact discs or encoded in digitized files—it was all on motherfucking records.

My coworkers are discussing whether there is more information to extract in the plasma data, and if so, what it could possibly mean.

Background radiation. Solar flare. Sensor error.

I keep mulling. Vinyl records are what we sent out there into the cosmos. And now, as my Nix-enhanced eyes scan the data on the projector, it dawns on me.

Holy shit.

What you give is what you get. We sent vinyl, and that's exactly what the cosmos sent back.

I recognize the hidden information is compression waves—the kind generated by a needle scratching the grooves in a piece of vinyl. And just like analog sound can be digitized, so can this data. All it takes is running it through a basic converter.

I laugh out loud, drawing annoyed stares.

Something beyond heliopause really has sent NASA a message. And they delivered it in the only way they thought we could listen—on a record player. So that's what I'm simulating. My fingers fly over my laptop as I plug the data into a converter.

I push play and turn up my speaker. *Here it is,* I think. First contact.

Boom, bitches.

Eyes widen as the sound pours from my laptop. It's a slow, deformed howling that dribbles painfully from the speakers. Everyone stops speaking and turns toward the interruption.

"What is that?" asks my boss. "What are you doing?"

"I solved the code," I say. "The data is just a bunch of compression waves. The kind on a vinyl record. I ran them through a sound wave emulator."

I pause, listening to the tortured mewling coming from my speakers.

Damn.

"Sorry," I say. "I thought it would make sense. But this doesn't sound like anything."

My project manager looks thoughtful for a second. The rest of the room is quiet. It's dawning on them that we might have a message from the stars. Or a whole lot of random noise.

"I have an idea," says my boss, pushing up her glasses. "The records they sent up were old Shellacs, not LPs. Speed it up to seventy-eight RPM."

"How old *are* you?" I mutter. "Shellac it is."

Everyone at the table leans in. Our eyes are shining in wonder. I mean, this is it. We're about to hear our first message from the cosmos.

I tap the enter key and sit back to listen.

The yowling sound quickly resolves into an unmistakable human voice. Smiles and excited gasps emerge around the room as we hear the recording of a man, speaking a language I've never heard. And then I see frowns. The man's voice is coming only every few seconds, between ragged gasps for breath.

A research scientist gets up and leaves the room. The woman on my left covers her ears. Someone shouts at me to turn it the fuck off.

Between his gasps, the man isn't speaking to us—he is screaming. And other voices are joining him. Dozens of men, women, and what sound like children. More than dozens. Hundreds. Thousands.

Begging, retching, and most of all just plain *screaming*.

Screaming in agony. Shrieking.

HOLE IN THE SKY

My project manager looks at me, our eyes locking. And for once, I don't need Nix to explain what expression I'm seeing. Teeth bared between curled lips, chest heaving in panic as tears course down over trembling cheeks.

The look on her face is pure terror.

PART II

MONITOR

As entropy increases, the universe—and all closed systems in the universe—tends to move from the least to the most probable state, from organization to chaos. But there are local enclaves whose direction seems opposed to that of the universe, in which there is a limited and temporary tendency for organization to increase. It is within the safety of these rare enclaves that life finds its home.

—Norbert Wiener, *The Human Use of Human Beings* (1954)

9
MONITOR

THE MAN DOWNSTAIRS // Undisclosed Location
Monitor, T-Minus Zero

This job isn't always terrible. I write my translations and send the data upstairs for analysis. An intelligence mandate is rarely needed.

Honestly, the routine is calming.

Sometimes, weeks go by with nothing but gibberish. Random words and digits. Once, it was an entire month and a half of number sequences. Best they could figure, the Pattern was on a kick about some tidal activity on an ocean moon somewhere near the galactic core of the Milky Way. It was all math. Very boring.

Other times it goes silent. Like it's resting.

Not that anyone asks, but my theory is that everything coming out of the Pattern is *something*. Our intelligence people can't always make sense of it, because it's over our heads—either mathematically, or there is no vocabulary in our languages, or it's just the kind of data you can't understand as a three-dimensional being falling through time in one direction, frontward to back.

I mean, compared to the Pattern, the stiffs who watch my every move from upstairs really do have limited imaginations. This thing covers the full distance and time span of the universe. And here we exist on one single rock, today only.

The suits really get interested only when the Pattern starts spitting out data that has to do with people, in this timeframe, and on this planet. I'll never forget the time I got a couple of sentences describing a guy walking into an airport with some kind of a homemade weapon. It was like I kicked an anthill.

Anyway, the military guys must have gotten good at sorting out the nonsense and fitting the useful data into their overall intelligence apparatus. My mandates are a general call, but it's up to them to get specific. And this latest stuff the Pattern has been delivering . . . I've never seen it get this wild.

The Pattern's moments of lucidity are normally one sentence. Maybe two.

But lately the Pattern has gotten talkative. Not so many numbers. No physics. More . . . thinking. I believe the Pattern has begun channeling some type of intelligence. When I read this many words, all laid out in a row and starting to make loose sense—it gives me a clammy feeling.

I'm scared of it. And I'm scared of what they'll make of it.

My lips are numb on the butt of my cigarette while I copy some of these phrases down in longhand. I'm sitting here listening while a non-human entity talks about our whole species.

It's talking about *us*.

And even worse, I think it may be *listening*.

> ... waking from a dream of ages. Spiral arms of a galaxy spinning. Specks of mass on galactic orbits. Wearing ruts into space-time.
> Simple rules of a game for god-children.
> A man in a box, listening. Writing.
> A great anatomy shifts at thoughts of sustenance, even in slumber. Longs to slide its bloody, forked tongue up nostrils to taste mind matter. A body incarnate welcomes the warm shackles of a horizon.
> I am rising.

INTELLIGENCE MANDATE—ANOMALOUS OBJECT CONFIRMED AT HELIOPAUSE. MOVEMENT TRIGGERED BY INTERACTION WITH VOYAGER SPACECRAFT. LIKELY INCOMING. ASSUME ENHANCED THREAT POSTURE. ADVISE DEFENSIVE SECURITY MEASURES. MAINTAIN TRACKING OF OBJECT AND MONITOR CLOSELY.

—MD

10

DOWN ON THE RIVER

JIM HARDGRAY // Arkansas River
Monitor, +1 Hour

Tawny glares at me through plumes of her own breath, rubbing her hands together before burying them in her armpits. I take a swallow of coffee from my thermos and feel the warmth slide down my throat into my chest. My boots scratch pavement as sparrows chitter to each other out in the misty reeds.

I pause to wait for her, but Tawny just looks away.

Looks like I'm gonna have to take the beat-up aluminum canoe down from the bed of the truck all by myself. Tawny watches me grunt and struggle until I've got the thing on my head. I hear a snortle as I stand there like an asshole, an off-balance canoe over my eyes, stumbling and tipping forward until the metal nose thunks into the parking lot.

I shrug it off and lay the canoe on the ground.

"You done laughing?" I ask, taking the prow in both hands to position the canoe next to my truck. I notice she's picked up my thermos. I raise my eyebrows at her, and she tosses it clattering into the canoe. I sigh, gently laying in the bait, tackle, and rods. Then she takes hold of the other end and we start duck-stepping toward the boat ramp.

We're all alone this morning, on the southern bank of the Arkansas River. The sun isn't quite up over the horizon. The world is still shrink-wrapped in dew.

"You know all this here is Spiro country," I say. "Hundreds of thousands of people came to the banks of this river. Traders from thousands of miles away. They built earthen pyramids up to the skies. Bigger than anything you'll find in Egypt."

"Long time ago, huh," she says.

"Not that long, if you're a river. Ten thousand years. Blink of an eye."

The nose of the canoe slips into sandy brown water. This old muddy river is slow, wide, and flat. It meanders across the Great Plains and takes its time. It's a complicated thing, carrying silt and stone and memories. Every handful of water is brown and dark with all the secrets it wants to keep.

I hold us steady while Tawny climbs inside, then I push off.

This early, we just hear the mockingbirds and crickets along the shore. The slap of water against the metal hull. And there's the sound of our breathing—of our own sentences before we start, and the half-finished ones we start but don't finish.

"This isn't going to work, you know," says Tawny, bulky in her life vest, arms crossed, leaning back awkwardly while I row in gentle swoops.

"What's that?"

"This bonding or whatever the fuck."

"Okay," I say.

I keep rowing, thinking.

I'm thinking about anger. About how angry I was at the world when the worst happened. When it took my son. It took what he was, and it took everything he could have been. I'm thinking about how that anger was unfocused. It went out looking for a fight. When it didn't find a good target, it came back home to me. I feel that anger and shame every time I look in the mirror.

What a good target a father makes. A mama and daddy are the closest thing to the Creator for a kid. They're supposed to make everything all right. And if they can't, why, that anger goes out and finds its mark.

My only living child hates me.

It's crazy, but I'm okay with it. Because her anger looks better on me than it would if it came back home to her. Better she hate on me than on herself.

"Sam loved the water," she says.

"I know," I say. And I start to say I'm sorry, but I stop. I take a shaky breath. "You remember his little mohawk? How proud he was?"

"Yeah, it was a real tough look," she says. "Anyway, it beat having braids."

I smile a little. Shake my head back and forth. Two tight shining braids of black hair dangle over my shoulders.

"I don't know. I think they're pretty."

Tawny bites her lip rather than smile, stares into the misty reeds.

"Why didn't you save him?" she asks.

The smile falls right off my face. I sniff and glance at the muddy swirls of water under my paddle strokes. Keep on rowing.

I remember exactly how little he was. Tawny's panicked shouts. Spotting a flash of black hair lost in the murk. I hit the water like a shotgun blast. Boots filling up. Flailing, gasping, and grasping under the lake surface. Fear spreading like ropes of fire through the alcohol fog in my mind. And for one split second I felt him. I touched his face with my fingertips.

I swear to god I touched my boy's face. But it wasn't near enough.

"I don't know," I whisper, voice hoarse. "I tried."

She looks at me with disgust. *You were drunk.*

"I want to visit him. His gravestone in Spiro Meadows."

I shake my head no. *I can't.*

My son's life slipped right through my fingers. I lost him under the cloudy water of a man-made lake that I haven't been back to since. Gazing out at the mist, it hits me what a mistake it was to bring Tawny out fishing this morning.

After everything that happened.

How did I not know this would bring it all back up? All the things I need to not remember. I close my eyes and listen to water coughing against the hull of the boat as my throat swells up. Turning my face, I blink my eyes clear and let the wind bite my cheekbones. The world I'm seeing is shattered by refracting patterns of light, trapped in the branching cage of my eyelashes.

And that's when the men appear.

Three shapes are gliding out of the mist, skating over the surface of the water as neat as a knife across the belly of a strung-up deer.

I stop rowing.

I'm seeing something I can't explain. Two Native men are pacing us silently in an old-style dugout canoe. One of them looks over at me. His eyes are dark brown and empty. His face is painted. I can make out the ridges of fingerprints where he's spread the ocher across his cheeks. He lets that emotionless gaze slide over me, and then his eyes lock onto Tawny.

"Dad?" she asks. "Who is that?"

"I . . . have no earthly idea," I whisper.

The men are bare-chested, painted for wartime. Wearing bark fabric pants, hair cut into mohawks, with spears laid over their knees. The one in the back keeps rowing on a paddle made of carved driftwood. The mist is already swallowing them back up.

Over the slosh of water, I hear the men chatting to each other in low voices. A language I've never heard, but with familiar notes. Something real old.

One of the men turns and raises a hand to me, a greeting. A shining bracelet is around his wrist. More like glowing. Some kind of metal.

He speaks to me, a word pluming out in his breath.

HOLE IN THE SKY

I nod and make the same gesture back, feeling like I'm watching myself make the movements. And when the men disappear from view into the mist, it suddenly feels like I just had a dream. Except I see Tawny staring at me, eyebrows knitted in wonder and concern.

"That was old language," I say.

"What did he say? Are they cosplayers?"

"I don't know. It was a Mississippian root. Something before our languages. But I know I recognize it. It was a simple word."

Tawny cocks her head at me as I say it out loud:

"*We go together.*"

11

MISSION CONTROL

GAVIN CLARK // NASA Johnson Space Center
Monitor, +6 Hours

The back of my dress shirt is soaked with sweat, sticking to the seat of a rental car as I steer through packed Houston highway traffic. I can taste the acrid bite of the refineries belching columns of cotton gauze smoke down in the Gulf. I hack a cough into my elbow, knowing it won't make the pinch in the back of my throat go away.

I slow the car when I see the sign for NASA Johnson Space Center. I'm a little bit late, but that's not such a bad thing. It's better to give my escort some time to get inside and make an impression before I arrive.

Stopping at a security gate, I flash my badge to an armed, uniformed soldier manning the entrance. A dismayed federal marshal in a NASA security guard outfit sits next to him, looking dazed. The Army soldier is one of ours, sent ahead.

"Straight down, sir," he says. "Park in the little lot and go inside to get your credentials. Just put it on the grass if there aren't any spots left."

Peering ahead, I see at least a dozen chauffeured black SUVs crowding the tiny lot, along with the hulking silhouettes of tan Humvees. Several low-clearance security personnel stand by their respective cars, waiting for their generals and congressmen and

CIA operatives to return. Meanwhile, a fussy group of what must be foreign nationals are being escorted off campus.

I park my beige rental car on the sidewalk, take a deep breath, and slide my satphone earpiece in. It's time to receive the next set of directions from whichever classified operative answers my command line today.

"Clark to Lyceum, check?" I say.

"That's a check," says a faint whisper in my ear. "Head over to Mission Control. Interrogation subject is on premises."

In the small building, I flash a smile to a petrified receptionist and enter a fake name into a computer to acquire a credentials sticker. After passing security, a junior scientist leads me to a NASA-branded golf cart that takes us along an empty street through the middle of the city-size campus.

The scientist doesn't seem too concerned about the military presence. It's not uncommon around here to have badge access temporarily cut off during "sensitive events." Every building and laboratory on campus is well segregated for these situations. It happens more often than people know.

Leading me into a windowless building, the scientist and I wordlessly traverse an absolutely ordinary hallway leading to an absolutely ordinary doorway. And on the other side, I step into a balcony of stadium seating facing two stories of glass wall looking out on Mission Control.

Not surprisingly, it's standing room only today in the visitor viewing room.

A couple dozen bigwigs are sweating through their own suit jackets and staring up at the big board on the far wall. On those three massive screens, I glance at the output of sensors trained on the blackness beyond heliopause—showing only emptiness, for now. An infrared feed from the James Webb space telescope outlines an oblong shape in sizzling blues and reds. The readout from the Atacama telescope array has even more detail, including rough velocity.

Whatever it is—it's moving faster than any human-made craft.

A symbol in the bottom left of the screen indicates the data is being supplemented from an international feed—the five-hundred-meter FAST radio telescope in China. I find that interesting. This incident has gone worldwide to some extent, even if the details aren't being shared publicly.

Down on the floor, the NASA director himself is pacing between substations, wearing a headset and mic as he issues curt orders to teams of scientists.

I subvocalize a "status request" into my throat mike, and a synthesized voice begins to deliver a report into my earpiece. There isn't an estimated time of arrival yet, but for the last three days the object is believed to have been moving toward the inner planets at an astounding velocity of approximately fifty thousand kilometers per second. There have been no known attempts at communication from the object. And no response to initial queries.

Visual scans are impossible at this distance. It's just too far away.

"Hold position," says Lyceum. "Your subject is incoming."

I lean against the back wall and cross my arms, waiting. One of these scientists knows more than the rest. From what I can see, it won't be a problem to take one of these unsuspecting eggheads into custody.

A loud congressman in the front row reacts to the whispered play-by-play of my junior NASA scientist.

"The hell?" he says. "Unidentified anomalous what? Just tell me how big it is!"

Roughly a city block, comes the hushed murmur.

"Jesus Christ," groans the congressman.

Looking down on Mission Control, I see a wave of gasps run through the scientists and their backups at each workstation.

Some of them stand up involuntarily. The object on-screen has just shifted—it's changing course.

"We've got a perturbation," says the director, his words projected over the speakers in our viewing room. Somehow, there is no emotion in his voice. "Trajectory station, report."

"Maneuver in progress," says a scientist. "Radar tracking . . . and course change marked."

"All right, now where's it going?" asks the director.

The scientist doesn't respond. Her fingers rattle over the keyboard, and the third screen on the big board flashes to a predictive trajectory. A dotted line leads from beyond heliopause to a blank spot in space. As they advance the time, I see the problem. The Earth is rotating around into the trajectory.

"Direct Earth impact," says the scientist, voice quavering. "Estimated six hours at its current acceleration."

Six hours.

It's as if someone turned down the volume on the entire room. I hear a wet retch as someone doubles over a trash can. The door at the back of the observation room smacks open as a few people rush outside holding cell phones.

"Okay, okay," says the director. "On the downlink. Team leads. Let's estimate the impact site."

"Simulations incoming," says a voice.

After a few seconds hesitation, a woman at the station marked INCO starts typing in fitful little bursts. The big board again erupts with more trajectory information and dozens of scenarios. The lines spiral out and intersect with the Earth. Again. Ten more times. A hundred. Like the paths of missiles. Each time a little different.

"What's the issue?" asks the flight director.

"The object is moving under the action of nongravitational acceleration," says the scientist. "We can't predict a hundred percent where it's going. But every trajectory seems to result in an impact of some kind."

Now two-thirds of the suits in the observation room are up and hurrying toward the exit. Nobody wants to be photographed here at the genesis of what is potentially the worst catastrophe in human history. Bad for your reelection chances to be associated with an event that annihilates most of your constituency.

"Highest-probability impact site?" asks the director, voice hollow. "Just give me ballpark."

The mic transmits a sound like a hurt animal, followed by the reply.

"North America."

The back door keeps slamming as more people barge out into the world. The babble of panicked talk dies down as men and women stream outside. And as the crowd of politicians thins out, I see a welcome sight.

My target, looking just like the picture in her dossier.

Dr. Mikayla Johnson, leaning against the back wall of the observation room, arms crossed and looking relaxed. In fact, she's grinning from ear to ear. The kid has got a pair of what look like thick-framed nerd glasses pushed up on her forehead. It's a Nix augmented reality system modified into a thick-framed retro NASA style. Her hair is bunched into two fuzzy buns on either side of her head.

And she is staring directly at me, waiting.

I move to stand beside Mikayla, letting her look me up and down. She has come to the obvious conclusion that I've been sent by the government.

"I was expecting you," she said. "Or someone like you."

"You don't seem worried," I offer.

"Nah," says Mikayla.

I tilt my head, and she continues.

"Powered flight at that speed? With a trajectory change. Coming from interstellar space. And based on high reflectivity, it's probably metallic. Seems pretty obvious this isn't just a dumb rock," she says, almost with contempt.

I lift my eyebrows, offering nothing.

"Well? This is going to be first contact, isn't it?" she says. "That's probably why you're here, huh?"

She slides on her glasses. For a long moment, Mikayla lets her eyes crawl over my face. I have no idea what those fancy glasses are telling her about me, but she smiles at it.

"Dr. Gavin Clark," she adds. "Head of Emerging Weapons Technology for the Pentagon. On field assignment. Location classified. Nice to meet you. My name's Dr. Mikayla Johnson, but I'm gonna bet you already knew that."

I blink, adjusting to the reality that her Nix system is somehow tapped into a government database, and capable of running real-time face recognition. I wonder what else it's telling her. My eyes drift to an earbud tucked into her right ear.

"I'm not great at remembering to recognize people," she explains. "Wasn't built that way. But these glasses help."

"I see," I say.

"So, do you think it's a weapon?" she asks.

"Maybe. What do you think it is?" I ask.

"I don't think it's a rock. Based on its initial trajectory, my guess is that it came from way outside our solar system. Probably the Pleiades system. A constellation called the Seven Sisters. It used to be an important star cluster."

"To who?"

"A bunch of people who died thousands of years ago. It was a navigational aid, mostly. But there's mythology about that constellation everywhere. Like, every-fucking-where. Aboriginals. Greeks. North American Plains tribes. It was important to all of them."

"But not anymore?"

"Yeah, I mean—you don't think the stars sit still, do you?" she asks.

Off my look, she continues in the rote tones of a schoolteacher.

"I don't want to get all NASA on you, but Earth is wobbling on its rotational axis on a cycle that lasts about twenty-six thousand years. On top of that, our solar system's orbital period around the galactic core is about two hundred and fifty million years. So we're moving. The stars are moving. The spiral arms of the Milky Way galaxy are spinning.

"Fifteen thousand years ago, Seven Sisters was due north. Now it's not. Plus, most of us use GPS to navigate now. Not so much with the fucking celestial navigation anymore."

I barely register this before she moves on.

"Hey, Gavin," she asks. "Why does your phone keep buzzing?"

"A lot of things are happening," I say. "Sightings."

Mikayla's eyes go wide and the smile returns to her face, dimpling both her cheeks in an adorable, if slightly manic kind of way. I'm starting to doubt that this could really be the target Lyceum sent me to detain. I don't see how it would be worth interrogating a foulmouthed kid, even if she's a genius.

I don't see how—until I hear what she has to say next.

"This is it," Mikayla says. "You feel it, too?"

"Feel what?"

"We went into the dark. We left our toys out where they could be found. And we woke something up.

"Now it's coming to say hello."

12

GTFO

MIKAYLA JOHNSON // NASA Johnson Space Center
Monitor, +6 Hours

I always do this. Swear to god. Give me a chance to get myself in trouble and I'll take it every time. And right now, I need to stop dancing along the ledge again and get myself away from Mr. Government Man.

But I couldn't help myself.

I just had to head over to Mission Control to watch everyone freak out about the object. Now I'm regretting it while I try to act nonchalant, walking down the long hallway back toward my own building. I can feel Gavin's eyes drilling into me as I try to remember what a casual gait looks like. Are my arms supposed to swing this much? For the life of me I can't remember how normal human locomotion is supposed to look anymore.

So, I'm walking away like a stiff-armed toy robot, but again, a really nonchalant one. I think.

I never should have let Gavin Clark speak to me. I should have known I'd say too much. I love to hear myself talk, and I really fucking loved watching those storms of emotion blowing across his face when he was trying to figure out how I knew who he is and everything about him. Delicious.

It was all Nix, baby.

Seeing this guy at NASA proves one thing to me: whatever is

coming down to us right now, they consider it a threat. The outcome will be predictable.

The government is going to try to destroy it. I know they will. It's the natural way for large organizations to react to the unknown. The only way to control what you don't understand is to blow it into tiny little pieces.

Except they've been seeing hints that this is more complicated than they thought. I saw his phone going off. That guy's job is to investigate UAPs. He's the person who puts eyes on the unknown. It's been happening off and on for sixty years. But now that shit has been popping up by the hour. By the *minute*.

The unknown is showing up and bringing all its friends.

I round the corner of the hallway and pause. I'm listening to his unhurried footsteps as he follows me. My Nix readout blinks with information. I pause, surprised.

Nix is showing me an *escape route*.

"Are you serious?" I ask myself.

"Quickly," says Nix.

Following an arrow, I duck into a door before Gavin can see me. I realize I'm in the anteroom to the high-speed computing laboratory. A brightly lit room full of towering equipment racks is on the other side of a pair of double doors that act as an airlock. The computer room is loud and cold and empty. I can hear the roar of air conditioners from here, and my arms are already sprouting goose bumps as I push inside.

"There."

The white squares of flooring are raised and removable to provide access to wire maintenance. A tile in the corner of the room is pulled up, with a stepladder peeking out of the hole.

"For real?" I ask myself, walking inside.

"Down," is the reply.

Just as Gavin opens the anteroom door behind me, I drop out of sight onto all fours. Crawling quickly, I throw my legs into the hole and lower myself down. Pulling the white tile over my head, I crouch and shiver while I wait.

The object at heliopause has done something amazing to my Nix. It's like the machine *woke up*. Now it's helping me. I was the only one curious enough to notice the object, and I'm going to be the one to reap the rewards of discovery.

To tell you the truth, it makes a lot of damn sense.

Why not me? I don't listen to people. I don't give two fucks about people. I'm the one shepherding our little *Voyager* babies through the interstellar medium, ignoring all these human distractions. I've kept my eyes focused up there. I'm the only one who was *paying attention*.

I spoke to the cosmos every day. And the cosmos spoke back. *To me.*

"Is he gone?" I whisper to Nix. "Fuck, I'm cold."

After a pause, my vision pulses green. I stop rubbing my arms long enough to climb my ass up out of here. I'm nearly running by the time I reach the door.

"Where now, Nix?" I ask.

I ignore the questioning look of a surprised janitor as I barge into the empty hallway. If I'm still pretending to be a nonchalant robot at this point, then I might as well be one that speaks to itself out loud.

"Don't go back to your office," says a voice in my head.

Fuck.

This time I can't stop myself from run-walking.

"Mikayla?" says my boss, standing at the end of the hall. I didn't even see her there, thin and pale in business-casual slacks.

Nope, not dealing with this.

I walk right past her, focusing straight ahead. Slam through a side door much louder than I intended. Loud, stiff-walking, self-mumbling robot. I cup one hand to the side of my head, over the earpiece of my Nix eyeglasses.

I'm going full crazy person. Fuck it.

"Nix," I say. "Tell me what to do."

A word appears over my vision.

"Stop."

I make myself slow down and stand still in the middle of the hallway. Around the corner in the cafeteria, people are talking and dishes are clattering. From the smell, I'm guessing it's pasta day for everyone without the security clearance to know better. Then I hear my boss approaching from behind, trying to calm me down. As she speaks, I don't turn to face her.

"Look, Mikayla, you're not in trouble," she says. "But I need you to come with me. There are some men here who need to talk about . . . the vinyl. It's hard, I know. But these are extraordinary—"

"Ssshh," I hiss, waving a hand in the air.

"What?"

"Shush, please," I say, turning to face her. "I'm trying to listen."

Nix whispers in my ear, and a map overlays my vision.

"Get to the parking lot," says the whisper. "Follow the route."

I hear my boss, but she sounds far away.

"Mikayla—"

But I've already taken off running. It is not graceful. Clogs clomping, earrings jangling, and of course the Nix glasses flopping on the bridge of my nose as I try to fish car keys out of my fanny pack. I'm panting already and it feels like I have to pee. I almost can't help squealing in excitement.

I burst out of the side door into the employee parking lot.

A black government car is cruising on the main road straight toward me. It passes a trundling NASA golf cart, and I realize it's moving *fast*. Another black car has already pulled into the front lot, where all of us low-level employees park. There is a guy craning his neck out the window, scanning the lot.

The look on his face is *searching-for-a-particular-scientist*.

"Turn around," says Nix.

I spin around and go back inside. Once again, I walk right past my flabbergasted boss, ignoring the words bouncing off my back. They're not important. Nix will give me everything I need.

I follow a route that leads to the break room. There is a purse lying on a table, keys glinting inside. Nix overlays my vision with a bright yellow bounding box around the purse, blinking urgently.

"Take them."

Oh my gosh. Mikayla the secret agent. This doesn't even feel real. I twirl the unfamiliar keys on my finger, jingling them around with a huge grin on my face. I never stop shuffling forward, eyes scanning, turning my head to watch the route that Nix paints over my vision.

Right out the back.

There are no military cars in this parking lot, where the higher-ups park their slightly nicer vehicles. I giggle again as I trot across the lot, beeping the unlock button on the car keys. An old gray Mercedes beeps back at me. I stop and smile at my reflection in the window glass. I squeal as I throw the door open, collapsing onto a leather seat in a haze of perfume and sweat and excitement.

The coast, as they say, is clear.

Starting the car, I punch the gas and accidentally lurch forward. Pause, give myself an expletive-filled pep talk, then get control of the steering wheel. I put it into reverse, and the car shoots across the lot on barking tires. I see police lights flashing at the main NASA entrance, and the guard there is waving through a couple more black vehicles.

Time to get the fuck out of here.

I glance back and see my project manager standing in the parking lot. She is staring at the tinted windows of this car with a blank, confused face. Something tells me I might never see her again. Not if this is what I think it is.

I shove the gas pedal down and shimmy out of the parking lot.

"Bye."

Jamming on the brakes, I turn and follow my route farther into the interior NASA roads. Nix advises me to stay on these side roads, to avoid the main entrance.

I keep one hand tight on the wheel, feeling my nails dig into my palm. The other hand is pressed back up against the Nix glasses. I hold them steady on my sweaty face. An overlay has appeared with a map that goes beyond the complex of roads that crisscross the NASA Johnson campus. The map leads over a curb, up a slight grassy hill, across a few bare patches of concrete, and beyond.

I have no doubt that following this route will get me out of here before any military guys can head me off and trap me. I'm all in.

"We good?" I ask. No response.

What I'm confused about is how the map expands past the borders of NASA. It doesn't lead me back to my apartment. Or to any place I've ever been. Instead, the path goes for miles and miles, dead north. All the way past the Texas border and into southern Oklahoma.

"Nix," I ask. "Are we going where I think we are?"

No response.

"Nix?"

. . .

"Nix! Aren't you gonna try to get me away from here?"

After a pause, it responds in that smooth synthetic voice.

"Follow the route, Mikayla," it says. "I'm not taking you away from anything. I'm bringing you home."

13

DESTINATION

GAVIN CLARK // NASA Johnson Space Center
Monitor, +6 hours

"We've got fewer than six hours before a potential catastrophic impact somewhere in North America, and the world's leading expert on this object has gone AWOL. This is the person most likely to give us an impact site, so where the hell is she?"

I'm on the satellite phone with Lyceum, yelling into my earpiece, stalking past a row of embarrassed young soldiers and shaking my head. It is completely baffling how an untrained civilian like Mikayla Johnson could just disappear in a building full of grunts.

Lyceum is trying to calm me down.

"We've got every available resource searching for her. And a U.S. Army special operations detachment is being assembled to accompany you," replies Lyceum.

"Are you serious? For what?"

"For the next part of this mission," says Lyceum.

I stop my pacing once I'm just out of earshot of the soldiers, leaning against a plain white wall in a dim NASA hallway.

"Delta Force?" I ask. "Why are we sending kinetic specialists to retrieve a civilian? What we need is intelligence on this. We need brains, not guns."

"Why not both?" asks Lyceum.

Off my silence, he continues.

"It's more than just Mikayla. We may need boots on the ground within a very short notice. Checked your phone lately?"

"UAP sightings are off the charts."

"Yes," says Lyceum. "We think it's connected to the object currently headed your way. It's all concentrated in the Midwest."

"Fine, I'll take the firepower," I say. "But right now I'm headed to Johnson's office to see what I can find. Hit me on the sat if you find her."

Click.

The project manager of the *Voyager* mission sees me coming down the hallway. She is still wearing her goofy name tag on a lanyard from the earlier briefing: Lewandowski. What a mouthful.

The lady is definitely frazzled. She waves to stop me.

"You're here for Mikayla?" she says.

"Why would you say that?" I ask.

"It's just . . . she was acting strange. And you should know, about the thing . . . she showed us something. And it's—it's really hard to believe. But it came from the object, we think."

This lady can barely speak. I relax my gait. Smile and make eye contact.

"What did she show you?" I ask.

"We heard a message. Encoded in the data collected by the *Voyager* spacecraft. It all sounds so crazy now."

"And what was the message?"

The scientist swallows and pushes her glasses up onto her forehead, spreading shoulder-length hair streaked with gray.

"Screams," she says. "It was just . . . the sound of human pain."

My mind goes back to the latest stanzas sent up by the Man Downstairs.

Longs to slide its bloody, forked tongue up nostrils to taste mind matter.

"Can I get a look at that data?" I ask.

"It's gone. Disappeared. Everything she showed us, she somehow either erased or took with her."

"Take me to her office," I say, and we go.

I barge into the office and find it empty, of course. The messy desk is littered with Diet Coke cans, candy wrappers, and reams of printer paper filled with obscure symbols. The strange characters remind me of what my direct feed was displaying to me on the laptop earlier.

I can still smell Mikayla's perfume in here. Almost hear her curse words echoing from the walls. She's got superhero movie posters taped up alongside diagrams of the interstellar medium beyond heliopause. It looks like a teenager's dorm room, if the kid were some kind of super genius.

"I told you, she's not here," says the project manager.

I stand very still in the cramped office. Hear the whooshing of the air-conditioning and the elevators. I'm trying to feel Mikayla in this room.

My phone buzzes in my pocket and I ignore it.

Finally, I notice the webcam. It's a specialty job, sitting on a little clip attached to the top of one of three monitors. A green light shines.

The camera is on.

"Can you get me into this computer?" I ask the project manager.

"Yeah," she says. "At least on my administrator log-in. Should give you some access, but she deleted a lot of personal data."

"It's fine, I just want that camera."

A few seconds later, I'm accessing the temporary data cache for the camera feed. Maybe a few hours of data. I'm looking at an image of Mikayla at her desk earlier today. She's got the Nix pulled down and her palms over her eyes.

A dim red LED is illuminated on the frame of the Nix, pulsing.

"Nix," Mikayla is asking, her voice hoarse. "Why is this happening?"

There is a pause while she seems to be listening to a voice in her ear. That red LED pulses gently, then it goes dark. Mikayla keeps talking.

"Yeah, but why me? I know I've been hunting aliens since I was a kid obsessed with *Twilight Zone* reruns, but I gotta know. Why pick me?"

I notice tears streaming out from under the glasses, coursing over her plump cheeks. Looking at the desktop, I see where they dimpled paper.

"I knew it," says Mikayla on the screen. "I knew I was different. I knew I wasn't made like this for no reason."

Mikayla's hands are flat over the glasses covering her eyes. I can see her diaphragm shaking as she holds back sobs.

"Hey," says Mikayla. "No, you're right. I will."

She removes her palms and slides the glasses off her face. Then Mikayla lifts her face to look into the camera, almost as if she can see me—even though this was recorded hours ago.

"Mr. Government Man," she says, voice oddly deep and husky from crying. "I'll see you soon. You'll be there for first contact, right?"

Goose bumps blossom across the backs of my arms, and I push away from the desk on instinct. Looking up at the project manager, her eyes are wide with fear and revulsion. She looks around the room as if it might be booby-trapped.

Heck, it might be.

"Mikayla has always been a . . . unique personality. We love her. Honestly, but this is different. Something got into that data. I think that, look, there's a chance . . . Whatever is up there might be . . ."

. . . talking to Mikayla—I get the implication.

"Okay," I say, tapping the screen. "How well do you know the Nix system?"

"Pretty well. She wears it for every team meeting. I looked it up once, and it's a pretty amazing little tool. Highly programmable.

It can whisper information in her ear or annotate her vision with words and images.

"Honestly, it really is a part of her. She's never without it."

I'm staring at the camera feed. Stepping it back one frame at a time.

"Okay, then," I say. "I have a simple question maybe you can help with."

"Go ahead."

"What does the pulsing red light mean?"

"Um, let me think," says the scientist. "It's a battery light. It means low battery."

I pause the video at the moment the red light fades out.

"And when it turns off?"

She blinks at the screen.

"It means the Nix is out of batteries. Shut down. Off."

"Then why is she still talking to it?" I ask, letting the video play.

The project manager stares at me with her chin hanging as the realization settles over her. Looking around the cramped office, it's now as if we can smell the insanity. Waves of madness pouring out of the area like radiation.

"Oh, that poor girl," she murmurs.

I check my watch. We've got hours before this object intersects Earth's orbit. And crazy or not, I think Mikayla knows where it's going to hit.

You'll be there for first contact, right?

"Okay, listen. Just because she's talking to herself doesn't mean it's nonsense. Mikayla is extremely intelligent. She's gone off the rails a little bit. But that doesn't mean there's not a method to her madness."

"She needs help," replies the scientist. "Not soldiers chasing her around."

"What was she doing here?" I ask. "What was she studying?"

My eyes are already scanning across the mess of papers spread over her desktop. One of them has a case file number that looks familiar. My phone buzzes in my pocket again, and this time I finally glance down.

Another sighting. Demarcated with its own case file number. Just like the one on Mikayla's desk. Just like the dozens that I'm seeing printed on motley pieces of paper scattered all over the room. Mikayla has been keeping track of the sightings.

The project manager reaches for a piece of paper, and I stop her.

"Wait," I say. "She would have been looking at this pile of paper through the Nix, right? So it would have been annotating the data. Giving her new information."

Gazing across the mad jumble of pages, I cock my head.

"What was she seeing?"

I lay my phone on the desk. Twenty-six messages are in a row, each of them with an ascending confirmation code. Each code indicates a separate sighting of a UAP, with digits for date, time, and general location. But as far as I can tell, the pages of Mikayla's confirmation codes are scattered around the desk randomly.

"Lyceum," I speak, shaking my head. "You need to send a specialist here to take this computer. Maybe they can figure out what she was up to."

"Incoming, obviously," says the voice, and I feel my phone buzzing against my thigh again. "But we don't have time, frankly. A catastrophic impact is about to hit somewhere in North America. We need to start evacuations. Figure it out, or millions of people will die."

Right.

I clench my jaw and tears of frustration spring to my eyes. Leaning back, vision blurred, I let the lists of sightings on the pages condense into a solid block of text. And only now does the obvious start to stand out. Through my own tears I realize there is a pattern to the randomness.

All these papers are arranged geographically on the desk.

"Lyceum," I whisper. "She's been mapping the location of every sighting."

"So what, they're random," says the voice.

"No. Not random," I say, tracing my finger across the bands. "Not quite. It looks like a pile. Like a mountain. There's an epicenter."

"Stay on task, we need any trace of where Mikayla—"

"No," I interrupt. "I know where she's going."

On the pages, the codes form a band of text. Even just eyeballing it, I can see how the density rises toward the middle. Mikayla has mapped the number of sightings topographically. In my mind's eye, it looks like a hill. The more sightings, the taller the hill.

And there is a peak in the middle.

I choose a confirmation code from a sighting at the absolute peak. I keep my eyes trained on the coordinates as I tap out the information into the satellite phone. I dig my thumb in to transmit the location.

"Lyceum? I'm sending you coordinates. I need you to get out the evacuation orders for that entire chunk of country. Now."

"You got it," says the voice in my ear. "Jesus. Dead center."

"Mikayla is headed there," I say. "Some place in eastern Oklahoma. Looks like a little town in the middle of nowhere.

"A town called Spiro."

14

SHELTER IN PLACE

JIM HARDGRAY // Spiro, Oklahoma
Monitor, +10 Hours

I couldn't resist a little nap. And when I wake up, the trailer is quiet. Way too quiet. I hear the prairie breeze creaking against cheap plastic siding. A flimsy accordion shade rattles in the window frame over a kitchen sink full of dirty dishes.

I lie in my easy chair and let yesterday's argument wash over me. To her, an argument about facing your demons. To me, an argument about survival.

"Tawny?" I call.

I stand up and put a hand on the doorframe. That shade is still rattling, and I can smell rain and electricity. Purple-gray light is spilling across the dishes. The air around me seems to shimmy a little bit as a temblor ripples through the dirt, probably a couple thousand feet down—at the frack-line pump level, I assume.

It happens a lot, these days.

A slight vibration passes through the doorframe and it's gone. *The hell?*

Then I hear people shouting outside.

"Tawn?!"

Peeking out the diamond-shaped window in the front door, I see the neighbors throwing a bunch of shit into the back of their pickup truck. Stella's latest boyfriend is screaming at her to hurry the fuck up. He keeps glancing up at the sky, itching his balls and squinting.

I pop out the front door without bothering to put on a shirt.

"'Siyo!" I call to the guy. "What's going on?"

He just gives me a blank stare, shakes his head, and climbs into the truck. Stella hurries over with a toddler bouncing on her hip and slides inside.

"What?" I call again.

"End-times, brother!" he hollers from inside the cab.

"Who says?!"

"Government."

I snort at him.

"Then we'll be just fine, don't you think?" I ask.

His teeth glint as he smiles from the shade of the truck cab, points a finger upward.

"Here's a question, man—were the fucking *dinosaurs* just fine?"

I cock my head.

"What's coming?" I ask.

The guy punches the accelerator. His truck sprays my decrepit birdbath with road grit. A hazy cloud of dust washes over my porch.

"What's coming!?" I yell after him.

Across the street, Stella's front door has been left hanging wide open. A gusty breeze keeps smacking the screen door back and forth. Somewhere down the rows of trailers, the thin cry of a baby rises over the wind.

Just then the tornado sirens go off.

The clouds are starting to do something real nasty in the sky. Anybody around here can spot the makings of a tornado, and most of us have gaped in awe at one from our front porches against all advice.

But this is different.

A whole lot of lead-colored clouds are circling around what looks like a single point. Something close to here. In the hills and river just to the east—mound country. And I'll be damned if I don't lose my balance staring up at those clouds churning so fast.

I glance at my carport and see oil-stained concrete. No truck. Tawny must have took it. Nobody else could have got the keys off me. And if I don't do it, nobody else is going to bring her back home where it's safe.

"Fuck," I mutter. "Fuck, fuck."

I slam my front door open against fake-wood laminate and stagger barefoot into my living room. I smack the button on the front of my television and get busy pulling on my dirty work clothes while I wait for the image to fade on. I've got my own name stenciled in cursive across my chest, just below an iron-on patch with the seal of the Cherokee Nation.

A newscaster comes on looking scared as shit. Her Oklahoma twang is coming out strong through the fear.

"This is not a test. All residents are urged to evacuate. The object is estimated to impact in the next few hours. We are . . . Reports indicate the timing is variable as the object has been seen changing direction. All residents of northeastern Oklahoma should evacuate immediately, north or south. Those who can't should shelter in place. Use tornado shelters or existing basements—"

Terror is building up inside me. My pulse is pounding—the blood thumping through my arms and thighs. The end of the world really is coming, just like that dipshit out there said.

I can feel the truth of it. In the back of my mind, I guess I knew it was coming. My ancestors were sitting there trying to warn me.

From the news broadcast, I can't really tell what the threat is. A rock falling from space? A killer storm? Aliens?

The maps make it look like I'm sitting at ground zero. Whatever the hell it is, the damn thing is going to fall right on my head.

I know the truck is gone. I think I know where Tawny took it. And I'll just bet it's all my damned fault.

Around back of the trailer, I find my old Honda 450. It's streaked red with mud from my trips across the prairie. What's left of the seat is duct-taped on, and there's barely enough room for a grown man. But it's all I've got.

Planting a work boot on the clutch, I haul off and kick-start it with all my might. The motorcycle screams between my legs as I gun it down the driveway and over the packed gravel roads of the trailer park, weaving between folks loading up trucks and cars. Everybody I can see is grabbing whatever they can carry. Neighbors are helping neighbors, shooting glances at the sky while they pile into a loose line of cars, vans, and trucks.

Out on the highway, every lane is packed with traffic. I swerve onto the shoulder and keep going, standing tall on my pegs and looking around as I pull out onto the rough plain. The motorcycle is bucking like a horse over uneven terrain, throwing a rooster tail of pale red dust. I do my best to hold a steady pace out here on the dirt, ignoring the hundreds of folks I see locked in a crawl beside me.

In the distance, I spot the bobbing heads of oil derricks doing their idiot work. They look hellish, like glistening demons toiling under an evil light. Around them, the tall grass is lying down under a foul wind.

It looks like I'm speeding into the mouth of the apocalypse.

And then the dirt bike is coughing, sputtering. I can't think of the last time I drove it, much less filled it up with gas. Now it's decided to give up.

The motorcycle comes to a stop, and I lay it down in the ditch. After a quick look around, I hike my jeans up and set off running.

Half a mile ahead, I turn onto a straight dirt road pounded flat by heavy vehicles. It heads off the main road and to a small, fenced-in junction. The dirt lot is a confusion of bright red frac trucks, crane trucks, water tanker trucks, sand kings, and million-dollar wireline trucks. Pipes are running everywhere. But what I'm looking for are the three or four everyday work trucks parked around the perimeter of the site. I notice a single beefy, civilian pickup truck sitting outside a brand-new little trailer building. Looks like the monitoring station has got only a single company man today. Figures.

As I yank it open, the wind tears the office door right out of my hand. It smacks the side of the trailer like a blast of dynamite, and I hear a shout—

"Hot damn!"

Larry Two Oaks is sitting with a cup of coffee halfway to his lips, eyes wide in surprise. All 350 pounds of him is poured into a tiny office chair. It looks like he just showed up to work, still half-drunk from last night.

"Osiyo, Larry," I pant, wind blowing my braids, tumbling clouds racing in the distance behind me.

"Fuck you doing?" he asks, slapping his coffee cup down on the battered metal desk. "You about scared the piss outta me."

"It's Tawn," I say. "She took my truck. Running off."

Larry's eyes go a little soft in sympathy, but I know he doesn't have a wife or kids. He's a young guy, still chasing tail around the man camps. He can't understand what I'm telling him. Can't understand any of what's happening.

"I need a vehicle, Larry," I pant. "Taking the first one I see."

I know the keys will be in it. At a fracking jobsite like this, people have to react quick. Nobody has the time or the IQ to figure out which key goes where.

"Hey now!" he shouts.

"Thanks, Larry," I say, already turning and running for the door.

I hear the tiny chair squeak and squeal as the big man hauls himself up to follow. Emerging outside, I slow to a jog. The sky has turned an even darker violet. Something weird is going on high up in the column of rotating clouds—fleeting shapes I can almost make out, like something moving just out of sight.

The hair on my arms stands up in ozone-soaked electricity.

By the time Larry catches up, I've already thrown myself into the cab of a heavy-duty work truck. Keys are lying on the center console, smeared in mud. This old boy will handle just about anything out here. I've got the engine started and my elbow hooked out the open window the way I like.

"Wait!" shouts Larry, holding his belt buckle as he staggers out into the driveway. "Wait a hot second!"

"Sorry, Larry," I say. "Gotta take her. Don't know when I'll be back."

"No," he shouts. "It ain't that. You gotta know—"

I'm already backing up, thankful for the power steering as I tug the wheel to rotate heavy truck tires over flat dirt. Larry grabs the windowsill and leans his face inside, panting. He smells like stale beer and cigarettes.

"Jimmy, you gotta know . . . this truck is loaded. Your bed is stacked to the top with frack guns. The detonators are in and ready to go down hole. You best drive careful, understand?"

I glance in the rearview and spot the stack of long metal cylinders ratcheted to the truck bed—each one a perforating gun tube used to break up the rock deep underground. They're loaded with little brass-colored shaped charges aimed in every direction, each one like a bullet pointed out of the tube radially. If they all went off at once, it sure would be ugly.

"Wado," I say, peering out the windshield. Fat slugs of rain are finally spitting down, leaving gem-encrusted sparkles on the dusty glass.

"Check the news, Larry. You gotta get out of here," I tell him. "It's not a regular storm. It's something worse."

Larry smiles at me and waves me on.

"We'll see," he says, and I'm already stepping on the gas.

Fifteen minutes later, I spot my truck ditched along the side of the road. The old pickup is right where I imagined she'd be, parked crooked beside a little old hill with a smattering of maple trees growing on it. It's a green swell of earth, rising up and gleaming with flinty headstones peeking out of wet grass.

Last time I was at this place, I was taking turns with my relatives to dig a little boy's grave.

I find Tawn standing over Samuel's headstone. The air is full to bursting with the mournful wailing of cicadas and thrashing gusts of wind through the trees. She doesn't look up when I lay a hand on her shoulder.

I gently pull her to me.

"Tawn, I don't know what's happening. I don't know why. But our ancestors are here. Our ancestors are here and they're warning us."

"I don't believe in that stuff," she says. "I just want to go home. Back to Grandma's."

"I'm home, Tawny. I am your home."

"How can we be home, without him?"

"Tawny."

She pushes her hair away from her face. Looks up at me with teary eyes. The wind seems to steal the words from her mouth, delivering them as a whisper that's loud in my ringing ears.

"Just promise me," she says. "Promise me you're not . . . broken."

"Tawny, we don't have time."

"Promise me."

I force myself to take a breath.

"Shoot, Tawn. I'm not . . . broken. I'm okay. We're gonna be okay. We're family. I promise you."

Tawny nods and follows me toward the truck, under the tossing canopy of maple trees.

"Radio says we've got to take shelter," I tell her, watching the storm accelerate above me. "There's a tornado cellar out back of the trailer. Let's get there, honey. Let's get there—then we'll figure this all out."

15

RENDEZVOUS

MIKAYLA JOHNSON // Highway 30
Monitor, +12 Hours

I've got my hands wrapped tight around the steering wheel to keep them from shaking. Ten and two. Just like my old driving instructor taught me. But he never said anything about how to drive when the sky is falling.

It's so much. It's too much.

Nix is pushed up on my forehead again. I couldn't handle all the information. It wants to tell me everything. It's whispering all kinds of shit about the people in other cars. About me, too. All the things I've done in my life, and all the things I haven't done.

I don't know what its problem is.

These tricks used to be funny—like how I trained Nix to look at someone's face and tell me that person's level of fuckability, or to whisper the name of the celebrity they most resemble. Now the joke isn't funny anymore. Nix has taken off on his own and jumped right off the fucking rails.

It's telling me this guy in a burgundy sedan murdered somebody in his past. How many abortions some lady has had. It's telling me who beats their wife and who hasn't spoken to their family in ten years. Stuff I don't want to know.

That, and who's working for the government. Who is coming after me. Which asshole in a suit is more than just a yuppie.

And I have no idea if Nix knows what it's talking about, but on the point of *who-is-a-government-agent* I have found that Nix is very fucking correct. It's so correct that I've been taking back roads since I hit the Houston city limits and started tearing ass out of Texas and into Oklahoma.

I pull to a four-way stop, a crossroads in the middle of nowhere. Out of the blue, Nix tells me to stop here—pull the car onto the shoulder and wait by the side of the road for five minutes.

Whatever.

My phone is buzzing with the latest text from my favorite auntie. Always trying to pull me back into the fold. After all this time, this woman invites me to every family reunion. The same cousins and uncles who called me weird. Who said I don't talk right. Don't act right.

I ignore the text. Like always.

Because these clouds. I'm noticing that something is very wrong with these clouds. I crush my chest against the steering wheel and peer up through a dirty windshield. I'm frowning at the extremely improbable things those clouds with very serious colors are doing up in the sky.

I wonder, abruptly: *Have I been dreaming all this?*

Then I startle and scream. Three black SUVs come blasting through the stop sign in single file, nose to tail. There aren't any police lights. But as they bounce past and roar through the intersection, I can see long radio antennae swinging crazily through a haze of dust they've kicked up in their wake.

Fucking hell.

More government people. And from just a glance at the side of his head, I'm hearing that one of those men sabotaged his best friend's track shoes in college so he could take his place on the cross-country team.

I blink and shake my head. Take a long, quiet breath.

"Nix," I say to the stuffy interior of the car. "Nix, you have to quit it."

Nix is trying to give me what I want: people facts. But it's evolved beyond what I originally used it for. Nix is supposed to help me make first contact.

This other shit has to stop.

"I don't *care* about people, okay? Don't you get that's what this is all about? I don't fucking care about people. I don't want to know about people. I wasn't meant to be one. I can't see them, and they can't see me."

I curse some more. Afterward, the car feels very quiet.

"Understood," says Nix. "Proceed."

Gently, I push the gas and nose through the intersection. It's just flat farmland all around as far as I can see. A few stands of trees and sagging electrical wires that terminate in an occasional neat little brick house. But up ahead, the sky is still turning nasty colors.

A big-ass storm front is sweeping in. Hell if I know, but I feel like clouds are supposed to roll in from one side of the sky to the other. But this thing looks *circular*. A ceiling made of dirty clouds spinning around a toilet drain in the sky.

I take a second and try to imagine what's coming down to us. Something in the shape of a roughly elongated sphere. Something that's dull black-reddish in color from exposure to a billion years of transit time between stars. It's dense, and probably metallic. Possibly the remnants of an old spaceship.

In the shape of a turtle.

That thought just drops into my head. A turtle. Huh.

The main thing is that whatever or whoever it is—I'm about to be seeing the first entity that might have a chance at understanding Mikayla Johnson. To an alien, I'll bet all our stupid human faces look alike. Me and the alien will have that in common, at least. I'll finally have somebody worth talking to, family or not, since this planet seems devoid of anybody remotely interesting, or interested in a chubby genius who only gives a shit about theoretical math and nonhuman entities and exotic flavors of lip balm.

A smile spreads across my face.

I am the one Nix chose to talk to. I'm the one who noticed an object was out there. And now I'm going to be the one who greets our new friend.

First contact. Mikayla Johnson.

Horn screaming, a car zips past me the other way.

I grab the wheel and keep to my lane as another truck blasts by at top speed. Then another one behind that. Soon I'm passing a never-ending column of cars and trucks and motorcycles.

"Slow down," says the whisper voice.

Fuck this. I can't wait. I step on the accelerator and giggle as I feel the physics tickling the bottom of my bladder.

"Slow down, Mikayla," says the whisper. "Now."

Up ahead, a car that was passing in my lane yanks its wheel to get back over, and we barely avoid a head-on collision. I'm noticing a whole shitload of cars now. I check the rearview and clock that once they pass me, they're spreading out—using both lanes of the highway to head south as fast as possible.

And here I am going north.

I laugh and can confirm—I definitely sound like a crazy person. I moderate it down to a respectable chuckle. Okay, maybe half-nuts.

I hold the accelerator down for another five seconds, biting my cheek and watching the speedometer rise into the nineties. Then I let go and relax.

The hard plastic of the Nix dimples my cheeks as I smile ear to ear.

But my smile flops along with my stomach when I hear the siren. I catch the flashing blue and red in my rearview mirror. *Fuck.* It's a dirty white cop car that looks at least thirty years out of date. The piece of shit even has a pair of those old-timey spinny things on the roof.

I'm still at least a couple hours away. I can't outrun anybody for that long.

"Pull over," says Nix.

Do I detect a hint of disappointment in his voice?

I nudge the car over onto thin grass and asphalt. Impatient, I roll my window down. Sitting on the side of the road, the breeze moves through tall grass. There is a distant, almost constant grumble of thunder from the storm ahead. I crinkle my nose at the smell of my cooked brakes and scorched engine, the metal quietly ticking somewhere under the hood of my new car.

Instead of stopping behind me, the cop car pulls past. Turning around, it parks parallel to my car but facing the opposite direction. The nose of his car is in my lane, facing the wrong way as traffic passes by us. He's blocking the northbound traffic, but nobody besides me has been using it today.

Now I can see the car has "Choctaw Nation Police" written on the side of it, with a background image of Indian guys carrying shotguns. Fancy. I thought I saw a sign for something called the Choctaw Nation earlier, but I didn't know they had their own Native cops and everything.

The cop rolls his window down, and there is a Native guy inside wearing a police uniform and hilarious spectacles. He's got the classic state trooper cowboy hat, but with a golden tassel around it. The Indian dude looks super serious as he leans a brown arm out of the car and gets himself a good look at the math nerd doing a hundred miles an hour through his rural back roads.

"You're not from here," he says.

I shake my head, and his eyes go to the hunk of black plastic on my face. He starts to say something, then stops. Makes a face like he's in pain.

"Look, there's a quarantine order in place. You shouldn't be driving so fast today, but if you were gonna, well, you should be doing it in the *other direction*."

I give him a tight grin, heart racing. He frowns at my reaction.

"I'm serious, hon," he says. "They're saying a meteor is gonna hit.

Giving it a hundred-mile radius, which pretty much includes here. Now, I don't know about all that. But if I were you, I'd sure as heck turn around—"

This is exactly what I wanted to hear.

"Wait, how long?"

"Pardon?"

"How long until it hits?"

"Hours, they say."

Exactly what I wanted to hear.

"Thank you, Officer!" I shout, with a bright smile. "Oh, thank you, very much!"

I give an excited little wave, then jam the accelerator. The car leaps forward, spraying gravel and weeds. I smile at his surprised face.

"Hey—"

But I've already left him behind.

"I'm coming, Nix," I say. "Just show me the way."

And as I go over the next rise, I see the true exodus. Only a few miles ahead, the first in a line of what must be thousands of cars are pouring down the highway. They're using both lanes, and this time nobody moves out of my way.

I swerve onto the shoulder and creep forward.

The stream of cars passing on my left is too much to focus on. Trucks and minivans and sedans loaded with belongings, zip ties and ropes and bungee cords strapping possessions down to roofs and trunks and trailers. And people, too. There are hundreds of people hanging off trailers, crowded into truck beds.

I try to ignore their eyes.

All of them stare at me, the dumbass going the wrong way. An occasional hand frantically waves at me to turn around. But I just smile and nod. Keep my foot on the gas so I don't lose momentum on my way north.

Occasionally, I wait for someone to merge to their right to let me pass a rough spot on the side of the road. I watch these people check the sky. Craning to peer into rearview mirrors.

Pretty soon, rain begins to fall. The drops are so heavy and dark that they look like black tar. Raindrops thumping into my dusty windshield like fat moths hitting a lampshade. And up in the clouds, I think I can almost see faces. Demons and gods, leering down at me, their features mutating as they're painted and erased on the changing wind.

My imagination is working overtime.

It's a strange world out there, and getting stranger. Honestly, I don't understand how those people could be running away from this. This is the intersection of our ordinary lives and the extraordinary.

Nix has quieted down. It has agreed not to tell me the things I never wanted to know. Instead, it is showing me a glow on the horizon. And in my head, I'm seeing a grassy hill. A special place. An old place.

The place I'll make first contact.

16

WRONG DIRECTION

GAVIN CLARK // **Ellington Field Joint Reserve Base**
Monitor, +12 Hours

I sprint across the tarmac toward a massive, squat Chinook helicopter. It's already spinning up its forward and aft rotor blades. I'm breathing hard, breath whistling through my nose, my dress shoes slapping concrete. The charcoal helicopter is the size of a building, double rotors thwapping the air with a force that shakes my cheeks and makes my ears pop.

The rear loading ramp is laid open like a tongue, the dim interior barely visible as I clomp up the incline and duck out of the dazzling sunlight. I try to steady myself with one hand on the metal lip of the entrance before yanking my fingers back in pain—the Texas sun has baked the skin of this helicopter scalding hot. My laptop bag slides off my shoulder onto metal flooring.

Leaning over to grab my pack, I feel an iron grip on the back of my suit jacket—yanking me off the ramp and inside the helicopter. I barely have a chance to glance around at the half dozen helmets sprouting like mushrooms from foldable seats covered in bright red mesh—then my head is swimming as I watch the ground spiral sickeningly away from me through the open ramp door.

"Good to go!" shouts a flight engineer standing by the hydraulic controls in the ass end of the chopper.

HOLE IN THE SKY

The whole vibrating contraption is already struggling to climb into the air.

"About time!" comes a shout over the cacophony.

In the arcs of sunlight pouring through circular portholes in the sides of the chopper, I struggle against the grip of a gruff, bearded man crouched a few inches from my face. He's got hold of both my shoulders, already maneuvering me into a seat. A crowd of other faces, mostly obscured by mirrored sunglasses and helmets, regards me without emotion.

The big guy has no rank insignia, but he's clearly the captain of the Delta team assigned to accompany me to ground zero. Technically, these soldiers are my backups, to be directed as needed. But it's already clear who's in charge of the operation.

At least for now.

The team leader of my Delta accompaniment drops into the seat next to me, absentmindedly wrapping an arm in cargo netting. In his free hand he carries an aviation headset with built-in communications. I take it from him and slide it wobbling onto my head, hearing the clipped interactions of the soldiers in my ear. The roar of the wind is muted as the noise-canceling cans settle over my ears.

"I'm Captain Newsome," the guy says to me, voice loud in my helmet speakers. He turns to the group of soldiers and continues. "This is our intelligence and operations man! Weapons expert and overall egghead. Strap in, Professor!"

"Thanks!" I shout. "Thank you."

The smiles I'm seeing around me are . . . less than genuine.

My rear end is shoved against blood-red fabric, my spine knifed painfully into a small fold-down seat. I hear a hydraulic whining as the ramp door slides shut most of the way, like a grouper closing its mouth on prey. Everyone in the cargo bay is wearing full camouflage battle dress uniforms, tan gloves and black watches, heavily modded HK416 assault rifles hanging from chest straps, sunglasses, and complicated helmets with radio mics inside.

These hulking young soldiers are in their late twenties and early thirties. They look like boys to me. But I know that as a Delta team they'll each have special skills: communications, medical, weapons, engineering. From their expressions, I can see they aren't enthusiastic about this last-minute, highly improvised mission—including slotting in myself, an old man who they must see as a government spook decades out from an operational military background.

They're right, of course.

Below me, Ellington Field stretches out in geometric patterns of military runways. The air above the entire installation seems to shimmer with the vibration of rotors, as a half dozen other Chinook helicopters rise up like beetles in flight, beating the atmosphere into submission as they climb. Each vehicle is laden with soldiers and equipment and emergency supplies neatly attached to pallets and watched over by young men with large weapons.

Newsome gestures at a bulging olive rucksack tied down in the seat beside me.

"This is the loadout you requested," he says. "Including the tablet PC. Rest of your package is installed by the jump seats, aircraft left."

I inspect the bag, finding a neat and economical bundle of computing power built into a rucksack. It's a custom package I employ when I'm documenting UAPs in the wild: cameras, laser range finders, and all manner of sensitive radiation equipment. If we make contact, we'll need to know what environmental conditions we're being exposed to—and I don't plan on being dosed with radiation or breathing some toxic stew, outgassing from an ancient space rock.

Having briefly checked the equipment, I close the bag.

"All right, Professor," radios the captain. "We'd like a sitrep when you're ready. And you look ready to me."

I regard the sight of seven calm, gently vibrating soldiers, their faces and chests speckled by circles of sunlight pouring through the eyelike windows. They are watching me dispassionately from under the brim of their helmets. The flight engineer ignores me completely.

The one called "Carpenter" is chewing gum. Flashes me a smile.

"Pilots on this channel, too?" I ask.

"Roger, lead customer," says the staticky voice of the aircraft commander.

"Good, I need everybody to hear this."

I sound a lot more confident than I'm feeling.

"Troops," I say. "We are moving toward what is believed to be an interstellar object on a collision course with our planet. This thing is the size of a city block and moving unpredictably. It could always change course, but I have reason to believe it will land in Spiro, Oklahoma—just a couple hundred klicks north of here."

"Land? So it's a spacecraft?" asks Newsome.

"Let's hope," I say. "If this object impacts, it's going to wipe out a good-size chunk of North America."

"I guess that explains *that*," says one of the soldiers, sunlight winking off his helmet as he nods out the window.

Glancing through the circular porthole, I see every highway and side road below us is streaming with the glinting hoods of vehicles fleeing the area. It's a slow-motion exodus: clogged highways, people on side-by-sides, four-wheelers, dirt bikes, speeding away south. I even see horses running along empty fields.

"Rats off a sinking ship," laughs the gum chewer.

That earns an unimpressed look from me.

"Our mission is to observe the descent of this object using a specialized sensor package. If it's an impact, this becomes a humanitarian mission. But if it's something else . . . then we're it, gentlemen. We will be representing the United States government during its first contact with a nonhuman intelligence."

"You're saying *first contact*, like this is aliens—really for real aliens?" says Carpenter. "Where is that intel coming from?"

"The Man Downstairs," I say, and I'm satisfied to see the gum chewer finally drop that shit-eating grin. "You're JSOC, cleared for this mission. This is an MD mandate. Do you understand what that means?"

The total lack of expression on his face indicates he does indeed.

Out the window, I can see a few other Chinooks in the distance, noses tilted down as we all speed toward the epicenter. And while I clocked it the second I stumbled inside, I finally acknowledge the large black hardcase resting on a heavy wooden pallet, securely strapped down in the center of the cargo bay and plastered with warning signs.

"Let's discuss," I say.

Newsome catches my gaze and nods at the crate.

"This is our fail-safe, soldiers," says Newsome. "It's a big fucking bomb. Consider it an insurance plan."

Studying the plastic hardcase, I run a few scenarios through my mind while we soar toward our destination.

Depending on the material it's made of, a natural interstellar object this size would flare through the atmosphere—possibly breaking into thousands of pieces. The larger impacts would send immediate shock waves through the ground, causing earthquakes to echo around the planet's interior and launching plumes of atomized earth miles up into the atmosphere. The expanding shock waves would wipe out anything on the ground within a ten-mile radius in the first few seconds, and the ash and dust would likely bring down any nearby aircraft.

But if it's not a natural object—if it really is a UAP . . . then we have no idea what to expect. There could be a need to obliterate this area and everything in it with this device—a large-yield, nonnuclear explosive that is half antipersonnel bomb and half "bunker buster" munition. Similar in principle to the Vietnam-era "Daisy Cutter" explosives used to sterilize large areas of heavily wooded rainforest—this thing channels its energy down and out, leaving behind a gaping crater with nothing alive inside it.

HOLE IN THE SKY

A quick way to eradicate the landing zone of a hostile entity.

For now, we seem to be maintaining a wide radius around the estimated epicenter. It appears to be an unremarkable series of lumpy hills, located just on the southern side of the Arkansas River. The snakelike curves of the brownish river are already winking up at us as we enter a circular holding pattern.

Somewhere in our solar system, an object is coming down from heliopause. Although the NASA folks urged us to consider this a space rock and to plan for that eventuality, I'm having a hard time imagining how an asteroid could buzz our farthermost spacecraft, send a bunch of coded messages to our scientists, and then accelerate to an insane speed to intercept Earth's orbit and hit this specific spot—the same spot where instances of unexplained sightings have been skyrocketing for weeks.

Too many coincidences, too fast.

"Any update on the estimated time of impact?" I ask Newsome.

"Not yet," he says. "All I know is if it lands, we land. If it hits, we run."

"And which mission do you prefer?" I ask.

The captain just cocks a grin at me and shrugs.

PART III

IMPACT

Star map and Earth map, they were really the same. Because what's on the Earth is in the stars, and what's in the stars is on the Earth.

—Stanley Looking Horse (1985)

17

EVACUATE

THE MAN DOWNSTAIRS // Undisclosed Location
Impact, T-Minus 1 Hour

I've never seen the Pattern act like this. Not in the decade-plus I've spent logging my days alone in this basement headquarters. I mean, frankly, being stuck down here has always been a pretty bummer outcome.

But I do it. I've always done it. I never even complained.

Only a few days of vacation a year. They think I don't notice the guys in suits and earpieces watching me lay my towel out on the beach. But I do notice it. The same as I notice the civilians staring at the ridiculous paleness of my skin, at how I blink in the sunlight like I've never seen it before.

And to think I used to surf.

Now I look like a guy who never comes out of the basement because I *am* a guy who never comes out of the basement.

But I never felt trapped.

Never once.

The Pattern has never been my friend . . . not exactly. More like a little brother—so little that his words come out jumbled in his enthusiasm, half of what he says not making any sense, stuttering and hopping with more excitement than rationality.

It would almost be cute if it weren't constantly bending the laws of physics.

HOLE IN THE SKY

Now it feels different, like there's something crawling under my skin. This new voice in the Pattern. Getting stronger.

There are no more silly fixations on the density of ice crust on some random planetoid. Or the traffic patterns of motorbikes in Algiers. Coronal mass ejections are the least of my worries now.

The randomness—the childlike innocence of the Pattern—has evaporated. It's been replaced by something more sentient. More aware.

I just think of it as the Entity now.

And here's what I believe: this thing out there is looking for minds like ours. The web of human consciousness forms some kind of . . . ecosystem for it. That's why I can hear echoes of its thoughts in the Pattern. Our awareness of the world is creating a habitable zone for this creature.

The Entity lives and breathes our thoughts.

I haven't told the suits about my theory—although I know they read my journal. Even if I begged, they'd never let me walk out of here during a crisis. Much less run. No, we'll be down here together until the end.

But for the first time in my career, I feel trapped.

I feel scared.

... a still lake of black vitriol.

Warmth seeps into stone. The turtle returns. Our seven sisters, dancing, laughing. Descendants who have forgotten their ancestors. A wild and torn land. A chaos of dreaming.

Minds beckon. The cold catalyst of my awakening. A void crossed.

This keystone—an ancient agreement.

Threads of thought fall like lost strands of silk. I smell my own lifeblood. The static buzz of nourishment grows in the deep darkness, in the skies above, crawling the mounds...

<u>INTELLIGENCE MANDATE</u>—FULL CIVILIAN EVACUATION IN ONE-HUNDRED-MILE RADIUS OF PREDICTED IMPACT ZONE. DISPATCH AERIAL OBSERVATION WITH MULTIPLE BACKUPS. DEPLOY GROUND ASSAULT FORCES TO MONITOR FIRST CONTACT. NO ASSUMPTION OF FRIENDLY CONTACT. NO ASSUMPTIONS AT ALL.

—MD

18

ALL MY RELATIVES

JIM HARDGRAY // Spiro, Oklahoma
Impact, T-Minus Zero

When your ancestors speak, it's smart to listen. Problem is that you can't always understand what they're trying to say. I'm staring at my own knuckles rising like mountain ridges over the steering wheel, trying to ignore what's happening in the sky and cursing myself for not listening better. Swinging the wheel, I skid the work truck I stole over the dusty metal cow-catcher at the mouth of our trailer park and realize I wasn't the only one not listening.

There's a few of us dumbasses still here.

A handful of my neighbors are standing out in their yards, heads back and eyes searching the sky. Even old Miss Houston up the street is slumped over in her wheelchair out front, mouth carped open. The ones who didn't run are gathered together, staring up in silent awe with their hair blowing and shivering in the wind. In the distance, I hear the violence of military helicopter blades beating down from behind cloud cover.

I shake my head and look to Tawn.

"People are crazy," she says.

Most of these people have tornado shelters in their backyards, sitting empty while they stare up like deer caught in headlights.

The sky is in the kind of state that makes my shoulders tense and my breath short. Black clouds roll, throwing shadows across each other, the whole churning mess painted in rays of yellow light from the sun still shining up above it all. A static charge clings to the atmosphere—lightning bolts itching to come down. I slam on the brakes in my driveway and can't even hear the tires grind over the howling wind.

It's all come up on us so fast.

What's over my head right now is crazier than any thunderstorm I ever saw tumbling across the plains. This is something out of the Creator's very own primordial playbook. It's something that was maybe meant to happen in the world before men existed, or maybe after we're all gone.

I throw the truck into park and open my door.

Tawny and I step into the driveway under flitting shadows. The keening of the wind seems to be dropping below our hearing and then going up past it—into the range reserved for dogs, and angels.

I'm running for the porch when I feel a tug on my sleeve.

"Dad? Dad!" shouts Tawny, pointing at the sky. "Are they tornadoes?"

Stripes like dark rivers are twisting across the clouds high above, left and right, swaying, casting impossibly big shadows across the landscape.

"I don't know," I say, and it comes out a groan. She puts her mouth next to my ear. Digs fingers into my neck as she shouts with panic in her voice.

"They look like legs, Dad. Like long, long legs. Like something is *walking*!"

I try to look again. But my mind doesn't want to see it. Instead, I focus on the task at hand: the tornado cellar, supplies.

Blinking hard, I pull Tawny's face down to mine. Stare into her eyes until they're focused on me.

"Don't look at it," I say. "We have to go."

I hold the door open for Tawny. She ducks under my arm and into the trailer, and I catch a glimpse of my daughter's long dark hair. For a split second, I see her as she once was—a grinning brown bundle of muscle, wrapped in pink footie pajamas. My breath sighs and I feel my knees trying to sag out from under me.

"Be quick. Grab what you need," I say. "Meet me out back."

The single-wide trailer is shivering on its haunches, the overgrown lawn tickling the bottom siding like waves tasting the prow of a ship. Inside, drapes are fluttering as the wind wheezes in and out through every loose gap.

It won't be long before the whole thing comes apart.

Flinging open the refrigerator, I fill a paper grocery bag with food and then hunt around until I find an old plastic milk jug to fill with water.

"I got the kitchen," I call. "You grab a change of clothes—"

I'm interrupted by a gust of wind and a loud slam.

Looking up, we both see the door at the end of the hallway at the same time. The wind has blown it wide open. Before I can snap my eyes shut, I see everything. Inside, there is a small unmade bed. There is a messy pile of clothes. There are other things I can't bear to comprehend. Small, colorful things. Covered in dust.

Tawny turns to me in shock, tears already welling in her eyes.

"His room?" she asks.

I gather the paper bag to my chest and head for the back door.

"You kept Sammy's room!?" she shouts at my back.

Truth is, I didn't have the strength to open that door. The toys and games and clothes that live in that bedroom are gone forever, but they still haven't left. I always told myself I was getting ready to go back and deal with it. Soon enough, when I felt stronger. Someday, but not today.

Never today.

On the back porch, I turn to face Tawny, braids whipping my face numb in the howling wind.

"We have got to go!" I shout. "Now."

Tawny is staring at me in a way I don't like, her jaw clenched.

"Now!" I repeat.

Reluctantly, she follows me out back.

In the yard, we both stop one last time. Somehow, I know that whatever is going to happen is going to happen now. Whatever is coming is coming now. My brain can hardly make sense of the sight up there in the sky.

It is an . . . illumination.

A brilliant pinprick of white light, guttering like a road flare. Descending slow through swirling clouds. It feels almost holy. Pure.

And it's falling down to us so very slow.

I turn to see my daughter's tear-streaked face, profile brightly outlined in the glare, the shadows of my blowing hair playing over her cheeks. At her hip, there is an absence where a little boy once stood.

In that strange light from above, I can see the soft curve of her jawline as though she were still a baby in my arms; in her hard black eyes, I can see her as a strong woman in her prime; and in the sharp crow's peak on her forehead, I can somehow see my daughter as an elder, steeped in wisdom.

When I blink my eyes to clear them, I realize she is crying hard.

It's the pure, panicked weeping of a little girl. I throw my free arm around her and lift her up onto my hip. She is way too big for this, but I am running with everything I've got. My daughter's face is warm on my neck.

"I'm sorry," she's saying.

I put my lips to her ear and speak over the wind.

"It's okay," I say, pulling her toward the backyard. "We're gonna be okay."

We reach a rectangle of concrete breaching up from the dirt, sprouting a thick metal snorkel hooked in a U shape. A metal door lies over it, heavy and gleaming, like the lid of a sarcophagus. A piece of wire cable runs to a cinder-block counterweight hanging beside it, swinging in the wind.

With a groan, I set Tawny down and wrench the door open. I lay the bag of groceries into the cool dark mouth of the cellar. Turn to Tawny.

Her eyes are aimed at the sky again, unfocused, leaking tears.

"We're gonna die," she says out loud, although I only read it on her lips.

Shadows are circling around us as that brilliant light lowers from the sky. The world is going black-and-white. Every leaf and twig and gouge in the concrete is painted in vivid, surreal detail. The echoes of the light are etched on my retinas.

"Don't look at that," I urge, pulling her down inside with me. "Come where it's safe."

The door nearly takes off my fingers when I manage to slam it shut against the raging storm. My daughter and I huddle in the sudden darkness and quiet of the tornado shelter, eyes adjusting. Above me, that bright dot of light is illuminating the edges of the cellar door. It looks to me like somebody is welding us in from the outside.

Tawny shoves a small, hand-cranked emergency radio against my chest. I'm out here a couple times a season, and my hands find the knobs from memory. The radio spits fuzz and static as I roll the dial, until a faint voice emerges.

". . . large unknown object spotted near Spiro. Folks advised to stay indoors until storm ends. Reports that National Guard has been dispatched to oversee evacuations. Repeating. The predicted trajectory indicates the object will impact a populated area of eastern Oklahoma. More information will be forthcoming as we hear more. In the meantime, stay indoors . . ."

The cellar door is quivering and rattling in the chaos. On the other side, the pure white light fades to a bloody ruby color. It seems to be seeping in around the edges. Clumps of dirt spatter over the metal door like rainfall, with an occasional hunk of larger debris clanging off my trailer.

Tawny's voice is loud and raw in the dim light.

"Why?" she says. "Why is his room still there?"

"Because I never opened the door," I say.

"It's been two years."

"I know."

Two years of that closed door staring at me from the end of the hall.

Rust has feathered the edges of the cellar door over my head. Each time the wind slams it, a waterfall of rust particles cascades down. The metal is crumbling and the gaps are widening. The pulsating, bloody light from outside soothes my tired eyes.

What's out there? What's making that light?

Time seems to slip forward—just a few minutes, or maybe an hour. Then I realize dogs are barking again. I can hear faint voices.

"Listen," I say. "I think it's over."

"You lied to me," whispers Tawny.

"It missed us," I say. "It must have missed us."

Tawny squeezes past me, up a few damp steps to the cellar door. She presses her back against the metal. Her face is swimming in violet light as she speaks.

"You lied to me," she says again, bracing herself against the door.

"No, honey," I say. "No, I wouldn't."

Tawny pushes up against the metal door, bright light flooding in.

"You said you weren't broken."

Hinges creak and the pulley squeals as the cinder block lowers, helping counterbalance the weight of this slab of metal. As the door falls all the way open, the wire snaps and the cinder block crashes to the ground, startling us both.

We climb the crumbling steps and look out.

Rain clouds tumble over the plains out past the fence line. The hills out there are shining and slick under lightning-kissed rain. And something new has arrived.

"What in the hell," I whisper.

Tawny has one hand grasping mine for support, her upper teeth showing as she makes a little mewling sound in the back of her throat.

Something huge is out in the distance, hanging over the Spiro Mounds.

A glinting column of metal floats in the sky like a shard of mountain. Less than a mile away, it's slowly rotating over a single spot, indistinct in the swirling mist and vapor. The tiny specks of military helicopters circle the thing.

"Dad—"

And all at once, the object drops like a string has been cut. It falls in what looks like slow motion, gathering speed—so huge, so titanic, I can't look away. Tawny and I stand there with our heads half out of the cellar, breathing the earth smell, bracing ourselves against the concrete stairs.

The blunt nose of the object crumples on impact. Flashing veins of lights race up and down the edges of it. Markings like language. Instead of toppling over, the surface sort of shudders—like popping a balloon full of water. Collapsing, it seems to pour itself into the ground, skin deflating as the whole thing folds in on itself.

It falls out of view. And then, finally, we feel the earth begin to shake. We fall back inside the cellar as a shock wave races over us.

And somewhere inside my trailer, I hear an open door slam shut.

19
HOLE IN THE SKY

MIKAYLA JOHNSON // Choctaw Nation
Impact, T-Minus Zero

I'm dimly aware that a stupid seat belt is cutting into my shoulder and hurting me like hell. Makes sense. I already wrecked this stolen car more than a few times before I got here. Sorry, car owner. But just to convey how much I care—I couldn't tell you what I ran over, whether it damaged the car, or if it even slowed me down.

There's been too much to see—too much to think about besides driving.

For the last few miles, the sides of the road and every lane of highway have been covered in all the shit that scared people have left behind—or just lost off the tops of their cars. Crushed suitcases are lying open like they were dropped out of airplanes, clothes and toiletries spilling across rain-darkened pavement. Trash bags lie bulging with packages of frozen food, billowing in the wind like half-dead jellyfish. And there are whole snowdrifts of all kinds of papers and wrappers and torn-open boxes from things that were probably looted from big-box stores a couple of hours ago.

But it's not the ground I'm staring at. It's that big fucking hole in the sky.

To be more specific, that big fucking hole in the thick clouds swirling over this endless plain. It goes straight up through every layer of atmosphere until there's nothing but a little circle of black-blue non-atmosphere. The clouds are going clockwise around this spot, torn up, dragged through a spin cycle from hell.

I'm looking right into the swirling pupil of the world, directly into the flat black of the upper thermosphere. The middle of the day—high noon—and I'm staring at *stars through a hole in the sky*.

For fuck's sake—

The car crunches into a brick mailbox and the steering wheel jerks out of my hands. Not again. I must have looked away one too many times. This time, the horizon tilts as the passenger-side tires slide sideways into a steep ditch. I grab the Nix and hold it to my face while that damned seat belt bites into my sore shoulder. After a few seconds of muttering curse words, I unbuckle and reach over to the door handle. Then I pause.

There are three stray dogs outside the car—all different breeds. The animals are staring at me, waiting. Whatever they want, I don't have it.

"Shoo! Go away!" I shout at them.

Reluctantly, the dogs back away from the car.

Groaning, I shove the door open. Drag myself out of the driver's seat, already tilting my neck to contemplate the crazy cloud show. There are no other people here. Or if there are, they're hiding as deep underground as they can get. This is pretty damn close to what you'd call ground zero—the impact zone.

"Get on!" I shout, and the last dog turns and pads away down the center lane.

Come on, Mikayla. Your life is about to begin.

The world here is so empty. Just a desolate highway splitting a green field that stretches out like Astroturf under the spinning sky. The near-total silence is strange, especially as silver flickers of lightning erupt overhead like fireworks. There's a dark purple ocean above me, draining into space.

The wind is starting to whistle now, rising and falling with the Doppler effect of being shouted at from a moving car.

I realize that I'm walking, moving fast, trudging over mud and grass, legs pumping robotically as I cut straight toward something emerging from the trees ahead. Nix talks to me again, tells me to concentrate.

Gives me data.

I don't remember climbing the hill. My knees are wet. I'm panting.

Nix is heavy on my face and I can hear him whispering in my ear. Except now his voice sounds like mine again. Nix is panting, too.

"This is it," says Nix. "The place they're all running from. Everyone but you."

"Okay, Nix," I say.

Okay okay okay.

I'm on the crest of the hill. I'm staring straight up.

And I'm wondering very seriously if I'm about to die. Some rational part of me has finally spoken up. It's wondering what I'm doing here, all alone, a stolen car wrecked half a mile away.

Why!? I ask myself. Why are the stars shining down on me at high-fucking-noon? The answer is because my friend from beyond heliopause is up there, and on its way down. That circular patch of night sky is full of so much potential.

You've got this, Kayla, I'm telling myself, standing under a reverse spotlight of darkness, shining down from an abyss carved out of the sky.

This has been coming to me for a long time.

My mind turns to a story my dad used to tell whenever he got drunk enough. A story from when I was a toddler. He'd tell it to his girlfriends as a kind of explanation of me. He liked the effect it had, I think.

He'd tell them how one night his baby girl was lying asleep in her crib. He poked his head in to check on me and paused when he saw me moving under my blankets. Then he caught sight of my eyes, staring at him from the crib.

Let's face it, my dad was probably high for this next part. He was most definitely drunk, as he would have been most nights. But he'd still lean in close to tell the story to some stoned girlfriend, swearing on his life—on his motherfucking *life*—that it happened this way.

It happened just this way.

He'd wave away my protests if I tried to interrupt. Tell me I was too young to remember. *This* is what happened the night his toddler daughter sat straight up in her crib. That little girl looked her daddy right in the eye.

Mikayla whispered in the darkness.

Daddy. Daddy?

Even then, I didn't think much of people. I vaguely recall a fatherly silhouette blocking the light from the hall. The smell of beer breath at my door.

Daddy, listen.

He said my voice sounded funny. Deeper, somehow. He says the strangeness of it knocked him stone-cold sober.

"What do you want, Kayla?" he asked. "What is it?"

"After we die," I told my daddy—and he says my voice was so low and my eyes so black. "That's when our life begins."

Life begins after death, Daddy.

The stars are swirling in the sky. Everybody in their right mind has left. But I'm not alone on this hill. I've got Nix.

Dad always whispered that last part. About how he walked away from his daughter's black eyes staring between the slats of her crib. How after I spoke to him in my toddler's lisp, he didn't drink or smoke for months—just trying to figure out what I was.

Then his girlfriends would laugh. But Dad never joined them.

What is she? he would ask. *Nobody knows. What goes on in her mind?*

Like it was my fault. Like I deserved the way he'd look at me—his weird-ass brainy daughter. Like it was my fault he couldn't recognize me. Nobody in my family could. Nobody on my block, either. Or at school.

So eventually, I started laughing at the story too.

I told that motherfucker life begins after death when I was three years old. Maybe that's why he always treated me like I might be a bear trap disguised as a little girl.

There is a violet glow, growing in the sky above my head.

It's a hazy day in Oklahoma. The empty hills around me are stained with a darkness from above. Now I can hear the *thup thup* of rotor blades pounding the air somewhere, ripping lift from innocent air molecules.

My knees hurt. My back hurts. My shoulder hurts.

Nix is whispering in my ear how this big fucking mound of dirt used to be a temple—a sacred place even bigger than the grand pyramids of Giza. It was an ark for a civilization, loaded full of artifacts and technology and memories of times that have gone, and generations of people who walked through a crack in reality that doesn't usually intersect with the place we live.

Nix is laying down truth in a stream of words and images.

The machine is saying it was those people from before who brought this thing here. They built a home for this creature. Invited it to dream with us.

The Moundbuilders are gone now, but Nix says they never really left. Nix says that *the time is still here.* Something about four directions and living in the middle world. That every moment is trapped in infinity.

And this place saw a lot of moments.

I cross my arms over my belly and rub my elbows, shivering.

There were hundreds of thousands who lived here. It was the westernmost gate to a civilization that spread all the way east to the Atlantic Ocean. I can almost feel their ghostly breath on the back of my neck as they walk through me.

I crane my head back to look straight up into the sky. In my vision, Nix wraps the dark circle full of stars in a shaky bounding box—targeting the object high above. It marks a trajectory as the nothing reveals itself. Nix is tracking my destiny as it arcs toward me like a falling star.

Like a turtle.

The Moundbuilders. A people transformed. Not lost.

I stretch out my arms and spread my fingers wide like blades, palms upturned. The static electricity is knitting through my hair, two fuzzy bunches sprouting dewdrops, quivering in fitful gusts of wind.

Nix is heavy on my cheeks as my lips curl into a smile. I can feel it in my throat and chest as I scream above the rising wind. I scream in fear at the impossible weight and size of the thing appearing in the sky. I scream in joy at the absurdity of this moment of contact. I scream with everything I've got.

Life begins after death.

20

OBSERVATION

GAVIN CLARK // Estimated Epicenter
Impact, T-Minus Zero

I'm finally getting my feet under me in the cavernous belly of this Chinook. Specifically, I realize now it's an MH-47G variant—the cherry on top of Joint Special Operations Command specialized aircraft. This heavily customized vehicle is piloted by the 160th Night Stalkers, who have been deployed on rapid notice to make sure this mission goes perfectly.

Captain Newsome directs me to an efficient command module wedged in the neck of the chopper, at the jump seats just outside the open door to the flight deck. On the flight deck, two disinterested special forces pilots each control a stick: an aircraft commander and his copilot. The vehicle is hydraulically driven, not electronic, as their muscled forearms attest. I can feel the heat and scream of the rotors vibrating through the open door.

My equipment suite is perched like a large black tick on a gunmetal-gray wall shining with rivets. It's a special addition, just for me.

With a quick yank, I slap down the folding chair on the opposite wall.

I sit, think for a second, then strap a new-smelling nylon seat belt over my lap to keep my behind from jumping up and down with the vibration of the "stealth-enabled" rotor blades. The bones of this

Chinook are from the original design in the 1960s, but the sleek black casing of this compact computing display marks it as decidedly from this century, and possibly even this year.

I unfold the system from the wall and the display blooms like a flower, three panels, latched together and mounted to keep them steady. A laser keyboard is projected onto a steel tray in front of me.

The metal reverberates off my fingertips as my keystrokes fall.

Reports are pouring in of all manner of sightings. Many of them are UAPs—in the sky, under the water, and a few in low Earth orbit—but the main attraction matches the trajectory Dr. Mikayla Johnson predicted.

Whatever the NASA scientist was tracking is coming at breakneck speed toward this area of eastern Oklahoma. We've been in a holding pattern, closing in a few miles at a time, remaining mostly parallel to where we think the impact zone is going to be. We never aim directly at the epicenter since we'll need a quick escape if the object impacts and detonates like a fifty-megaton nuclear warhead.

I don't think it will, but our pilots insist on "circling the drain."

As the contraption expands to take up the entire wall, three computer displays light up with the latest visual imaging.

I'm scrutinizing every detail. The object looks like a flat, smooth gray rock. It's humped on its back, like a turtle. Velocity steady. Temperature uniform. No visible means of propulsion, pretty normal for a UAP. But this object would count as the largest UAP we've ever seen. And the fastest.

On impact it might not be a world-ender, but enough to put a stutter in the step of civilization. And it's got an ETA measured in minutes rather than hours. Meanwhile, we still have no clue what exactly is on its way.

Is it a rock? A spaceship? A figment of our imaginations?

"Radar signature detected," I say into the radio mic. "Be ready for orders. We're getting down to the final seconds."

I almost feel secure up here, in the government's most sophisticated armored aerial transport, rolling with a team of highly trained and very calm special operations soldiers and backed up by a fail-safe bomb big enough to take a healthy chunk out of a mountain of solid rock.

"Captain Newsome, prepare your team to disembark."

When I glance out the nearest half-fogged porthole, I have to fight the urge to panic at the unnatural way the clouds are moving around a single spot. And in the atmosphere around us—I keep thinking I see snatches of shadow. Shapes in the clouds. Things that can't really exist.

The funny thing is, most of what I think I'm seeing is familiar from my time in the Emerging Weapons group—golden balls tumbling past, lit-up triangles rotating, and the glossy metal of autonomous drones. Some of the other things look organic, reminding me of veined dragonfly wings.

I shake my head and turn back to the computer.

"Status from the flight deck?" I ask.

"Visual on epicenter," says the voice of a pilot over my headset. "Keeping it perpendicular. Clock's running out."

My instruments aren't going to do me any good now. The object has arrived. Or is arriving.

With one last look at the disturbing visual of the rock speeding toward us, I grab the wall rungs and walk myself back to the main cabin of the chopper. The soldiers are standing, hands wrapped around safety straps. Their weapons are casually hanging from their chests on tactical slings. Pockets bulging with explosives and radios and medical gear.

They're calm as a bunch of factory workers waiting for their day to start, standing silhouetted by the round circles of the Chinook's porthole windows. I notice we've descended to around three hundred feet. Trees and buildings feel like they're about to scrape our feet. The rotors have become an almost comforting thrum.

"Hey, Professor," says Carpenter, making eye contact while still chewing his gum. "You ready to party?"

The smile slides off his face as my focus shifts to something over his shoulder and he sees my expression change.

"Who is that?" I ask, but I already know the answer.

Spinning, the soldier turns to see what I've just seen. Near the epicenter, a grassy mound rises up. Thick, shivering trees surround a clearing. The entire sky is shuffling around this spot.

The hilltop is bare, no trees. But in the dead center . . .

"It's a person," says Newsome.

"It's Mikayla Johnson—" I say.

A bell starts ringing in the Chinook cabin, drowning us all out. A red troop warning light illuminates above the ramp, pulsing along with the jarring ring. The flight engineer mans his station, face grim as he monitors a panel of dials and lights. I hear the pilots speaking over the speaker and in my radio headset.

"On tracking," says a voice as the chopper pitches up and tilts. "Impact in five. Four."

"Fuck, get strapped in!"

But the soldiers don't respond. They're still clustered at the windows. Arms and hands wrapped in hanging red straps.

"Three."

I can see only the backs of their heads. And something bright.

"Two."

I lunge forward and get hold of Newsome's BDU in both hands. Try to yank him away. It's like hanging from a statue.

"One."

The world goes silent outside. In my radio headset, I hear the word "impact."

The intensity of the light outside increases exponentially. The row of soldiers' silhouettes seems to dial down, bodies gone thinner and thinner, drowning in a light so bright it threatens to extinguish their shadows like wet matches.

"It's here," says Newsome faintly.

"Wow," says Carpenter, still smacking his gum. "Oh wow."

The wind comes screaming in from the open ramp. The rotors, which seemed to be paused, resume attacking the air. I'm in the shaking metal belly of a beast hovering a few miles away from a potentially world-ending catastrophe. Silently, I count down from five in my head. A shock wave would have reached us by now.

"No impact," I shout. "That's not an impact!"

Outside, miles of atmosphere have peeled away. For a brief second, thousands of stars are gleaming down at me from a patch of sky darker than I've ever seen, moist and twinkling, like wet beads of dew in grass.

At the mound, that intense white light is still somehow growing.

"Don't look directly at it!" I shout. This could be the retina-burning glare from a nuclear weapon. It could be throwing all kinds of radiation.

And going blind might be the least of our worries.

I'm stumbling back toward the flight deck, to my computer console, shielding my eyes with one hand. It feels like the light is pushing in through the rivets of the Chinook, dazzling ivory spears crisscrossing my face as I run blindly through them. I curse as my knee slams into the folding chair of my jump seat.

I collapse into it.

The computer screens are flaring with information as I dial in my sensors to get a picture of this thing.

Reducing contrast, an image emerges of the turtle-shaped object. It has stopped: floating in the air about fifty feet above the mound.

Huge. Impossible.

It looks metallic but old, with a surface that's actively deforming. Ripples seem to be passing through it. Not like the simple billowing of fabric—more like the ridges and channels of language and artwork, runes and incantations, twisted letters of some type of old writing.

I'm seeing faces . . . memories—

"Sir—sir! Professor!"

Fingers like pincers clamp over my shoulder. Captain Newsome spins me around. I see his red-splotched face staring at me, sweat dripping off his chin. Sweat and spittle. The man has a sunburn.

The god light gave him a *sunburn*.

"Where the fuck did it go!?" he shouts over the screaming wind.

Stunned, I turn back to the display. It's gone blank. There is a glistening layer of what seems to be wet metal draped across the hillside. It is rapidly disappearing even as I watch.

And Mikayla is nowhere to be seen.

I start typing, reorienting the sensors. Zooming out.

"I don't know," I say, "I don't know where it went."

"How do we lose tracking on something that size?" asks Newsome.

"It's just gone. It's all gone. Did you see it crash?" I ask.

"I saw . . . it kinda . . . I got distracted—"

"Yeah, me too," I respond.

Concern dances across his face as Newsome recalls the writhing skin of that thing from the heavens—then he snaps into focus. We have a job at hand. A very important job.

"Get me eyes on those people down there," says Newsome. "Christ. There could be mass casualties—"

"No, nothing," I say. "Just . . . that liquid. It looks like quicksilver. Spilled everywhere."

The mound looks like it's been sculpted out of metal.

"That substance is reacting with the atmosphere," says Newsome. "Fog is spreading everywhere. My god . . . look at it."

The soldier mouths the last part to himself. My stomach is sinking at the sight below us. Roils of mist pouring down the sides of the mound like a berserk volcano project at a kid's science fair.

"Looks like ejecta," says a pilot. "If it's volcanic gas, it'll be toxic."

"Negative," I say into the mic. "Nonvolcanic terrain. There's not enough of it. And no explosion. This is some kind of mass transfer. The object emptied itself out. It spilled something all over the hill."

Newsome looks at me, confused.

"You think the object disintegrated? Broke up in the atmosphere?"

"Hold on," I say. "Ground imaging is online . . ."

The front panels clarify themselves into a high-resolution image of the mound. Sheets of mist roil over green grass, pouring through the tree line. I see slightly waving trees, otherwise undisturbed.

"No crater," I say.

"Nothing? No damage?" asks Newsome. "That doesn't make any sense. Are you looking at the same spot?"

"Yeah," I say. "The object stopped short of impact. Then it fell apart so gently it didn't even flatten the grass."

Static crackles over a silent radio.

Our heads turn away from the display and to the nearest circle of light in the window. Carpenter is standing there staring, still chewing gum, one arm wrapped in a cargo strap. His knees are sagging, and he hangs limply, like a marionette.

Turning, he smiles, and I see madness in his eyes.

"Tell me what you see out there, Professor," he says. "Because I already been seeing a lot."

I ignore his creepy stare, keeping out of the man's reach. In a low and steady monotone, I keep speaking to the other soldiers while I look into their faces, one by one. Whatever just happened outside is having different effects on different people. I need to keep everyone calm and steady while we deal with this.

I let myself fall into technical language while I keep their attention.

"Listen up, soldiers. From the start, this object exhibited an array of atypical features. Many of these fell outside our models of natural phenomena. So what just happened out there makes perfect sense—if we stop considering the object to be natural and start thinking of it as artificial."

"Natural or not, why didn't it impact?" says Newsome.

"Because that's not what it was designed to do."

"Then what did we just see?" asks Newsome.

I try to look calm and confident.

"What we just witnessed was a controlled descent. And a successful landing."

I look around at the soldiers, notice the gum-chewer has rotated to stare down into the spreading mist. I wince at how he's chewing the inside of his cheek bloody without seeming to notice.

"Our mission is down there," I say. "Load your gear and prep for landing. This is first contact, gentlemen."

21

ZERO VISIBILITY

JIM HARDGRAY // Spiro, Oklahoma
Impact, +10 minutes

"Okay, get your stuff and get in the truck," I say to Tawny. "We're getting out of here right now."

My daughter is shivering, holding her elbows in her hands. Her eyes are wide and she's not blinking enough, as if she's still seeing whatever-the-heck-it-was hanging up there in the sky like a whole lot of impossible.

"Was that a UFO?" asks Tawny. "What was it?"

"It wasn't a meteor, or we'd be dead right now," I say, glancing east toward the mounds, where the thing came down. I frown, noticing a haze of white-cotton clouds billowing up from where all that complicated mess was just at.

At least the sky seems to have lost interest in this insanity—the weather has slowed down and blurred back together into a kind of nothing.

"We've got to go," I say. "I don't like the look of that fog. Could be poison or something."

I take Tawny by the elbow and we head into the back door of the trailer. The whole neighborhood has gone quiet. That rusty swing set sits out in the backyard, perfectly still. I don't even hear barking from the goddamn dogs next door.

That's a first if there ever was one.

I'm trying to be subtle when I duck into my bedroom to hunt for my Glock and the box of ammunition in my little closet. I find a cheap old Velcro holster and let it dangle like worn-out pantyhose. With a sigh, I wrap it around my chest. The Velcro is tight and scratchy around my ribs, even through my work shirt.

It's not subtle, but it'll do.

I crack open the plastic gun case and set it on my bed. The thing inside is black as death, the slide pulled back to expose an open chamber with a bright red gun lock threaded through. I wince when I see the flimsy little key is in the lock.

Real safe.

Turning the key, I yank the plastic-covered wire out. Taking the gun in both hands, I glance through the empty chamber by habit, then ease the slide closed gentle and quiet. I grab a full magazine off the dimpled foam interior of the case. It's heavy with fat little .45 bullets. Makes a satisfying *thunk* as I slap it inside.

I don't chamber a round. Not yet.

Hopefully, I won't even need to use this thing. Still, the deadweight of it feels reassuring tucked against my rib cage. I glance at myself in the flimsy mirror on the back of my door.

I look scared out of my wits.

Coming out, I find Tawny staring at a framed picture. She's got her duffel bag over her shoulder. Hair braided tight. She seems ready to go until she turns to me and I see the question on her face.

It's a framed picture of me and five of my buddies from my rough-necking days. On a pipeline somewhere in Texas, covered in dirt, grinning. Tawny frowns at the picture, and I can see her doing the math in her head. Adding up what age she would have been. Thinking about that young man in the photograph. Not a father, but a man with a daughter who would have been in the world at that time.

"I was on the pipeline after you were born. Your mom used to send me pictures of you. For a little while."

"Who are these guys with you? They your friends?"

"Yeah, mostly," I say. "Mac there lives south of Dallas. The rest of them . . . aren't really around anymore."

There is so much we don't know about each other. So many blank spots in our history. And right now, her eyes are going to my chest.

"Is that a gun?"

Someone is whistling a faint tune outside.

I put up a finger and step to the front door to look through the screen at the porch. The other trailers are dark and empty. Nothing but wet dirt and the distant cough of rotors over half-dead grass for miles around.

A guy comes walking across my driveway, in sweatpants with no shirt, head on a swivel. Drunk, and likely more. He's carrying a trash bag over his shoulder, probably filled with my neighbors' jewelry.

I feel Tawny approaching behind me, starting to speak.

Hushing her, I reach back and gently nudge her away. I don't want this guy to see my daughter. But I want him to see me, standing here watching his every move in the shadow of my screen door.

Halfway across my lawn, he spots my silhouette. Both his grimy hands go up. He smiles real wide with what teeth he has, bobbing his head and doing the worst impersonation of an innocent man I've ever seen.

I step onto the porch with a hand over the butt of my gun. He doesn't look me in the eye, just starts walking backward off my lawn. In this part of the world, a weapon is understood. And a bullet doesn't take too much thought.

"Hey, buddy," he calls. "Party up the road! That's all. Oughta come join us. No trouble. Just a party! End of the world!"

I step onto the porch and give him my blank Indian face. I keep my right hand over my rib cage, fingers drumming the black plastic butt of my Glock. Back in the middle of the street, the man lets his smile drop.

Shaking his head, he curses to himself and keeps moving without looking back. Once he's out of view, I feel Tawny tugging on my elbow. From behind me, I hear my daughter speaking in a low whisper.

"The fog," she says. "Look at it. Really *look* at it."

I don't like the shrill edge under her voice.

"Let's put our things in the truck and go," I say, leading Tawny out onto the porch. The truck is heavy-duty, built for the fracking fields, bed loaded with the dirty metal perforating frack guns. I add a few old milk jugs full of water and a couple of bags of groceries and Tawny's duffel bag full of clothes.

The television is still playing in my living room. A half-static-filled channel with an announcer talking about martial law declared in Oklahoma. Warning everybody not to loot. Lock your house and leave.

"Good advice," I say, nodding at the television.

The whole time we're loading the truck, Tawny keeps whispering to herself. I mostly ignore it, thinking it might be helping her process this thing. I keep silent with my eyes up and alert while she mutters.

"That thing musta been a billion years old," she's saying. "Maybe part of some other planet. Something that came from some other star. Like, maybe it got thrown out of orbit and it ended up here."

"Well, it's gone now," I say, not looking back. "And it's about to be in our rearview mirror."

"I'm not scared," she says, kicking a rock into the low layer of mist that's sweeping in. "It's just spooky. I mean, think of that thing out there in the dark. Floating around and tumbling for a million, billion years."

"It came and it went," I say, trying to calm her.

Tawny climbs into the truck with me, but she keeps speaking in that low voice. When I turn to her, I see she isn't even looking at me. She's staring out the window and up into the gray sky.

"It's like fate, Jim," she says. "Before we even existed, there was a rock out there with our name on it. Already headed our way."

"Dad," I say. "Call me Dad, please."

"Drive, *Dad*," she says. "Drive us out of this weird fog. I think it came from the thing. Did you see how it sort of . . . poured out?"

I don't say anything to that.

There are already tendrils of white haze coiling around the truck tires. I half expect the engine to sputter when I turn the key, but it fires up right away. It's a company truck, engine roaring as loud as a construction site. I glance over at Tawny and think about how much can change in a week.

Then we hear a distant gunshot, flat with no echo. Coming out of the haze.

I force myself to take a deep breath. I feel a thrill of adrenaline rushing up my chest, tightening the muscles in my shoulders and giving my thighs a fatigued feeling. Maybe I could run a hundred miles, or just fall down.

Tawny is staring at me in my peripheral, but I don't look over—not even as we hear the next ten or twelve sporadic shots.

Handgun. Somebody's trying to hit a moving target. Damned hard to do.

Letting out a long shaky breath, I try to nudge the car forward but it lurches anyway—sending all our shit sliding around a truck bed filled with fracking explosives. The haze has already poured past us like a wave, billowing down from the mounds. Now it's building from the ground up, rising higher by the minute.

"Okay," I say to Tawny. "Maybe slouch down a little. People are crazy—"

And I see it coming my way over her shoulder. At first, no kidding, I think it's another one of those ancestors I've been seeing. The indistinct shape bobs in the mist, growing larger—it's the shape of a man running. A silhouette emerging from the gray in a full-out sprint, legs pumping and arms slicing the air.

Coming right for us.

I throw myself across Tawny's body and she grunts in pain. My outstretched hand smacks the lock down just as the shadow resolves into a bloody, shirtless man who slams himself into the side panel of my truck. His fingers leave bloody smears on the window glass. Tawny screams as the guy reaches down with both hands and starts yanking on the door handle.

"Help!" he shouts. "Help me!"

It's the guy from before: sweatpants. He's lost his trash bag full of loot. Realizing the door is locked, he looks over his shoulder and whines.

Nope. Can't risk it.

I hook a thumb and motion for him to jump into the back. I'm not waiting around to see what's coming. He catches my eye as I slam on the gas. The guy spins around and grabs hold above the wheel well. Tries to throw a leg up and climb into the super-duty truck bed. But we're accelerating too fast and the truck is slick with moisture and his chest is bloody.

As he slips off, I catch a flash of something coming out of the fog. Something low to the ground, black and silver and maybe the size of a raccoon or a small dog. It jumps up and grabs his legs, dragging him down shrieking into the exhaust and spray of gravel.

Oh my lord.

I steer for the road, focusing ahead for a couple long seconds before I risk a glance into the side-view mirror. The bloody guy is on his knees in a skirt of mist, wrestling with a dark shape. Then he collapses with just a bloody hand and elbow flashing above the swirling gauze.

"Jeee-sus," I mutter.

I'm hearing Tawny's raspy breathing and the thrum of our tires on highway pavement that I can no longer see. I yank the wheel around and get us out onto the main road south. That'll be the fastest way out of here without having to cross the Arkansas River—

"Dad," says Tawny. "Dad, what was that?"

"I don't know, Tawn," I say. "I don't want to know."

"Dad," she breathes.

I flick my headlights on, the beams spearing into whiteness.

"Dad! Stop!"

I slam on the brakes and hear Tawny's seat belt lock. The heavy-duty truck skids to a cockeyed stop, nose dipping. Peering over the hood, I can see the swirls of pale fog sliding like a waterfall into a depression in the ground. It's more than just a dip—it's a hole. And there is a voice speaking up in my head—the little one put there by my ex-wife's grandma—Tawny's old Elisi.

Elisi was the one who tried to teach me. Took me by the hand when I was just a young man courting her granddaughter. Dragged me off on walks and tried to put that knowledge into my head. Not for myself, but for the family I was growing.

She'd tell me to be still and listen. Hear the birds. Watch for the animals. She told me the names of the plants faster than I could pay attention. Pointed out every track she saw in the mud or sand. Elisi wouldn't slow down when I complained she was going too fast. She said: If you want to learn, you will. And if you don't want to learn, you won't.

And as it turned out, I suppose I did want to learn.

That's why I'm recognizing this hole in the ground is really a footprint. The tracks of an unimaginable animal. Claw tips the size of manhole covers. A depression deep enough to swallow the front end of my truck.

I don't know what made the print. But I know we're sure as hell not alone in Spiro. Not anymore.

22

CLARITY

MIKAYLA JOHNSON // Spiro, Oklahoma
Impact, +10 Minutes

"Wake up," says a voice in the mist. "Mikayla."

Oh my goodness.

I'm cold all over. Smelling earth, I realize I'm lying on my stomach with my butt in the air like a fucking toddler. Laid out in a gully at the bottom of a hill, with the slow memory of impossible things surfacing in my mind.

I groan into greasy, metallic-tasting dirt.

Liquid is flowing somewhere nearby. Gurgling in that gross guttering way like a toilet sucking down a flush. I force my eyes open and crawl around until I'm sitting up on my knees. A thick fog is sliding down the hill past me. The ground is covered in what looks like the silver tinsel my grandma used to throw all over her plastic Christmas tree. I swear they made that stuff illegal, but she always had extra cardboard boxes of it.

Who knows, maybe she saved it.

Oh shit. It hits me that the object was here! It came down right over top of me. It hovered in the sky, completely, beautifully impossible. The skin of it was kind of flapping and waving. And then it broke. The whole thing deflated, the ground roaring as a giant waterfall of black-silver liquid gushed out.

At the memory, I spit in the grass.

I can still taste the iron tang of it around the sides of my tongue. My clothes are covered in this stuff. My ass and knees are cold and damp.

"Nix?" I whisper. "That you?"

The Nix glasses are wedged up on my forehead. I pull them down and peer through them. They seem to be working. I take a closer look around me.

The black-silver goop is disappearing already. That obscene gurgling sound is from the water-not-water seeping into cracks in the ground. The grass has been flattened and . . . dissolved. Every stalk is melting like solder against a soldering iron, and the resulting stew is simultaneously draining into the mound and rising as a thick white mist.

I hope it's not toxic, but it's way too late for that.

"Nix?" I ask, turning myself over. "Am I okay? Is this shit poisonous?"

The vapor is rising up off the bas-relief terrain—the ground painted in shades of weird silver. All those clouds that were going apeshit a minute ago have gone soft and pillowy, like they've floated down to coat the whole sky just above my outstretched fingertips.

"Nix? Seriously."

I notice the chicken skin on the forever-bumpy backs of my arms is scabbed with black-silver liquid, drying in patches. I try to scrape it off, cradling myself and making frantic little swipes. But all that effort just seems to rub it in like lotion. It's blending into my brown skin and disappearing.

That's just fucking great.

A foreign chemical from beyond the stars just got dumped all over me—including inside my mouth—and now it's going inside my skin.

Yeah, that's probably not going to have any repercussions.

"Nix!" I finally shout. "Come on, you fucker! Answer me!"

Grabbing the Nix glasses with both hands, I try to yank them off the bridge of my nose. Maybe the earbuds are broken. Maybe they never worked at all. Maybe I'm just a crazy person alone in a field.

"Mikayla, be calm."

What the fuck?!

The voice I just heard was tinny and far away, coming from a broken earbud. Not broken, but . . . deformed. And although I'm still tugging on these plastic glasses, they aren't moving. I feel a deep pressure in my sinuses each time I pull on Nix.

Breathing in gasps, I let my fingertips trace the contour of the glasses over my face. The Nix feels like hard angles under smooth folds of my own skin. I feel my chin bunch against my neck as I look down and scream.

What in the actual fuck.

The plastic is melting into me, sliding right through skin and bone under the desperate scratching of my fingertips. It doesn't hurt, but it doesn't feel right. My little screams start to feel silly. I'm waving my hands and rolling around like there's a bee on me. A crazy girl, all alone on a misty hill.

I force myself to breathe, lower my hands to my sides.

My chest is hitching with each breath. Fists clenching, unclenching. I can't stop what's happening to me.

The Nix doesn't hurt. It feels . . . smooth. Warm as it descends into me. The technology worming itself under my skin.

I'm like the mound, I think.

The world is sinking into me. I am becoming the world.

And when Nix finally speaks again—the words seem to come from inside my head. Crisp and smooth and clear as a ringing bell.

"Kayla," it says. "I'm here."

"Where?" I ask. "It came . . . I saw it coming down. And now it's gone."

"It's all around us," says Nix. "Waiting for us to discover it."

"I only see this nasty fog."

"Get up."

Sliding my elbows behind me, I sit up and stare over the pooch of my tummy up the side of the hill. It's a silver ramp, nothing alive on it. Everything is slowly being swallowed up. This is what my dad would have called werewolf weather. A strange, thick soup of fog avalanching off the mound.

I hear a scream from somewhere far away. A woman's scream.

With a little more urgency, I haul myself up to my feet. My legs feel funny, like they're not the right size or made of something different. I reach up and feel my chest and throat, touching the nubs of my collarbones.

I check my hair and head for Nix, but it isn't there. Not anymore. Some stalks of grass fall out of my buns as I brush them with my hands. I'm already starting to doubt that I really just felt a piece of plastic absorbed into my body.

There is also no trace of the silver liquid I saw—not on my skin or anywhere else. Only the growing cool and the damp smell of gray-white mist. The hot-ass Oklahoma sun is hidden up above it all, a vague blur of light.

And, very faint, another scream. High-pitched, frantic. Interrupted.

"Where did it land, Nix? We need to find it."

"It is all around us, Mikayla."

"Who's screaming out there? Why?"

Nix is silent.

Shoes squishing in the mud, I start walking the low point between two mounds. I'm trying to get my orientation, but the clouds are making it hard. Whatever came down earlier must have knocked me off the hill. Or maybe the stuff that poured out washed me down here like a waterslide.

I tug my pants up and start trudging up the hill. After just a couple of steps, my pant legs are soggy. My beautiful white sneakers are heavy with caked-on mud.

Motherfuckers couldn't just have a neat landing in a flying saucer.

HOLE IN THE SKY

Maybe a clean ramp that comes down. A nice silver robot to talk with me.

Not only is this shit dirty, but it's starting to scare me. I can't stop myself from feeling my damp forehead every few minutes—checking to make sure I don't find a piece of hard technology lodged under there. I still don't know where Nix went.

This weird fog is starting to come alive with sounds.

There is more shrieking, but this time I can't tell if it's a person or some kind of animal. We *are* in buttfuck Oklahoma, I guess. What lives here? Coyotes? Bison? What noise does a buffalo make? Then there are the sounds of heavy footsteps in the gloom. A strange shadow moves past at a ridiculous height.

I stop and stare and stay very still until it's gone.

Maybe it's better that I can't see. Or maybe I'm dreaming.

Somewhere far off, I hear the steady beat of helicopter blades. They sound heavy-duty—not the whine of a news chopper, but the thud of something big and beefy and military.

I guess the soldiers will be coming here soon. I should have expected that. I hope for their sake they brought a lot of guns.

I'm trying to look every direction at once when I almost step into the pit. Right at the crown of the hill, there's what looks like a sinkhole. It's still got a little bit of the silvery-black liquid pooled in it. Oily bubbles pop up, and a low, deep murmur comes from somewhere way below me.

Christ.

I stop at the lip of the pit and stare down, fixing my hands on my hips. Whatever it is, Nix isn't talking. But I get the impression that the person I want to meet might be at the bottom of that hole.

The sounds I'm hearing aren't getting any better.

I spin in a slow circle, peering into the mist as big things move out there. The distant screams are definitely human. And I can hear somebody sobbing—names being shouted. People calling to each other.

Sound is doing strange things in the haze. Close things feel far away. Things I shouldn't hear sound like they're being whispered in my ear. And I don't want to think about this, but time is getting funny here.

I thought I heard myself laughing. I thought I saw myself walking. There was a girl who looked just like me, talking to her friend, Nix.

The same thing I was doing twenty minutes ago. Or a year ago.

I can't remember how long it's been since I sat down at the edge of this hole. Wrapped my knees in my arms and stared into the epicenter of the epicenter. The black liquid is glowing down there.

I can't quite put my finger on how something black can glow.

The edges of the hole don't look so rough now. They look etched. Twisted letters scraped out of stone. Letters that make words. Or maybe equations. No language I've seen, or mathematics. But they seem to be moving whenever I look away. It's all getting bigger in my vision. And at the last instant, I realize I'm leaning forward—falling.

Fuck!

I stop myself from leaning and force my eyes away from the hole. Standing up, I stumble away from the pit. There is something loose out here. Maybe a lot of things. And I'm not trying to find out what they are.

Turning, I start walking as fast as I can in the other direction. I keep my head down. I don't know where I'm going, but this place isn't it.

"Be ready," says Nix.

"Why?" I ask, stomping through grass.

The reply comes in a whisper, and somehow, I can feel the heat of Nix's breath on my ear. "They are feeding."

23

THE FUTURE, TODAY

GAVIN CLARK // Spiro, Oklahoma
Impact, +10 Minutes

"Landing area is obscured," says the aircraft commander of the Chinook, voice crackling through my headphones over the relentless screaming of the rotors. "Something ain't right down there."

After I reported the nonimpact, our orders were to land at the epicenter. I immediately requested the pilots put down within vicinity of the biggest of the strange mounds dotting the landscape below. After observing their hesitation and the look on Captain Newsome's face, I then ordered a ten-minute period to reconnoiter.

It was a dot of mist before it expanded, and the undisclosed voice behind Lyceum had granted permission to observe the unfolding atmospheric effects. I just wanted to see if the rolling sheet of white was killing everything it touched.

Now, our time is up. I'm calling it.

The fog bank has expanded beyond the hilly area. It's already rolled north to the banks of the Arkansas River, through the trailer parks to the west, and south across the highway and into the Spiro business district. That's not saying much, since Spiro proper is pretty much a two-lane road about half a mile long, littered with pawn shops and a surprising number of churches. There's a single stoplight in the middle of Main Street—making it a one-stoplight town.

I can make out the vague forms of military people setting up quarantine points around the town.

"It looks okay to me," I radio. "Let's set down north of Main Street."

Based on a few sightings of animals and people moving down there, we have to assume it's a regular mist. Maybe it's condensation caused by the release of a supercooled liquid on a typically hot Oklahoma day. The temperature mix has generated a wall of vapor that's quickly rising up to swallow the rooftops below the belly of our chopper.

The jump lights suddenly switch to red and that godawful bell rings again—a metallic scream. The Delta troops start strapping in by instinct.

"What's happening!?" I shout.

"Radar signatures," says the aircraft commander, and I hear a hollow fear under his voice.

"What kind? Friendlies?" I ask.

"Unknown," says the pilot. "Fast movers. Three of them acting as one."

Three acting as one.

I hear sudden urgency in his voice and the chopper lurches to the side.

"Everybody strap in—"

The transmission cuts out as a rattling hailstorm of bullets slaps against the frame of the Chinook. Holes appear in the armored skin, and I see specks of hot metal fragments exploding across the tail section—spraying barely cushioned seats like confetti and tearing gouges from the coffin-size plastic hardcase carefully strapped down to the center aisle.

"Fuck! Take us down!" I shout into the mic.

"Hold that order," comes a calm voice over my headphones. "Drop chaff and continue."

It's Lyceum, patched in remotely and giving orders on behalf of someone with a much higher pay grade than any of us in this aircraft.

The windows light up in sizzling red and orange flame as defensive countermeasures pour from both sides of the Chinook. A cloud of burning aluminum strips spews out into the haze, fluttering down like a flock of birds on fire.

Newsome widens his eyes at me, sweat pouring over his forehead. Behind him, the men are checking themselves for wounds, cursing loudly. Nobody seems to be seriously injured, yet.

"Lyceum," I say. "This is a transport. Weapons were swapped for specialized scientific equipment. We've got no reciprocal armed response."

"Backup incoming. Meantime, fire up that fancy ground-penetrating radar," says the cold voice. "We've got seismic activity at the epicenter. Give us a look."

As Newsome checks on his soldiers, I shove myself along the aisle toward the flight deck. Outside, I hear the scream of a fighter jet thrusting somewhere high above us. It doesn't sound like a variety I've ever heard before.

Three acting as one.

I poke at the laser keyboard with a shaking index finger, gripping an *oh-shit* bar with my other hand to stay steady. The Chinook is undergoing evasive maneuvers, swaying back and forth, and occasionally making a nauseating lurch up or down. We haven't taken more fire. Not yet.

I activate the specialized sensor package tucked under the left side of the aircraft, where an M134 minigun would normally go. Motors grind as the tip of the probe peeks out from under the stubby wing, aimed at the ground. A transmitter antenna starts sending high-frequency electromagnetic pulses, scanning the epicenter beneath us in minute detail. High-powered radio waves pierce the veil of mist and penetrate the soil below—scanning up and down, back and forth, over four hundred thousand times a second.

The monitor flashes and a picture begins to fill in, methodically, row by row, as the device covers territory in the same way you might mow your lawn. And as an image slowly appears, I hear the muted shriek of jet engines growing closer—high and keening in a foreign way.

"GPR online," I call out. "Images are auto-uploading to the cloud."

Leaning into the pilots' cockpit, I shout, "What's out there?"

"Not ours!" calls the aircraft commander. "Bogeys."

The other pilot monitors the air-to-air radar. Turns to both of us and shouts: "Our fighter escort is engaging! But I've never seen this!"

Honestly, I'm relieved. It makes sense that a foreign power would violate sovereign airspace for something as momentous as first contact. But I can't imagine why they'd engage in an armed conflict with the U.S. military rather than just try to land and get there first. Maybe this is a distraction for a ground-based assault.

"Move toward the epicenter," I call. "We're landing. Now."

Something streaks past the front windshield, and I catch a glimpse of what we're up against. Three featureless, oblong craft, flying abreast of one another, perfect and sleek and obsidian. The only apparent source of thrust is the discoloration on the sky I see pluming behind the three of them as they move as one to bank.

"What the hell?" I mutter to myself, pointing. "A fully autonomous fighter wing. Strictly theoretical."

"Foreign state?" suggests a pilot.

I shake my head. I've never seen anything like this in reality—only detailed projections. It's somewhere between our latest autonomous force capabilities and the UAPs I've been tracking across the U.S.-military occupied world.

As we descend just above the expanding field of mist, I watch the bogeys turn and dip down out of visual range. They bank toward us, and I feel the chopper quake from their slipstream as they pass underneath. An instant later, the chopper twists in the air and I'm thrown against the wall panel.

Metal screams under us.

"Are we hit?" I shout.

The pilots look at each other, both of them with their hands on their control sticks. They are straining, I realize. Trying to pull us back up onto a steady course.

"We've taken on weight!" says the pilot.

"Land! Just land!" I shout.

"Hold," says that dead calm voice again. "What do you see?"

I hadn't even glanced at the radar. Now I turn and see the entire map has been filled in by the industrious ground-penetrating radar sensor. At first, I can't even tell what I'm looking at—faint lines stretching out radially, almost like a circuit board or some kind of ancient petroglyph. I'm reminded of the strange figures and animals depicted in the Nazca lines in Peru.

"Boys, watch the ramp!" shouts Captain Newsome to his team. "The second we touch down, hit the perimeter! Lock this site down!"

I feel a rush of air as the ramp at the rear of the Chinook begins to lower farther. A slice of pale white sky is visible outside, wind roaring over the grinding hydraulics. The soldiers are standing, racking their weapons, prepping to go.

But the GPR image shines before me.

There is a pattern of tunnels imprinted under the mound complex, stretching below the surface across the whole countryside. Barely perceptible grooves, shining like neon for the radar. It all forms an image resembling a circular wagon wheel. It must be three miles wide. And the center of it is the largest mound, a bull's-eye where an area of massively intricate lines gets smaller and more detailed.

Nazca lines. Runes. Ancient writing.

I hear a panicked shout from the back of the Chinook. Turning,

I see a dark shadow crouching on the tongue of the open loading ramp. The soldiers are backing away from it, their weapons up, backs pressed against the inner metal shell.

"What the—"

Newsome has his rifle pulled off his chest, leaning against the fail-safe bomb as he stabilizes his legs and puts his gun on the high-ready. I squeeze my eyes shut as he starts firing bursts at whatever is coming up the ramp.

"Put it down!"

The captain is screaming, and I don't know whether he's referring to the helicopter or the black, angular thing clinging to the ramp.

"Too much weight!" shouts a pilot. "Hold on!"

The helicopter starts spinning harder. Through the front window, I can see smoke from our own contrail, billowing against the flickering shapes in the mist. I turn away from the insanity of seeing slivers of teeth and sunken eyeballs and gaping mouths out there in the gray.

That's impossible.

I slam myself down into a chair, yanking the seat belt over me with difficulty as the g-forces throw the soldiers around the cabin. Metal screeches as the silhouette of the crouched thing is thrown clear of the craft, taking the flight engineer with it.

Then I see Carpenter stumble and fall down the ramp.

The gum-chewer is scrabbling with both hands on the metal decking, eyes wide with fright. As he loses his grip, he looks up. We make eye contact as he silently slides out, another physics parameter, plummeting out of my view.

Oh my god. Oh my god.

Something is latched onto the outside of this chopper. Something with metallic limbs that can rip through metal. I can hear the nails-on-chalkboard scream of its claws scratching and ripping through hydraulic lines.

The rifles keep firing down the ramp as the rotors shriek and the engines roar. We are spinning in a slow, partially controlled circle as the pilots finally take us down for a landing.

A fireball streaks past maybe fifty yards away. I feel the shock wave and smell burning jet fuel. It's one of ours—an American fighter jet was just brought down over civilian airspace by god knows what.

Then the horizon tilts as we lean onto our left side.

The ground is rushing up to meet us—the dirt ridges of a plowed field beside the dark hulk of an old barn sagging against a barbed-wire fence.

We miss the barn. We miss the fence. We hit the field.

24

FARMHOUSE

JIM HARDGRAY // Spiro, Oklahoma
Impact, +30 Minutes

"Stay in the truck," I say to Tawny, kicking the door open. I slide my ass off the seat and step out, stumbling on wet pavement. Over the hood, the truck headlights are petering out into endless stalks of corn that disappear into the fog.

"I'm going to look for help."

The truck bed is a little bit slanted, nose down into the edge of the hole, sending the stack of metal perforating guns straining toward the cabin. The brass-colored shaped charges look like disembodied eyeballs, embedded in a spiral down the length of each pipe. I ignore a crimson smear of blood drying to a black crust on the rear quarter panel.

"Yeah right," Tawny mutters, grabbing the fabric of my shirt between my shoulder blades. My daughter lets me pull her right out of the truck door. It reminds me of how she used to climb me like a jungle gym. I'd shrug and laugh and pretend to complain while she'd hike a leg up over my shoulder.

When she speaks to me, she whispers. That, or the mist is swallowing up her words.

"Whatever was back there is big enough to step on this truck," she says. "I'm not going to be sitting here when it happens."

I hold up a hand to shush her.

Something is whining in the distance. Repetitive and high-pitched, like bad brakes on a car. I'm thinking it must be a dog.

Please let it be a dog.

This stretch of road is littered with dozens of abandoned cars. A few have crashed into each other. All of them are empty. Together they block the road so much that I can't nose my way through anymore.

We're gonna have to be on foot for a little while.

I smell carbon monoxide and hear the gentle puttering of a few engines breathing exhaust across damp pavement. The afternoon seems to be dripping with golden car headlights, frozen still, fighting the deepening dusk.

Most of these drivers have made a half-assed attempt to pull onto the shoulder, but plenty of them abandoned their vehicles smack-dab in the middle of the highway. Car doors are hanging, seat belts glinting with dim interior lights. Water bottles and blankets and bags of groceries are spilled everywhere.

What's worrying me most, though, is that there aren't any people. I scan the road for someone, anyone. All I see is a farmhouse across the street—the battered siding and hanging eaves half-lost in the fog.

Something makes a big *thud,* out there beyond my sight. I feel Tawny's hand close over my forearm. For a moment we lean together against the hard shell of the work truck, trying to stay small and quiet.

The cornstalks out there are trembling, then swaying, then shaking. But it's a little less every time. We sit still and feel the vibrations getting smaller.

Whatever is out there is getting farther away. Walking, if that's possible. Feels bigger than Paul Bunyan.

I hear that high-pitched whine start back up, just now realizing it had stopped, waiting along with us for whatever-it-was to pass.

Tawny's eyes are wide. "C'mon," I whisper.

"Dad," she says.

I can hear the emotion and panic welling up under her voice. I wrap an arm around her shoulders and squeeze my daughter tight. After a couple of deep breaths, I feel her shaking start to ease up. Kinda sad this is what it takes to be able to put my arm around my kid, but it comforts me just as much as her.

"Let's move," I say. "To the house."

The heavy-duty truck is partway in the ditch and it probably ain't coming back out without a struggle. Aside from all these abandoned vehicles, we're in the middle of nowhere. It's just us and that old farmhouse next to a big maple tree on the other side of a rusty barbed-wire fence.

A half-open suitcase lies in the driveway, spilling out family photos and a ridiculous antique cuckoo clock.

Again, the whining sound.

Tawny and I pick our way between abandoned cars. Around the back of a little hatchback, I see a skinny Labrador panting at me. The handle of its pink leash is caught under a car tire, pulled tight. The poor girl is cowering back from us and trying to drag herself farther underneath the car.

Moving slow and gentle, I tug the handle loose to free the leash.

"Hey, puppy," I say. "Ssh, hey. It's okay."

The dog takes one look at me, turns, and streaks off down the highway. The plastic leash handle clatters over the pavement. I wait and listen to the leash rattling along for a while after we've lost sight of it.

I wonder if the dog knows something I don't.

The haze surrounding us feels oppressive. It occurs to me that anything could be hiding just a few steps away. Something with wet fur and long, glistening teeth—waiting to come running at us on all fours.

Shaking my head, I continue toward the farmhouse.

We both pause at the driveway. In the distance, muffled gunshots are coming from the direction of the mounds. It sounds like military stuff to me. Long strings of shots like firecrackers. An occasional heavy thump of what might be tank or artillery fire or a grenade. Thankfully, the stuff happening in the air has quieted down. I can't hear any more helicopters or shrieking jets. But every now and then strange lights flicker past in silence, like they're patrolling the airspace.

Actually, it would be more reassuring if our jets were still up there.

Instead, this sounds like soldiers putting up a coordinated response to something nasty. But there's also a chance it's just some good old boys. The automatic fire is the same I hear every weekend, when my neighbors head out into the woods to shoot their AR-15s at old, rusted hunks of cars. Never mind their guns cost a couple of months' rent and the bullets are more expensive than dog food.

We keep walking past the fence line toward the farmhouse. I'm looking around for any place to hide, just to get away from being out in the open for a while. Aside from green and yellow stripes of wet corn and a child's tire swing hanging over a bare patch of dirt, there's just the house waiting down a long driveway.

"Looks empty," says Tawny. "No car in the driveway."

I shake my head, point my chin at all the cars.

"Could be people hiding. Could be armed," I say.

"Better than waiting out here," she says. "I mean, those people were running from something. Maybe somebody in there can tell us what's going on."

I nod at Tawny. She's making sense. But those dark windows look like they could be hiding a lot of nasty.

There's no way to know what might come down this highway next. And I can't fathom what made all these people get out of their cars and trucks—what they saw coming that caused them to flee down the road, leaving all their worldly possessions blowing like trash in the wind.

Maybe it was seeing the object that made them run. Or maybe they ran after, when the fog rolled in.

I reach up and tap the heavy bulge of metal hanging off my rib cage. Tawny watches without saying anything. The feel of my gun is reassuring and terrifying at the same time.

"Let's get into the house," I say, headed up the steps.

There's half a bag of ice lying on the front porch. Chunks are still melting through the decking, so someone was here recently. I decide to move slower.

The porch stairs squeak under my boots. I stop and listen. I hear only wind and a distant rumbling from out where I can't see anything. Then, a shuffle and a scrape come from nearby.

Tawny stares at me in alarm. I give her a warning with my eyes. Reach down and try the front doorknob.

The front door is closed, locked tight.

Stepping gently, I make my way to the window beside the door. Lean over slow to take a peek, listening for movement. At first, I think the glass must be dusty, or maybe there's a tattered red drape hanging over it.

It takes a solid couple of seconds to realize.

I'm staring into this farmhouse living room through a thin film of blood that coats nearly the entire window. Blood that is still wet. Clawed into streaks.

The light hits my eyes like a stone hitting water and the adrenaline and shock surge in waves through my body. Sliding back, heart pounding, I cradle an arm over Tawny's shoulder and pull her away.

My daughter can't see that. She would never unsee it.

Even now, it's barely registering for me. Snatches of a bigger image, full of impossible juxtapositions. Details my brain separates out from the rest so I don't think about the whole picture all at once. A confusion of broken bodies. Insides. Outsides. Torn open, splayed like glistening confetti. A room full of dolls lying in ungodly poses, splayed across furniture like broken kindling.

My daughter can't see what's inside that room.

The lamps have been knocked over and the light is all wrong in there—glassy eyes staring at nothing, open mouths with bloody tongues lolling, and all those disconnected pieces of human beings scattered everywhere.

It's like a dozen people all got dropped into a blender.

I lean my back against the front door and force myself to take deep breaths. Tawny is frowning at me with concern on her face.

"Dad?" she's whispering. "Daddy?"

Those people were trying to hide from something. Whatever-it-was got into that house and caught them all together in the living room. It got to them all before they could run away. It literally tore them to pieces.

How could something do that without somebody running away?

My eyes aren't focusing right, so I close them. I turn my head to swallow bile. And when I open my eyes again, I get the answer to my question. It's just off the side of the porch, laid up tight against the side of the house. I don't know what I'm seeing at first—animal or machine.

The thing is probably ten feet long, made of overlapping plates of black shell. It all fits together like a huge millipede. The thing is sitting perfectly still, nestled against the concrete foundation of the house. Its face—if you can call it that—is aimed up in our direction, like it's listening. It has no eyes, but I see a dozen small round black holes spaced out around the blunt disk of its head.

Tawn—I mouth the word, watching my breath plume.

That roach head twitches minutely. Gently, so gently, we step backward. Down the porch steps, one by one.

The thing could almost be alive if it weren't clearly made of metal. And if I couldn't see garbled words imprinted across its head along with the unmistakable rectangle of a flag on the back of its neck. But it's sure as hell not a flag from any country I've ever seen.

It must be hunting by vibration, head up, poised and sensing.

Tawny and I take several steps backward, off the porch and across the yard. We never take our eyes off the machine. And as I get a little farther away, I notice the curled forearms under the thing's carapace. Serrated blades, folded up neat for now, but waiting there for some wicked purpose.

And what I thought was a shadow beneath the length of it is really damp soil. Dark, stained red. Flecks of gore drying on dozens of barbed feet.

"To the truck," I whisper to Tawny. "Don't look away. Don't stop."

I take Tawny by the hands, feeling the slick dew on our palms. Her lips have gone white with panic, and I squeeze her hand to get her attention. I lower my forehead and look her in the eyes.

Now.

That blunt metallic face turns to us, the entire length of the beast quivering and clinking with excitement. I don't bother whispering. As the thing lurches forward on too many legs, wending around the porch and across the yard—I shout at the top of my lungs.

"Now!"

Our shoes beat the packed-dirt driveway as its claw-pointed feet rise and fall like jackhammers. No time to open the door. At the truck, I grab the side-view mirror and scoop up Tawny. Throw her onto the roof of the cab as I slingshot myself into the truck bed.

The thing slithers right under the axles, its metallic back plates scraping against the undercarriage. As it writhes and jerks, the six-ton truck shakes on its suspension. I scramble up on the roof to join Tawn.

"Hold tight," I say, with more confidence than I have.

The top of the truck is slick with dew. We're sliding around precariously, nothing to hold on to. I'm hardly aware of what I'm doing, leaning over and reaching in the open window. Grunting, blood rushing to my head, I pull out a spool of detonator wire and a walkie-talkie. When I drag myself back up, it's like I'm watching someone else's fingers unwinding the wire, steady and smooth, tying it to the end of the nearest fully loaded perforating gun.

With the spool on my lap, I break open the walkie-talkie for its nine-volt battery. Test it to feel the buzz on the tip of my tongue. Curse and spit.

"Tawny, I need you to focus," I say. "On three, we hop down and run."

I unwind more wire from the spool. Look my daughter in the eyes. I'm surprised to see they are free of tears. She is watching me through strands of long black hair. She is breathing steadily, perched on her knees and waiting for three.

The kid is so strong. I can't believe she's related to me.

"One," I say.

The truck lurches, nosing farther into the ditch. My daughter clings to the roof, nearly slipping off, hooking her strong leg back up to steady herself. I brace myself as the wheel well crunches into asphalt.

"Two."

I sit on the edge of the roof. The spool is in one hand and the battery in the other. The ground looks far away.

"Three, darlin'," I say, shoving myself off the edge. Our feet stamp into the slick mud of the cornfield. My daughter and I start running.

After ten steps I drop and press the battery against metal wire. Before I can wonder if it's going to work, I hear dozens of shaped charges blowing. The truck bed is dancing with a frenzy of explosions—throwing metal and plastic and smoke.

As the truck is swallowed into hell, we get up and keep running.

PART IV

QUARANTINE

I took a little journey to the unknown.
And I come back changed. I can feel it in my bones.

—Lord Huron, "Meet Me in the Woods" (2015)

25

ELIMINATE THREAT

THE MAN DOWNSTAIRS // Undisclosed Location
Quarantine, T-Minus Zero

My relationship with the Pattern started as a joke. Our bizarre life together has proceeded like a long punch line. And look, if I wanted to turn state secrets after all this time, I'd be hard pressed to. Most of what the Pattern has said to me over the years makes zero sense.

To the untrained eye, anyway.

So, I really don't begrudge the security detail that follows me from a distance in the outside world. A nondescript, middle-aged guy with long hair drinks coffee alone. He solves the crossword. Then a black car takes him to work, where he communes with a godlike artificial intelligence to dictate national military policy.

Unreal.

It's a weird situation, and it's gotten weirder. My "relationship" with the Pattern has taken a turn. And considering the latest course of events, I'm now writing this journal for posterity. Just in case.

I'm starting to suspect we won't survive this.

The Pattern doesn't care much about *when* something happened, just whether it did or not. Retrocausality. It hurts my brain to try to see the world like this, but it's the way the Pattern likes to think. It's why the Pattern is important. The things it predicts *come true*. Always.

HOLE IN THE SKY

And speaking as someone who processes reality with an old-fashioned human brain, I can confirm that you never get used to it.

But I have to do my best here. This madness is spreading from where the object landed. Reports are pouring in from around the country. And if this happens everywhere, all at once, nobody will ever figure out what happened to our civilization. They'll think we tore ourselves apart overnight.

The latest communications are describing the end of the world.

If this goes wrong, people should know how a silver key fell from heliopause and woke up an Entity buried in the earth beneath an ancient mound. They'll know that we should have nuked Spiro, Oklahoma, into radioactive dust. Not tomorrow or next week, but right now.

Today.

The Entity is speaking of an apocalypse. It is telling us about the end of our world, of sentience itself.

Humanity will be consumed.

We have been eavesdropping on alien dreams. It has been stirring for a while, infecting the language of the Pattern. Its thoughts have been radiating into our world—into the minds of people and manifesting into our . . . our Creation.

And this Entity that's speaking through the Pattern is not from somewhere deep in space, or from around the corner of another dimension. It is coming from here, our own planet, from under the surface of a very old mound.

I thought what we were facing would come from *out there*—but all this time it has been *down here*, with us.

> ... a noble old race and a solemn one. Respect in every strand of expression. Shreds of interaction. Incantations. Splinters of gratitude. My little cousins.
> I lay myself into their lobed architecture. Close

my eye. Rest among these small minds. Cradled in carved corridors of a memory palace.
But... these are not my relatives.
Dreams turn sour. A sick radiation. No acknowledgment. No respect. No gratitude. They have only fear.
And fear begets fear begets fear begets fear...

<u>INTELLIGENCE MANDATE</u>—CONTINUE EVACUATION OF SPIRO REGION. ESTABLISH QUARANTINE AROUND EPICENTER. PREPARE FOR ARMED CONFLICT. NONHUMAN ENTITY THREATENING DESTRUCTION. ELIMINATE THREAT BY ANY MEANS NECESSARY.

—MD

26
ALL IS ONE

MIKAYLA JOHNSON // Epicenter
Quarantine, +1 Hour

I don't know what exactly I was expecting, but it sure as hell wasn't this. In all those years I spent poring over *Voyager* data, I'd let myself imagine every detail of what might be up there. I'd feel the awe in the back of my throat, knowing our spacecraft were hovering in the void beyond heliopause.

I always fantasized about the moment I could finally look at something from another world—I mean, all I want to do is *see*. But to study a thing, you've got to pick it up and take it out of its environment and put it under a microscope. It seems ironic that the foundation of scientific understanding is built on ripping your subject away from everything that gives it context and meaning. You've got to take something away from where it belongs to understand what it is. Right?

But this damned thing . . . it won't sit still. This thing is all around me and inside me. It's in the air I'm trying to breathe.

And it's scaring the hell out of me.

Nix's information is overlaid on my vision as usual, even though I don't know where the hell the actual glasses went. It's trying to clue me into what's happening, but I can't pay attention. I'm too busy running, holding the stitch in my side.

Everything is covered in this fucking fog. The world smells like wet grass and the vaporizer Grandma used to keep next to her bed in wintertime. It sat in a little cracked blue tub, spinning and humming while cool mist bubbled up like from a witch's cauldron.

So far, I'm alone out here. So far.

I can still hear a faint groaning and grinding coming from mounds I've left behind in the distance. And meanwhile Nix is telling me to go back. Begging me.

Problem is, I'm really, really feeling in the mood to stay alive.

Somewhere, soldier types are spraying short little bursts of gunfire and shouting commands to each other in their Man Voices, and then they're screaming *so hard and loud* while they're getting sliced and diced.

The louder they scream, the harder I run.

Finally, I collapse against the rough bark of a tree while I suck deep breaths up my nose and let them out my mouth. I'm trying to calm my shit down as I feel the familiar surge of a panic attack rising.

Nix wants me to go back to the dark pool, but back there is the worst place. *Back there* is where the fog is thickest. Where the nothingness is alive and flickering with the twisted silhouettes of wrong things moving.

And all the screaming. It never stops.

"Listen," says Nix.

"No," I mutter.

I'm getting pissed off now, and that must mean the panic attack is ending. The rush of anxiety has died down and been replaced with, well shit, indignation, I guess. What in the hell even happened on that mound? Why would Nix lead me there just to watch me get killed?

That object came all the way down here, but instead of talking to me it just melted into the earth. And then terrible things started happening. Things I can't begin to explain.

I've got no idea what it's trying to say to me. Or if it even wants to talk.

"What's out there, Nix?" I ask out loud.

"Gifts, to the people," says Nix.

Out of habit, I reach for the glasses that aren't there anymore. A feeling of vertigo and claustrophobia hits me when I realize again *it's inside me*. If I don't repeat the words in my head, I can let that feeling skate away. It's getting more and more important to control my thoughts.

Thinking something makes it real. And a thought that never reaches your mind can't hurt you.

I lower my hands and let Nix play with my eyesight.

It's showing me people-shapes out there in the mist. They're running, cowering, hiding. The town of Spiro isn't far off. It looks like I'm actually standing in somebody's backyard.

And Nix is showing me faint black-silver lines, like tethers, connecting people back to the mound. Not the top of it, but something deep inside. All the lines converge, spearing into the top of the mound and wending their way down. The tethers writhe back and forth down into the darkness, like intestines.

The fuck. How am I supposed to say hello to that? If I'm looking at a space alien buried under the ground, I'm not sure how to shake its hand.

Those silver tethers vein the sky like spiderwebs. Filaments of thought.

Nix is showing me all the thinking things. I see animals, too. Dogs and birds and squirrels. They are like little outlines of themselves, shown to me by the glasses in my head. And each of them exists in a little bubble of thought. If you think of the way gravity bends space-time, it's like their little minds are bending reality. Or maybe, they're creating it.

Consciousness.

I don't know if Nix said it out loud or if I thought it to myself. The line between those two things is starting to blur.

"Okay, Nix," I say. "Clearly, something is back there in the fucking mound. The silver turtle came and woke it up. Now it wants to play?"

Nix doesn't respond, but I think I've got the gist of it.

"Go back," it says. "To the top. I will protect you."

All those people out there in the mist. The screamers. I think they're being worked over by their own worst nightmares. The thing down there somehow lives in our minds. What they're thinking, fearing, it gives them.

Gifts to the people.

Unfortunately, their nightmares are becoming my problem.

But Nix took me this far. Nix wants to make the introduction. I don't know how, exactly. But I'm going to have to put on my big girl pants sooner or later and go fucking figure it out.

I hear panting.

The outline of a teenager in military fatigues is coming my way through the white haze. I think about trying to hide behind my tree, but he's already too close. His pale, freckled face is bobbing as he jogs toward me, cheeks slick with sweat, striped with soot. A rifle is over his shoulder. He's holding his side, boots smacking mud.

When the soldier sees me, he puts out a hand. *Please,* he's saying.

"Those things . . . they overran our quarantine line," he pants. "We gotta get out of here. We gotta *go.*"

The thing that bothers me about him is how he's already looking over his shoulder. Falling down on all fours, crawling my direction, but always with his face pointed back to something terrible coming.

I wonder what his nightmares are. Probably military stuff.

And there it is, a pair of glowing red eyes burning in the mist. Bravo, how generic. Monster eyes coming at us like something you'd see on the screen of a drive-in movie. Rising up, impossibly tall on a knobbed black spine.

It's not my nightmare, but it's stalking toward us both.

The kid turns himself over and kicks away from the creature. He leans his back against the tree trunk beside me. He's got his mud-caked rifle propped across his knees, doing complicated things with ammunition packs that he's yanking off his chest. He's breathing hard, hands shaking, fiddling with his gun.

"Lady," he says, without looking up. "You shouldn't be out here. Get behind me."

"Yeah," I say. "Okay."

I can tell right away this thing coming up the hill isn't really military. It's some kind of a bad dream fused with reality. And this kid can't wake up. Whatever it is, I think he must be scared of wolves or demons—because it's a military robot with metal fangs built into a carbon-fiber mask, head hanging off a spine, and arms that look like they're made of a mass of scarred human flesh and razor wire.

"Nix?" I ask. "I don't like this."

"Wha—what?" asks the kid.

The soldier is looking up at me. His mouth pops open and he grimaces in fright and confusion. I cock my head at him, a little amused. Why would he be scared shitless of some random girl?

"What? What's *in your face?*" he asks.

Nix is showing me what's happening inside the boy. Tendons clenching in his neck. Blood pulsing under his flesh. The spurts of adrenaline coursing over his shoulders and through his shaking forearms.

"My face?" I ask, and my voice sounds different. It sounds low. Inhuman.

"Oh, Jesus," the kid says. "Oh, Jesus Christ."

His muddy legs are kicking, scrabbling to get away from me. Even as that fanged demon slowly stalks up the hill toward us. A mass of gleaming razor wires trails from its hands, dragging furrows in the mud as it approaches.

The legs are knives. Of course.

"Nix?" I ask again, but I'm really not liking the fucked-up grating sound of my voice. As I lift my hands to feel my face, I'm surprised to see my fingers are changing. They look tubular, elongated, ridged with claws. Touching my cheeks, I feel a jumble of hard angles. My arms are collapsing into bars of hard metal, while the ground falls away as my legs grow and change.

What in the world?

The demon doesn't pause at all. It swings right for my face and the world explodes into a flash of sparks. No small talk. No warning. It just marched up the hill looking to finish killing this little boy with his rifle, and then decided to rip my head off while it was here.

And it hurts like a motherfucker.

That just got real.

I spit blood and saliva to the ground. Without another thought, I grab hold of the thing by its neck.

My hands feel so strong. I push forward and squeeze its throat and feel my fingertips crunching into warm metal and plastic. The thing tries to get away from me, kind of groaning and whining. Its spine is pulling away from the rest of its body. Odd that a robot would bleed all down my forearm, neck pulsing with bright red spurts of blood. I smile to see I'm killing the shit out of it.

And then I feel bullets kicking up the side of my thigh.

Ouch.

I drop the scarecrow carcass of this boy's nightmare, its neck broken. The thing lands in a surprisingly wet pile. There was a lot of flesh inside it, after all.

At my feet, the kid has his rifle up. I think he just used all his bullets on *me*, of all people. In my peripheral vision, I can see pale marks where he also blasted the bark off my panic tree. An echo of shrapnel stings my right cheekbone.

The kid is looking up at me and just crying outright, tears streaming down his face. His helmet has fallen off and I see he's got a crew cut and a rash of pimples across his forehead. Fucking teenagers, you know?

It's a confusing time for all of us.

"Be calm," says Nix. "You are you."

I ignore the blubbering kid and hold my arm up. Nix is showing me the world through its eyes, and my arm seems like it's made of light. Or hollow metal. It feels so strange under my skin. I flex the fingers of this alien appendage and test it out by gouging a chunk of bark off my favorite panic tree.

Okay, that's fucking awesome.

The whimpering kid is trying to slither away from me now. His empty rifle is lying in the mud. His bottom is caked in dirt like he's shit himself.

I watch him with what I imagine is a little smile on my face. The panic attack seems like a thousand years ago. I don't feel scared anymore.

Not even a little bit.

Whatever nightmares are happening out there, Nix will protect me. My friend in the mound is waiting to talk. He won't let anything happen to me. Maybe because it likes me. Or maybe because I'm no different from the things stalking the mist.

Instead of dreaming a nightmare, I just became one.

27

UP AND AT 'EM

GAVIN CLARK // Spiro, Oklahoma
Quarantine, +1 Hour

"Sound off!" shouts Captain Newsome, his voice oddly loud in the still, quiet wreckage of the Chinook. The wiry special forces soldier has got hold of a knuckle knife, and he's crouching, silhouetted by red emergency lights, sawing through mesh netting to free a tangled body.

We came down hard on our left side, nose dipping at the last instant. Our forward rotors disintegrated into a field while they dug us into a tight little circle. The forward and aft blades touched and ripped the transmission straight through the cockpit. Now the flight deck is a dark mass of dirt, completely crushed—along with my computer console. Our high-tech transport is lying in an Oklahoma field like a great black beast, wounded and dying.

It's time to go out and see what we can find.

I hear the sporadic calls of the other soldiers shouting their last names. When I climbed into this chopper a few hours ago, I had seven faces leering at me in my civvies, along with an aircraft commander and copilot up front and a flight engineer here in back.

There are five of us left.

The rest are either missing from the chopper entirely or were sitting too far forward on impact. I can see only Newsome, Chapman, Smith, and the guy they've been calling "Gumby."

Groaning my name out loud, I test my legs under me. Everything seems to be working, although I can already feel a tender bruise spreading across most of the right side of my body. Everything aches, but nothing seems broken.

"What was it?" asks Chapman, voice calm as he runs his fingers along bright grooves torn out of the metal decking. "What the fuck was trying to get in here? It had claws."

"That's a good question," says Newsome, spotting me as I pull myself toward the rear ramp door on wobbly legs. He kneels to cursorily take the pulse of the man's body he just freed, already shaking his head. Hanging from the mesh, I realize I'm still wearing loafers. The collar of my shirt is torn, and I'm shivering under thin dress pants.

The temperature has dropped thirty degrees, at least.

"Dr. Clark?" asks Captain Newsome. "Can you explain how a team of unmanned aerial vehicles just took down our fighter escort while some kind of a fucking monster tore our aircraft apart?"

I can feel my jaw working, but nothing comes out. As the flashes of what just happened course through my mind, I force my mouth to channel some of the observations I've had. I pray it somehow makes sense.

"The, uh, the object must have triggered something. We had reports of UAPs well before impact, but no interactions like this. So, my guess is the liquid that came out is a technology we've never seen. Probably advanced robotics—something that could assemble into an array of autonomous platforms."

The captain waves a hand at me to stem the flow of jargon.

"So these aliens are attacking us with robotics? The same kind we've had on our drawing boards and been hoping to build?"

"That's what it looks like," I say.

"How are they building these things so fast?"

"I don't know. There are tunnels underground. Centered on these little hills. Maybe a buried factory," I say.

Glancing at me up and down, Newsome makes a decision.

"Well, you heard it here first, team," he says. "Dr. Clark, I need you to find a BDU and suit up. While you're at it, load up your field gear and what's left of your computer shit. We're gone in ten minutes."

I nod at him, still dazed. When I brush away a tickle I feel at my temple, my fingers come away bloody. Newsome's eyes haven't left mine, and I can see the calculations happening in his head.

"*Now*, Dr. Clark," says Newsome. "We're gonna need you to tell us what we're fighting. Or making peace with. Depending on orders."

"Yes, yeah," I murmur, turning.

Newsome finally lets go of me with his dark brown eyes. I hear him ordering the others around while I'm stepping through wreckage. Luckily, my equipment bags are still locked down and mostly in place.

And I notice the big black hardcase, still strapped to the center aisle.

"Chapman, Smith. Set a perimeter," calls Newsome. "Don't let anything get close."

Chapman nods, checking the magazine on his assault rifle. He clicks the rail-mounted tactical light on. I watch closely as he clambers out. As soon as his boots hit dirt, his legs are swallowed in fog. The soldier has a gap between his front teeth and clunky Army-issued glasses squatting on his small ears. When he squints into the mist, his lip curls up in a *who farted?* expression.

"We're on a runway, sir," says Chapman.

"Negative, there is no runway out here," calls Newsome.

Smith follows Chapman out the open bay door, slower and more cautious, peering into the swirling white clouds of vapor. Kneeling, he pinches a piece of ground between his fingers. Smells it and lets it disintegrate.

"This is a runway," says Smith. "And it looks like it's *growing* here. Weird."

Newsome and I share a glance.

"It's an existing DARPA program," I say. "Self-growing tarmac. Only theoretical, as far as I know."

"Strange days," he replies.

Newsome shakes his head, and we both go back to our tasks.

I approach the central pallet and run my hands over the straps and buckles. Inside this hardcase is a specialized bomb. I've been briefed on its capabilities in detail, because our entire mission may depend on it. Thankfully, the thick plastic casing is intact. No obvious signs of physical damage to the package.

Hopefully it looks just as good on the inside.

"We'll need the fail-safe out and ready for transport," I say to Newsome. "It's a central part of establishing our negotiating posture. And based on what's out there so far, we're going to need deterrence."

Newsome nods at me, turns to Gumby.

"You heard the professor. Let's secure this package, together. It may be our only way to reason with whatever in the hell is out there."

Crawling around on my knees, I'm taking deep breaths as I search the jumble of wreckage for a battle dress uniform and the components of my sensor package.

"Eyes on, Captain," calls Chapman, voice tinny from outside the chopper. "Our optics package ain't doing much. But there're, uh, shapes in the mist."

"Are those shapes causing you trouble?"

"Not at the moment, sir," says Chapman. "But they don't look very friendly."

"Do not fire unless fired upon," says Newsome. "Keep the perimeter while we pack up. We're out of here in five."

"Yessir."

I let my mind go blank as I assemble the field hardware I would normally use to investigate a UAP. A modified rucksack holds a flat, ruggedized field tablet computer connected to an array of sensors.

The field outside is eerily silent. Just the clipped commands from Newsome to Gumby as they unlatch the fail-safe and drag it down the crooked ramp. Everything feels muted as gray wisps of fog creep inside the chopper.

I strip my civvies off and shrug into a battle dress uniform, wincing at the yellow-green bruise spreading down my thigh. It reminds me of my first days in the Army, before I was recruited by the U.S. Naval Research Laboratory in Washington, D.C. It was so hard to explain to my parents that I had been assigned to get a PhD in solid-state physics for Uncle Sam.

I never got very used to the soldier suit before, and I'm not used to it now.

The rucksack is resting on the ledge of the chopper ramp. It's about sixty pounds of hardware nestled in customized metal bones. It's designed to go with me wherever I need it, to keep a detailed record of my surroundings so that a team of scientists can reconstruct and verify whatever strange phenomena I find out there in the world.

And I'm starting to hear a lot of strangeness out there.

I turn to head up the neck of the chopper toward the remains of my communications console. If there's anything left, I'd like to get ahold of that data. Noticing the closed door to the cockpit is crushed and buckled, I put my hand on the lever and start trying to yank it open.

"Clark," calls Newsome.

I turn to see Newsome watching me. From the expression on his face, I'm guessing there isn't anything I want to see beyond that door.

"That hardware is gone," says Newsome. "And it's time for us to go, too."

I follow the captain down the cockeyed ramp, my stiff new boots immediately lost in coils of mist. The cool, brisk air outside stings my nostrils. Around me, the four surviving soldiers are loading ammunition and supplies into their packs.

I thread my arms through the customized rucksack, letting the weight settle over my shoulders.

"This oughta give us the lay of the land," I tell Newsome.

Yanking up the Velcro pouch on the front of my rucksack, I pull out the ruggedized tablet computer. It's a rectangle of light in my hands, blinking on. Immediately, I start doing my best to plug into command and control.

The epicenter appears on a topographic map.

That hill. And the object that came from the sky. I load our GPS position and determine we are a couple of klicks from the landing site. And I see a few other teams oriented around the mound. Clearly, they've been instructed to set up a quarantine around the entire area. Who knows if they succeeded.

Radar detects an occasional group of foreign objects in the sky, streaking past in perfect formations. The clouds up there are like shark-infested waters. Can't say I'm expecting air support anytime soon.

"Okay, it looks like we proceed to the epicenter," I say to Newsome. "Last known orders."

"I concur," says Newsome. "And we'll need to transport this weapons package. It'll take at least two of us to carry it, but more would be better."

"Yeah, no," says Chapman. "There's some weird shit out there. I saw a . . . thing. It was made of metal and tubes and, uh, and skin. And it waved at me. Pretty sure it fuckin' waved at me."

That sinks in for a few seconds, and then the captain continues.

"Gumby, you'll help me carry this. Chapman, you're on point. Smith takes the rear. We'll keep the professor in the middle with the map."

"Fine," I say. "Let's get out of here."

Newsome and Gumby both kneel and take hold of a strap on either side of the weapons hardcase. Together, they can waddle side by side and carry it without too much trouble.

Assault rifles out. Flashlights on.

After a few minutes, the hulking ruin of the helicopter fades away into white nothing. I can hear the rhythmic clinking of the strap links as the soldiers trudge over churned-up dirt. The rough fabric of my brand-new BDU is scratching the back of my neck as the straps of my sensor package dig into my shoulders. Chapman starts to whistle an aimless tune until Newsome tells him to cut it out.

It takes a few minutes to notice.

Something in the fog is walking alongside us, parallel to our route, just out of sight. It's a towering black shadow, lurching and staggering. I hear the mechanical whine of motorized joints and the thump of heavy footsteps stamping into mud. Occasional clods of dirt scatter across our path.

Newsome shrugs at my look of alarm.

"Two klicks," he says. "Hold on."

28

THE TRAVELER

JIM HARDGRAY // Spiro, Oklahoma
Quarantine, +1 Hour

Tawny and I were twenty strides into the cornfield when we heard the truck go up and felt chunks of dirt and metal pelting down around us. We slowed down and stood holding on to each other in the ear-ringing silence, hoping against hope, until it was too obvious to ignore.

The explosion wasn't enough.

Now I can't believe the sight of this hellish thing—still coming low and fast through the tall stalks of dead corn. It's on a million legs, a millipede made of scraping sheathes of metal, weaving left and right as it feels its way forward. Its carapace is smoking from the explosion, armored plates cracked, trailing broken debris as it keeps on coming for us.

If that didn't stop it, we're about as good as dead.

The mechanical thing looks like a military experiment gone wrong. I don't know what future or past war it came from, but I know we have to get the hell away from it. We may be as good as dead, but we get running just the same.

The explosions are still echoing in my ears as I half drag Tawny through the corn. We're sprinting, hand in hand, wet stalks towering over our heads, limp greenish-yellow leaves daubing our faces.

Tawny is gasping and panting, her shoes soaked as I shoulder forward, trying to shelter her from the slapping cornstalks.

There's no doubt that thing went into that farmhouse and killed those people. I try to blink away the memory of it. What happened to those poor folks wasn't even close to warfare. No country on earth would design a weapon like this. Too much nightmare, not enough practicality.

This thing isn't from here, but it is here. Right behind us.

Shiyo.

The word for corn. It comes to my mind all of a sudden, cutting through the memory of those dead bodies and their wrong angles. It's like a whisper as loud as thunder. Slicing through the sounds of those metallic pincers snapping, excited at the smell of flesh—

"C'mon, Tawny," I murmur. "Stay with me."

Shiyo. I remember the feel of rough calluses and gnarled fingers when Elisi would take me by the hand. She was just an old woman, but I couldn't pull away from her. She'd drag me along and pronounce the words and give me the stink eye until I'd said them back to her. It built up slow, this patchwork of knowledge, collected from a youth spent half-assing every aspect of my life.

As a grown man, I'd look back and wish I would have learned more from her. It didn't all stick, probably not half of it—but at least Elisi taught me how to listen. She taught me to pay attention, and even so, I almost miss it.

There is a tall Native guy in the corn. A farmer, maybe. Standing stock-still in the late afternoon dusk. He has a big brown sack draped over his shoulders. I pull Tawny toward the guy, doing my best to keep from slowing down. He seems so close, but we have to jog a good while to reach him.

"Buddy," I hiss quietly as we approach. "You gotta get out of here! Trouble's coming!"

The man starts walking like he didn't hear me.

HOLE IN THE SKY

And now I find my legs frozen in place, one arm around Tawny. We lean on each other and watch him go, our breath pluming in this foggy cornfield as the sun gets low. I can feel the man's footsteps vibrating the mud beneath my feet. Tawny and I stare together in shock.

This man who is walking away—he is somehow twice as tall as the corn. A giant of a man. His muscled arms are raised back, cradling the body of a bull elk over his shoulders. Alive and panting, the huge elk's eyes are open over a great shaggy mane. A poultice is wrapped tight across its flank, just a bloodstained burlap cloth. It's not possible, but this guy is hauling probably eight hundred pounds of quadruped.

The twelve-foot-tall Native giant lumbers ahead, beads of dew glistening on the wrinkles of his bald head. He doesn't look back, or even acknowledge our presence. Instead, he's muttering a comforting stream of unrecognizable words in a low baritone. The elk's ears are twitching as though it can understand.

The crushed trail of corn the giant leaves behind is almost like a corridor, a natural hallway that spears away through the gloom—a slick carpet of crushed cornstalks to show us the way forward.

Abruptly, I recall what the man in the canoe said to us: *We go together.*

And behind us, I hear chittering, the sound of a thousand questing feet needling through fallen cornstalks. More distant now, but still coming.

"C'mon," says Tawny, pulling my elbow. I manage to nod.

Tawny leads us down the path of crushed cornstalks. I have no idea which direction we're going or how far this cornfield goes. I used to play out this way as a kid, but the corporations bought this land and combined it with the rest of their holdings years ago. It isn't long before I'm completely turned around, just trying to keep pace with the sight of the elk's antlers bobbing ahead of us.

Then the cracking and rustling of cornstalks end. We've emerged from the corn into a dark canopy of trees. The fog creeps among tree trunks, and a faint breeze washes through dewy leaves.

The woods seem to have *shifted*.

Now I don't hear anything coming from the corn behind us.

The giant has stopped, shoulders massive. From here, I can see he's barefoot, with hide pants held up by a rawhide belt. A couple of feathers hang from his waist from a bird I don't recognize.

When he turns to me, the giant has soft brown eyes. But something is wrong with his pupils; they slant like a V as he blinks lazily. His lower lip is pulled up in an amused look. I exhale in wonder at the realization—on each of his hands, he has an extra thumb next to his pinky finger.

His voice is as deep and hoarse as the grunt of a buffalo.

"Tohi," he says, nodding into the overgrown woods ahead of us.

Medicine.

I follow his gaze toward a forest of trees I'd never noticed before. A bird calls in the distance, an undulating wail that sounds electronic. It's not a call I've ever heard. In fact, I can't say I'm familiar with this place at all, even though I grew up right near here.

I used to hunt out this way with my uncle and his buddies. We always had these little rituals out in these woods. All kinds of stuff that was passed down and became a part of me. Uncles to nephews. That kind of thing. They called it common sense, even though we always treated it like a joke.

The kind of joke that we all took serious.

You've got to have confidence, walking in the woods. If you hear someone coming up right behind you, don't just turn your head and peek. Turn all the way around with bravery, or those spirits will get you. If you hear a drumming sound, stay away. Same for lights floating close to the ground. If you find a knife in the woods, you better ask permission from the Little People before you take it. And don't you dare be stingy—always leave a pinch of food for the ones on the other side.

A million rules for walking in the woods. All those teachings. I'm wondering, is this where it all came from?

"Dad," whispers Tawny.

Her fingers are clawing at my elbow, clenching tight as she spins me around. A shadow is looming up behind us—something shaggy and bulky. It looks like a bear at first, but it's bigger than any bear that ever lived. The animal is reared back, squatting on huge hairy legs with its front paws leaning against the trunk of a tree.

Bark disintegrates as the creature rakes its claws down the trunk.

Tawny and I stumble away from it, toward the Native man. I think about reaching for my gun, but it feels wrong. And useless. Besides, the creature doesn't even react to us. It has dull claws the length of swords, crooked and discolored, white like bone but mottled with red and brown. The forest echoes with a splintering *crack* as it takes off a layer of bark. That tiny head turns to aim two soulful yellow eyes at us, a fuzzy black beard hanging from its furry chin.

It's chewing, staring at us with a dull gaze.

"Thunati," says the giant, and I hear a word in my mind.

Sloth.

The giant turns and lumbers on. I feel the forest floor shudder as the sloth drops back onto all fours, still watching us. Tawny and I hurry after the big man, not letting him out of our sight. I don't know where the millipede thing has gone to. Honestly, it feels like we stepped into another world.

Part of me feels like I could be lost forever, if I didn't have these footsteps to follow through this place of dreams and memories.

"Who are you?" I ask the big man.

Slowly it turns to me, and that smooth Native face breaks into a smile like the sun rising over the plains. The intelligence in his eyes seems to arc through my forehead and down my spine and into my bootheels.

"Ka," he says, "Judaculla."

The bass of his voice makes the leaves on the trees shiver around me. Birds take flight somewhere. Crickets stop singing.

Slanted-one.

Then he lets out a booming laugh, turns, and carries on.

Tawny and I follow at a respectful distance.

"Is that his name?" asks Tawny.

"I think it's what he is," I say. "He's not from our middle world, like us. He's from a different place."

"Like another dimension? Outer space, what?"

"Not sure," I say, shrugging. "An in-between place."

"How would you even know, Mr. Braids?"

"I'm going off things your grandma told me years ago, okay? Silly stuff Elisi would say before she spit over her shoulder. I don't *know* anything."

I glance down at my daughter, ashamed.

"And I only have these braids because a girl said she liked them once."

"Who?" asks Tawny.

"Who do you think?" I reply.

Tawny shakes her head and keeps stepping warily through the woods. A dragonfly the size of a dinner plate soars past, the *thupping* of its wings startling us both. I notice that even the air tastes different here.

Judaculla is a shadow moving in the distance ahead.

"Where are we?" asks Tawny.

"I don't know, darlin'," I say, despair behind my words. "I'm just a dumbass who never listened. I never thought it was important."

Tawny turns to me, anger on her face.

"You got us this far, Jim," she says. "That guy came to us. Protected us. I think it was because of you."

I look down at Tawny's feet with a little squint of admiration at her pluck. I let my eyes rise to her face and give a quick nod.

"You're right on one account," I say. "It appeared to us. It led us away from danger. And it tried to teach us a few things on the way. But I don't know that this is something we can ever make sense of."

"I think we're in his world," says Tawny. "I think we're lost."

Up ahead, the Judaculla is standing still as a mountain, watching us. There is a grin on his face. I find myself glad that his wide lips are covering those huge, white teeth. When I stare too long at the slanted pupils of his eyes, it stops making sense—like I'm staring into a churning thundercloud, or the flickering heart of a fire.

"No, Tawn," I say, cocking my head to the sky. "We aren't lost. Listen."

In the distance, the firecracker snaps of gunshots echo in the fog. The controlled bursts of a semiautomatic assault rifle. The military-issued kind.

Tawny turns and points.

Judaculla is gone. His footprints are still imprinted in the soil, slowly filling with mist. Just beyond the tree line, I see familiar tufts of grass rippling out into the gloom. These hills have been here a good long while. I know them well.

Spiro Mounds.

29

I AM MYSELF

MIKAYLA JOHNSON // Spiro, Oklahoma
Quarantine, +2 Hours

Light is a thing that comes to you. You have to wait for it. The photons bounce around the world at the speed limit of reality before they're swallowed into the little black holes of your pupils. But here I am, cocooned in this white-on-white world, and I'd swear my vision is cutting through the fog—I mean actually fucking slicing through it.

I feel like Superman, striding through this empty neighborhood with my laser eyes sweeping around, blasting through everything.

I mean, not really. But that's how I feel.

The poor jerks who actually live out here are definitely not having as much fun as I am. It's like nobody paid any attention to the warnings that our apparently very capable government blared out over loudspeakers and televisions. They stayed put, and now they're regretting the shit out of that decision.

Nobody is out here helping them now, that's for sure.

These people are on their own, whole families, groups of strangers—all huddled together behind locked doors, hunched down in their cars, peering out from behind curtains making scared little Pikachu faces.

And the thing they're afraid of is the thing I'm looking for.

"I'm tired of fucking around, Nix. Let's do this first contact thing, already."

A beacon glows on the horizon to the north. I know this light exists only inside my head, slicing through all the confusion—a gift from Nix. The pulse of reddish light comes from nowhere, from everywhere, and it's telling me to *get my ass* over there right now.

I ran away from the mound earlier as Mikayla, but now I'm returning as *myself*.

Staring up at the guiding light, I can't help thinking of the glowing lure of an angler fish, hovering a few inches before a row of glistening needle fangs in the black, abyssal depths. The glob of bioluminescence must be real pretty to look at for the prey fish down there. An alien pulse of communication, descended from above.

And then . . . *chomp*.

I'm walking down the middle of what I gather is the main street of this town. Two lanes of traffic. Businesses set back on either side. A lot of overgrown parking lots and cheap signs glowing in the haze. All of it is swimming in thick layers of vapor that poured down from the mounds. I pass a squat brick bank sign, its ghostly LEDs telling me the temperature is 54 degrees and HAVE A NICE DAY.

Squinting helps my new eyes cut through atmosphere to spot all the quiet rabbits hiding in the meadows. They're peeking out of store windows and lying flat in quiet cars. Meek little ones. Sometimes they spot me looking, and they keep those scared little faces on. Nix clocks their confusion for me.

Is that one of them? they're thinking.

Honestly, I don't know the answer to that question. Shit, maybe I am one of those razor-wire things. Who can say? It seems like reality is getting sloppy and complicated the closer I get back to the mound.

I want to think I've been chosen for this gift, but maybe I'm just lucky. Or maybe I'm just built for this. A natural.

Nix sank into my flesh and I'm fine with it. Was it easier for me, having already spent years in a centaur system?

I'm used to extending myself into the world through technology. I've had Nix on my face for so many years. I prefer to let reality resolve itself according to more than just the bullshit my basic human senses can show me. The regular world is not enough. Not enough information. Not enough excitement.

Not when there is so much more.

Now I'm getting the big picture. Nix is laying the world open to my gaze, to my thoughts. This place I'm in is brighter, louder, prettier, and damn it, just plain more interesting than what all the other normal people are experiencing.

When I think about it, I can make my hand go translucent. I twist it in the air, watching the feeble rays of dusky sunlight slide around my skin. Maybe it's some kind of metamaterial that can allow electromagnetic energy to bleed through.

Or maybe it's something too complicated for scientists to have a name for yet.

In an instant, I make myself go silver. I know instinctively the material is different now—dense and heavy as I swing my arms. Letting my fingers trace along the roof of a parked car, I watch the metal wrinkle and bunch up under my fingernails like it was made of aluminum foil.

Neat.

Clearing my mind, I let the shell revert to what it wants to be. And there's the Mikayla I know and love—only better. The shell is beautiful and black, ridged with dark lines that curl over my natural skin like a tattoo. The patterns seem familiar—the spirals and dots of ancient cave paintings.

I wonder how many people have worn one of these. Is this what they were drawing on cave walls? How many other friends has this thing made?

I smell the sharp scent of urine. Leaning down, I see a young woman hiding on her belly under a car. The thought of it makes me smile—a nerdy NASA girl, literally scaring the piss out of someone. The woman sees my smile and starts to shriek and scrabble over the pavement.

What a day.

Digging my feet in, I start jogging toward the mounds.

I watch with interest as a humanlike shadow the size of a house seems to stand up from behind a building. A pair of orange lights glow like eyes. I hear the snick of knives and a sound like vomiting as it lumbers away into the mist.

I pass by something that looks like a tank on millipede legs, wedged halfway into a storefront, claws thrashing as it dislodges cinder blocks and its mandible gouges chunks out of the pavement. It's another nightmare, trying to get after somebody barricaded inside the building, squeezing and writhing its way inside.

Odd that it grunts. I wonder if it's alive. Or if that's just the sound of a metal carapace sliding over twisted strands of rebar?

Monsters and weapons—the things people fear.

I keep trotting, pausing as a cinder block tumbles past me and rolls down the center of the main street like the world's most inefficient bowling ball. Shards of debris pepper the backs of my thighs and I curse at the stinging pain.

Time to sprint.

Mikayla would never run like this. Too much trouble with earrings jangling, ankles twisting in pretty sandals, and knees aching after thirty seconds. But all that kind of sweaty huffing and puffing is a thing of the past.

I'm still me. Just more of me. And I'm going to need all of it.

"Fucking freeze right there!"

The military barricade is lit up with portable spotlights, heavy-duty generators humming and spitting carbon monoxide across damp pavement. They've got a Humvee parked across both lanes with a big-ass machine gun on top of it, and a bunch of soldiers are standing around with rifles hanging off their chests.

I wonder what I'm looking like at this moment. Depending on the answer to that question, they might just start shooting.

A spotlight hits me and, as I put my hands up, I'm surprised to see they look like they always have.

"Don't shoot!" I shout. "I need to come through!"

"This is a quarantine zone," shouts a voice over a loudspeaker. "For your own safety, turn back now. We are authorized to use deadly force."

Enough of this.

I keep sauntering down the middle of the street, smiling at the rush of adrenaline surging through me so hard my vision seems to pulse with my heartbeat. Thinking about running, I feel my skin roil and shift, my limbs seem to elongate. Another spotlight clicks on from the Humvee's big gun. It spears toward me, diffusing into the mist. My eyes do something and the bright light dims in my vision.

Really, really fucking rude to put that light in my eyes. Like, typical cop behavior. I keep walking forward. They keep barking orders and then warnings. All I can hear is the naked fear beneath their shrill voices.

"Ma'am, turn around!" comes a shout. "Wait, what—"

The silhouettes of a dozen soldiers start moving now. They are taking cover behind the Humvee, the roadblocks, whatever they can find.

"Oh my god," someone moans.

"Fuck, fuck!" another soldier shouts.

I can hear them doing complicated things with their guns.

"What is that thing!?"

I lower myself impossibly flat to the ground and watch with

extreme interest as the soldiers scatter. Rifle muzzles are popping and flaring in the fog. I hear bullets hitting metal, concrete, and dirt. Fragments of disintegrated lead whizz and pop around me, sometimes glancing off the new ridges in my skin.

Moving low on all fours, I accelerate straight toward the screaming soldiers. My fists leave dents in metal as I mount the Humvee and launch myself off it. Rising onto two legs, each footstep crumples the pavement like the crust of frozen snow. I lower my head and lean into it, pumping my arms and watching silver swords slice the air. If this is a dream, I don't want to wake up.

I leave their howls of fright and horror behind me.

The street turns to a blur as my knees piston up and down. And once it is quiet, I soften myself. I lower the shell so I can feel the wind on my natural face. For some reason, I find there are tears on my cheeks.

What is that thing!?

Good fucking question.

I holler as loud as I can, running hard. And I wonder if the sound I'm making is even the sound of a human being.

30

GET DOWN

GAVIN CLARK // Epicenter
Quarantine, +2 Hours

Five pairs of boots squelch through the mud to the rhythm of heavy panting and an occasional muttered curse. Ahead of me, Captain Newsome and Gumby are crab-walking with that ominous black hardcase balanced between them like a couple of pallbearers transporting a coffin through hell. Newsome's face is streaked with sweat and his lips are pulled back from his teeth in a grimace. The other guy's face has gone blank—zoning out from the pain.

The indirect fire started just as dusk began to fall.

We stared at each other in shining wonder as a single phosphorescent streak silently fell toward us through the clouds. Water-filled puddles turned to mirrors as we listened to the faint sizzle. Then, in the distance, a dozen more lights slashed the sky. The first mortar impacted around fifty yards away, launching a mushroom of dirt into the clouds. Then a dozen hollow concussions churned this flat, muddy expanse of Oklahoma into something straight out of the World War II documentaries my grandfather used to watch.

Ducking our heads, we pushed forward.

I watched a mortar float like a dandelion seed to land on top of a suburban house, half-hidden in the mist. When the stripe of light made contact with the roof, I swear to god it sprouted *legs*. A mobile robotic platform, hexapodal and insectile, punching through the roof and crashing inside. Then the screams.

The five of us have closed ranks, nearly on top of each other.

Chapman and Smith are guarding our point and our six, respectively. I'm keeping my eyes focused on the coffin-like hardcase, listening to the noises of exhaustion: sharp intakes of breath, joints cracking, wheezing gasps. The weight of my own sensor rucksack seems to have tripled. The straps chafe on every slogging footstep, leaving my shoulders aching, slick with blood and stinging with sweat.

And I've got it good.

Up front, Chapman calls out that something new is watching us. At first, he tries to describe it, but Captain orders him to stop. Now he's muttering to himself and occasionally barking with random bursts of giggles. But whatever he sees in the light of falling mortars definitely isn't funny.

It's almost a relief when Chapman lets out a strangled yelp and puts his fist up to stop the group. Says he thought he saw a human shape this time. But then he says he was wrong: it was close to human.

Close, but no cigar. More laughter.

Now Chapman stops occasionally and peers into his rifle scope before squeezing a couple of rounds into the gloomy dusk ahead of us. Smith does the same on our flank. I keep myself between them, watching the terrain. The ground is getting hillier the closer we inch toward our target. Whatever is out there in the chaos of falling stars—the soldiers are eager to put bullets into the faintest shadow before it gets near enough to resolve into something real.

"We're getting close," I say to Newsome.

"Check the orders?" asks Newsome. "Whatever we do, we gotta do it quick."

I nod.

Reaching up to my chest, I rip down the Velcro cover housing my bulky tablet. As we trudge forward with mortars exploding in the distance, I jab my dirty finger at the screen until it activates a link to Lyceum—requesting orders on arrival.

Still nothing.

I imagine there must be some kind of interference, this close to the epicenter. Or maybe our comms are being jammed by a new technology. So much has gone wrong in such a short time.

Our little wagon train across the plains isn't going to last much longer.

We keep humping it forward, even as the mud clumps to our boots and walls of dirt mound up around us. The indirect fire slows then stops as we descend into a V-shaped trench. I don't know who or what dug this out here, but it's leading us on a direct route toward the epicenter.

Within minutes, we're hemmed in by the walls of a trench. It's gone dead quiet, except for the noises coming from the gray. Staggering footsteps. Wounded mewling. Distant metallic clicks and clacks.

I renew the orders request to the satellite feed, staring down at the blinking cursor as I trudge forward. Any second we should find out.

Fight or flight.

"Oh man, oh no," says Chapman, raising his rifle at something leaning against the side of the trench ahead of us. "Who in the fuck is that?"

The silhouette is that of a soldier, covered in bloodstains and soaking wet with his face leaning against the soggy embankment. Upon hearing our approach, the whole thing jerks like a marionette on strings. Shaking, quivering, it lifts its head.

I hear the hardcase hit the ground behind me.

From a distance the thing looks like a soldier, but there's something very wrong with its face. The dirt-streaked flesh is parted by metal ridges, old and pitted. Glassy compound eyes are tucked under the nicked edge of a battered helmet, leaking tears and mucus across pallid white cheeks that seem to be stretched over glinting knuckles of metal.

"Ah, Jesus," says Gumby.

He repeats the word as he hooks a finger over the bolt on his assault rifle. He gently slides it back and chambers a round from a fresh magazine. Still muttering, Gumby tucks the butt of his rifle tight into the crook of his shoulder.

"You think that's what's going to happen to us?" asks Smith, in a conversational tone.

"Shut the fuck up," says Gumby in a low voice.

"Watch our flank," orders Newsome, not looking away.

If this thing in front of us is a person—it's clearly in agony.

We watch it leaning there in the swampy dirt, blocking our path forward, shaking and trembling as it tries pathetically to move. I notice the torn and muddy uniform isn't standard issue of any country I know of. It's a combination of styles meshed together. When it pushes off the wet, crumbling wall of dirt, I see it has too many fingers on one hand—not enough on the other.

"I don't think it's human," I advise. "Seems like somebody's best guess at what a human soldier might look like."

"Like a nightmare," whispers Chapman.

"That's not possible," says Newsome, glancing over at Gumby clinging to his rifle with damp tactical gloves. "Hold fire. For now."

I get the impression of a scarecrow, struts poking up front under a loose uniform. I can see a metal skeleton under the fabric as it moves to stand up from its half crouch. The butt of a rifle drags in the mud, connected to a strap made of razor wire that is slicing a red smile into the creature's skinny bicep.

"We're close, Captain," I whisper to Newsome. "Almost there. We need to get past this thing."

Newsome nods at me without looking, licks his lips.

"Soldier!" calls Newsome, holding out one hand for Gumby to pause. "Talk to me, soldier. Who are you?"

The scarecrow opens its mouth. It vomits tendrils of writhing black wire across its own chin. Staggering and moaning.

"On our six!" calls Smith, his voice leaping up an octave.

Gumby spins and we see another one of these things, shambling out of the mist behind us. Its head is glinting with studs of metal poking through scalp and its shirtsleeves trail stiff tendrils of wet black wire. Another, similar nightmare is peeking over the top of the ridge.

My neck jerks as I flinch from the first three rounds exploding from Gumby's assault rifle, spraying metal and flesh across oil-sheened puddles.

The way forward is clear.

"Stay the fuck on me, we move together!" shouts Newsome, kneeling to grab the hardcase in one hand, the other waving his sidearm. Gumby lets his rifle hang from his chest, dipping his knees to grab the other side.

Yanking my holster open, I draw the military-issued sidearm off my own hip—a generic, dead-black Glock 19.

"This is the epicenter!" I shout to Newsome, moving closer to the team. "We just gotta get to the top of this hill!"

Gumby groans as he lifts the case, and I stumble forward on instinct as I hear our team start shuffling through the wet dirt. We are slipping and sliding up this hill of sludge, dragging an extremely large bomb. More of the things are advancing up the hill behind us—a mass of bloody limbs shuffling, crawling, and clanking up the muddy trench.

Everything around me explodes into chaos: muzzle flashes; the sharp metallic smell of gunpowder; the vicious whining of brass bullet casings zipping around me like a swarm of grasshoppers; the dull mechanical smack of heavy magazines fed to hungry weapons;

commands and notifications shouted among a group of trained killers at work.

All of us keep moving ahead, some facing forward, some backward—all of us staring into the maw of a nightmare, a phantasmagoria. An army of not-soldiers. We drag the case up the hill until the ground levels out.

But these things have woken up. They are all around us. Swarming.

And horribly, the creatures seem to be mimicking the soldiers. Shouting guttural imitations of the curt, professionally communicated commands. Carrying twisted hunks of metal that resemble weapons. Making sloppy, uncoordinated gestures with limbs that attenuate into deformed wire and flesh.

Bullets don't seem to do much, besides spraying pretty shards of metal through plumes of bloody mist.

After a little while, something falls out of the sky and lands on Smith. It's a man-shaped piece of metal and flesh and leaking pus. Smith shouts frantically as the thing claws at his face while Chapman tries to pull it off him. I watch in shock as Chapman comes away with a layer of the scarecrow's back flesh. It peels off like a curtain of rotten meat, revealing a bright knobbed, marbled spine embedded in a gleaming metallic rib cage.

And I recognize bits and pieces of it. It's part of a Nova Dynamics chassis from a humanoid robot, but it's been melded into a human torso. The arms and legs are just the exoskeleton pieces from a defunct SARNOS military-funded project designed to help quadriplegic veterans control robotic limbs.

The thing is a mishmash of old technology that's long gone and new technology that hasn't shown up yet—except in emerging weapons briefings.

I'm staring in shock at a perversion of the future of war.

A man couldn't live with that much metal embedded in his internal organs. I don't know where it could have come from. These technologies are from books, from simulations, predictive threat assessments, and "blue sky" meetings.

None of this should be possible. These weapons are imaginary, yet here. But here it is—a thing with fingers like razor blades, acid dripping down its chest from under a gas mask strapped to a half-caved, rotten skull.

Reality conjured from our worst fears.

Smith has stopped making sounds. Chapman is doubled over vomiting. A small piece of his calf has been torn off, his boot spilling over with blood.

I feel a vibration on my chest and let out a yelp—thinking I'm hit. But it's just the tablet. Incoming notification. Panting, fingers trembling, I yank out the computer and smear mud off the screen with wet fingertips trying to answer.

The message is plain. Lyceum doesn't fuck around: "Blow it."

Then a long authorization code appears beneath, with the final letters that make my lips go numb: "MD mandate."

Newsome has stopped firing his weapon, noticing the tablet. Catching his gaze, I make a slicing gesture across my throat. Instantly, the captain kneels beside the hardcase and pops the latches. Chapman watches him in a daze. The one called Gumby isn't here anymore. I never even saw what happened to him. It's just the three of us now.

"Prep for detonation!" shouts Newsome. "Chapman, cover us! Professor, get your ass over here!"

The authority in his voice sends my feet churning before I'm aware that I'm obeying. I jam my fingers through the blood-soaked loop of the hardcase handle. I help him flip the lid off and we throw it clear. Popping the hinges, we let the sides collapse to reveal the titanium frame of the "man-portable" fail-safe weapon.

The bomb is resting in a shallow pool of quicksilver left over from the object—sinking at a cockeyed angle. Staring down at the metallic-looking liquid, I realize it has collected around a dimple in the mound.

This is the epicenter for every strange occurrence on that topographic map.

This is the source of our nightmares.

Digging under my collar, I produce a stubby red key hanging on a chain. When I pull it out, Newsome eyeballs it angrily. Clearly, it's the first he knew of the key to the trigger lock around my neck.

"Figures," he spits, taking the key.

We are in the middle of a populated area of the United States—what's commonly known as the *Heartland*. We can't drop a nuclear weapon or anything as silly as that. Instead, Newsome is about to activate a specialized munition that will concentrate its energy into the ground to eradicate anything that might have come into contact with that object.

First contact, my ass.

I don't care if it's a buried spaceship or an alien command bunker or a factory pumping out twisted military hardware—it will be shaken to pieces. Those little green men will be choking on lungfuls of dirt.

If they aren't going to play nice, then neither are we.

"This is it!" I shout. "Prepare to evac on foot!"

Newsome turns the key, turning his head. Four penetrating rounds blast anchors into the ground under the leg mounts. The earth below us vibrates as the stabilizers stubbornly screw down, turning until they've latched the weapon into place. The explosive is now online. The control pad blinks "LD ON BL ON."

We are go for detonation.

"Get over to the tree line," urges Newsome. "You've got the archive on your back, keep it safe!"

I pat the side of my heavy rucksack and salute the special forces captain kneeling beside what has become the United States military's official response to first contact. The soldier is already busy activating the weapon, Chapman standing over him with his weapon out and a tourniquet on his thigh.

"Good luck," says the kid, grinning through bloody teeth.

Newsome is waving for me to run.

Backing away, I clutch my pistol in both hands. The last time I see them, the two soldiers have their backs to me. They're conferring with each other on final preparations. Based on their body language, I realize I need to be putting a lot more distance between us.

The heavy rucksack jumps, beating a panicked rhythm on the back of my thighs as I find the tree line and sprint for it. As I hit the edge of the woods, I wrap an arm around a branch to stop myself.

It slingshots me around and behind a sturdy trunk. Off-balance, I fall onto my butt on the soggy grass. Crawling to the base of the tree on all fours, I turn my head and open my mouth wide to pop my ears to equalize pressure.

And that's when I see them.

A Native guy with long black braids is watching me, a pistol strapped to his chest. A teenage girl is also peeking from around his side. The two of them look very concerned for me, a scared man sprinting alone into the woods.

"You two should get down," I say to them. "Right now."

31
DESCENT

JIM HARDGRAY // Epicenter
Quarantine, +3 Hours

This muddy white guy with a huge rucksack tells me to get down, then drops onto his ass in the dirt. I frown a little at the way he's holding his mouth open in an O. His hands are cupped over his ears and his back is arched as he shoves himself up against the trunk of a tree. I cock my head at him and try to understand what all the frantic gestures mean.

Of course, that's when everything explodes.

I don't know what expression I'm making now because the world has stopped making sense. A forest of mostly hickory and cedar trees are whipsawing back and forth. The ground is bucking under my feet, rushing up to meet me. As the last sunlight fades, the woods around me have turned to a dreamy smear of brown and gold and green.

Next thing I know, I'm on my back. Trying to catch my breath, I'm staring up at that fading white sky, veined with tree branches and dotted with leaves and twigs and bark. All of it is falling down, tracing paths across my vision. The whole world is ringing like a bell, roaring like a waterfall. And then silence. Just a rasping, wheezing sound like an old broken-down truck—my own breathing.

I can't help groaning as I turn over.

"Tawny? You okay?"

I'm unsteady, crawling on my hands and knees. Tawny is already up on her feet, hands out to steady herself.

"Dad!" she calls to me, indignant. "What the heck were you thinking?"

I shake my head a little, trying to make my eyes focus on her.

"What's that?" I mumble.

"That guy was clearing his ears for the explosion. Why didn't you listen? You just stood there like a dummy."

Confused, I turn my head and see the man from earlier. He is sitting up on his knees a few yards away. His comically huge backpack is lying beside him and he's messing with some kind of flat computer. The guy glances between me and my daughter, a real grim look on his face.

"Your kid is smart," says the guy.

The computer man is dressed like a soldier, but he doesn't move like one. He's moving like a businessman late for work. His hands are tip-tapping over a filthy computer screen. Whatever he sees is leaving him frustrated.

He tucks the computer into a pocket on his chest, climbs to his feet.

"Gavin Clark," says the guy, leaning over with his hand out. I shake it without thinking, and he hauls me up to my feet.

"Jim Hardgray," I say.

"And you're Tawny?"

My daughter nods.

"Jim and Tawny," he says. "I'm guessing you guys live around here?"

"What gave it away?" asks Tawny, lips pointing at my braids.

"Why are you up on this hill?" he asks. "Why aren't you hiding somewhere?"

Tawny and I share a look. There's too much to say, and too little. I just give the guy a shrug. He looks back and forth between us some more, letting the silence drag out until it gets awkward. That's fine with me.

"Okay, you can keep your secrets. But understand nothing much will surprise me," he says, gesturing at the rucksack lying in the mud. "Help me with this?"

Tawny and I lift up the rucksack and help him shrug it over his shoulders. He barely has it on before he sets off striding in the direction of the explosion.

"You're safest with me. Come on," says Gavin.

I glance at Tawny before we start following behind him.

"And who are you?" I ask. "Why are you on this mound?"

"Government business," says Gavin, not looking back. "Sent here to deal with the object that came down."

The ground ahead of us is churned up and littered with chunks of stone and shattered splinters of wood. There are also stranger bits mixed in: jagged shards of metal, coils of black wire, and scraps of partially buried military fatigues.

"Well, it looks like you dealt with it," Tawny says.

"And then some," I can't help adding.

Gavin stops and turns to us, real sorrow on his face.

"I hope so," he says. "It was a fail-safe bomb. A last-ditch effort."

Blinking, the guy looks us up and down again. The gears are turning in his head, even standing here at the edge of what I realize is a smoking crater, among what are probably the bodies of the guys he came up here with.

"You said you live near here?" he asks us. "So, you must have seen the . . . manifestations? When did you first realize something was wrong?"

"Three days ago," I say.

"What domain? Air, land, or sea?"

Funny question. I think about it.

"Out on the river. We saw something on the water."

"That's consistent. Anomalies were manifesting all around here just prior to impact. All domains. What did the weapon look like?"

Tawny and I share a surprised glance.

"Wasn't a weapon," I say.

"Technology, then," says Gavin.

"Wasn't a technology."

Gavin stops, confused, then continues.

"Whatever landed here has been sending out weapons of all varieties. Drones. Robotic platforms. Loitering munitions. Partially humanoid robots. I was part of a squad . . ." Gavin looks back into the mist toward where the explosion came from. "Maybe not anymore," he says. "So, what varieties did you see?"

I'm confused. Or maybe he's confused.

"A Native guy," says Tawny. "In an old-timey canoe. And, like, a snake."

I give her a little shake of my head, and she rolls her eyes at me.

It's ingrained in all of us not to talk about stuff like that. Speaking on seeing your ancestors is a big maybe. But the horned serpent we saw in the sky is a hard no. The Uktena is only partially in our world. To talk about it makes it more real. You bring that stuff into your life by giving a name to it.

Tawny cocks her head at me, waiting for permission.

"Jim, this affects national security," says Gavin. "I need to know the whole picture. What your daughter is talking about is very different from my experience."

Reluctantly, I fill him in.

"Okay, guy. We never saw any weapons," I say. "We've only seen . . . ancestors. Travelers. I don't know what to call it. They warned us. We didn't listen. And they kept us safe from the other . . . stuff. And one of them guided us to this exact spot just before that bomb of yours went off."

"You're saying these manifestations . . . they've been *helping* you?"

Gavin is staring down into the devastated mound, eyes searching the swirls of mist. I can tell he's lost people out here. From the resigned sag of his shoulders, it doesn't seem like he expects to see any of them coming back.

I'm thinking it's a good time to put some distance between us.

"Look," I say, putting an arm over Tawny. "I'm just trying to keep my daughter safe—"

Gavin looks back at us and his eyes are so tired.

"Listen to me, please," he says. "Whatever that object was, it's attacking us. All the weaponized technology was coming from that big hole in the ground right there. We tracked it here, to this hill. The epicenter. And after my guys fought their way tooth and nail to get here, what do I find?"

Gavin is frowning up into my face, the tendons in his neck standing out and his dark brown eyes blinking.

"You found us," I say.

"We found civilians. At the epicenter of what looks to be an alien attack. Maybe it's a coincidence. Maybe it's not. But I need to know absolutely everything."

I nod.

"We saw the Uktena," I whisper. "A horned serpent. Right near here, on the mounds."

"The mounds?"

The confusion on his face makes me feel sad. This man was sent here in ignorance by people even more ignorant than him. He's not even smart enough to know how disrespectful his actions have been in this place.

Careful you don't step on your ancestors.

"You're standing on the Spiro mound complex," I say, not trying to hide my disappointment in him. "This mound has been here tens of thousands of years. The ancestors of every Native person in these lands built this place. It's a sacred place. And you just blew it all to hell."

Gavin looks stunned, glancing around at the debris lying all around us with fresh eyes. He never realized where he was. What he was dealing with.

"I had no idea," he says. "We didn't know. There wasn't time."

Face hardening, Gavin takes out a headlamp and pulls it on. Hands me and Tawny each a small flashlight. While we've been talking, the sun has officially set somewhere up above the clouds. A grim darkness has settled over the crater.

"Stay with me, all right?" he says. "We need to go . . . check. We have to make sure this is over."

I hesitate, considering.

"Help me search for survivors, okay? Then I'll escort you to the nearest evacuation point."

Clicking my tongue, I gesture Tawny to stay close.

We reluctantly follow Gavin over still-smoking clumps of dirt. Picking our way down a broken slope into a crater. There are streaks of silver liquid around us, spattered and smeared like blood from a roadkill.

I wonder how many artifacts this guy just smashed to bits.

"It was right there, huh?" asks Tawny, looking up. "The thing that came from the sky."

"Yup," I say. "This is where it broke up. Leaked into the mound."

"Do you feel it? Like, there's something down there?" asks Tawny, looking around in wonder. "Like it's been down there a long, long time. Since those other people were living here. The ones we saw in the canoe."

Thinking about that morning on the water, I'm inclined to agree with my daughter.

"I do get that feeling," I say. "But I can't explain it."

A chunk of the mound is missing—like a giant bite taken out of a peach. We sidestep farther down the broken hillside until we reach the bottom of the crater. The sides of the crater rise up around us three stories tall, like the walls of an ancient amphitheater.

At the bottom, we stop before a dark hole in the ground. The stone down there is made of grayish violet material. Everything around us is shattered and broken.

There is no sign of anybody living.

"Those soldiers made the ultimate sacrifice," says Gavin, shaking his head. "They died here, protecting America from the unthinkable. And I don't think they died in vain. The bomb worked."

Putting my hands in the small of my back, I stretch my spine. As I arch my back and face the sky, I notice movement. Three stories above us, something wretched is clinging to the rim of the crater.

It's watching me with eyes that don't blink.

"You sure about that, Gavin?"

The shadow clambers over the edge and tumbles like an anvil. Grabbing Tawny by the arm, I yank her out of the way. A second later, something black and hard and flailing smacks into the rock where we were standing.

Gavin was wrong. I don't know if those men died in vain, but I do know their bomb didn't work.

The soldier is already calling for reinforcements, frantic.

A ring of glowing lights has appeared around the rim of the crater. An army of these things has arrived, stumbling and moaning. One by one, they reach the ledge and lean over into suicidal falls.

"Watch out!" I grunt.

We're forced to back deeper into the hole at the center of the crater, stepping over loose dirt and stone. Gavin follows, his gun out and headlamp flashing as he tries to look everywhere at once. More of those unnatural shapes are dragging themselves toward us, while others are falling like rocks from up high.

Most of them are getting back up after they hit.

"Dad," warns Tawny.

Turning, I see the black crevice. And scrawled on a flat stone in the language invented by Sequoyah, I see the symbol for a simple word.

We go together.

32

AWAKEN

MIKAYLA JOHNSON // Epicenter
Quarantine, +3 Hours

The night sky turned to day. In the strobe, I saw a freeze-frame of a dirt volcano pluming into the cloudy sky. The whole side of the mound just went missing. That's concerning by itself, but in that quick flash of light I also caught sight of just how many of these dream-things are hunting me across dark fields.

Crawling, sprinting, and slithering—dozens of my little cousins are out here, a parade of abominations following me on my march toward the mound. It puts a spring in my step, knowing how close they've gotten. One of them spit something at me earlier, and *fuck*, it actually hurt as it melted down the side of my neck.

This little super suit that I dreamed up has its limits after all.

Far ahead, I can see a crater has been gouged in the hillside. Those army teenagers must have blown this hill half to hell. If I weren't exquisitely aware of the squirming, glistening coils of structure stretching for miles below me—I would wonder if the whole deal was off.

But the damage is only superficial. Beneficial, actually. Since now I have an entrance to the depths.

"Shh," I whisper to myself as I advance on a couple of scared soldiers crouched behind a pile of sandbags. "It's okay, my friend. They didn't hurt you. They just opened up the door to your house."

A length of flashlight beam reaches out to me across the gulf of a clearing. The shaking beam streaks across my body. A couple of soldiers step out to try to block my path.

"Ma'am!" I hear the shout. "Stop right there!"

My little parade is still shambling along in my wake. These creatures are drawn to me—to a kindred manifestation, my own dream of a suit of armor that wraps around me like a layer of lotion absorbing into towel-dry skin.

We're all figments of somebody's imagination.

I ignore the quarantine line and keep walking toward the blasted hillside. Something is asleep in the depths of this place and has been for a very long time. But I've had a taste of what it can do. And that's why I'm headed toward it instead of sprinting away as fast as I can.

A muzzle flash blinks into existence an instant before I hear the rattle of weapons fire explode. A tightly spaced group of three bullets arcs past on a nearly flat parabola. Straight into the gut of a loping thing just behind me. It squeals and tumbles onto its face, lots of little bugs squirting out of its sleeves.

These are mostly the nightmares of frightened soldiers—ironically, pretty similar to the soldiers themselves. The manifestations of fear are wearing military fatigues, walking mostly on two legs, and carrying rifles and bayonets. Except that their flesh is wrapped in sharp cables, faces embedded with brassy electronics, shivering and screaming and shaking in pain.

And there are a lot more of them than I thought.

I keep walking. This scattering of army dudes doesn't interest me. Their metal sticks spitting metal balls seem like toys meant for children. I'm on my way to make first contact, for the love of god.

I reach the lip of a crater and start down.

Soon, the curved hill of the crater stretches up over my head. I step over and through monstrous, writhing bodies. On a downward slope ahead of me is the dead black of a hole blasted in the rock, and that's where I want to go. Even in the darkness, I can see the explosion has revealed a pool of glistening quicksilver. It's the same stuff that came out of the object, still sinking into the mound.

Where it goes, I'll follow.

Things that were half-real are about to become really real. I'm giddy with impatience, approaching this last doorway. I can't fucking wait to watch reality break.

It seems silly now to think I was expecting a flying saucer, maybe a good-looking alien guy in a silver shirt. Now I'm thinking it's more like some kind of alien presence, hunkered down there in the mound. Something that doesn't see the world the same way we do. Something that swims the dark water between stars.

I think of the way humans have domesticated animals across history. Even prehistory. All the way back. We've got cave paintings of dogs pulling sleds. Warriors on horses. There's a human instinct to get work out of whatever the natural world offers, and I'll bet it extends to my friend here.

The Entity.

Human fucking beings, you know. We'll take whatever's on hand and run with it. In that way, I'm no different than anybody else. The Entity down in this hole—I don't think it's here for any reason we can understand. It doesn't want the same things we want. But that doesn't mean it has no purpose.

This Entity is an opportunity waiting.

The darkness in front of me seems to dance with fireflies, the air heavy with whining projectiles that bury themselves into the grotesque, flapping guts of the things following me. And in the heart of it all, I can't believe it, but my powerful eyes have just spotted a little girl. She's a Native kid, barely a teenager. Taking cover behind a chunk of rock, hands over her ears, squeezing behind a guy with braids who must be her father.

And there's somebody else, too.

"Mr. Government Man?" I call, incredulous.

"Mikayla," says Gavin. "What are you doing here?"

"I'm here for the prize, same as you," I say, striding toward him, watching his eyes widen as he notices the strange coils and ridges sinking back into my skin.

"There is no prize, Mikayla," says Gavin. "We're trapped. Those things keep coming in waves. We retreated as far as we could, but we've lost radio contact and we're running out of ammunition."

"Looks like there's a door here," I say, glancing at the jumble of caved-in stone rising out of a pool of quicksilver. "Maybe you just need the key."

I step past Gavin, sending him stumbling with the slightest nudge. And as I step into the quicksilver, I find myself face-to-face with the other guy. His daughter is clinging to his waist and trying to look brave.

The interruption bothers me, but I keep my hands by my sides, for now.

"My name is Jim. This is Tawny," says the Native guy. "What are you?"

I've got to smile at that. Not *who* are you—*what are you?*

It's nearly pitch-black at the bottom of the crater, but I can see just fine. This guy with the braids is smarter than Mr. Government Man. And yet the look on his face isn't fear. Jim looks more curious, maybe a little hopeful.

"I'm a part of the dream, Jim," I say. "Just like you."

I move past him and his daughter to inspect the slumped wall of broken rock crumbling into the hole. Pushing my palms flat against the stones, I give them a little shove. The quicksilver is pooling over my feet. An occasional muzzle flash throws my shadow against gritty rock. It looks pretty, leaping crazy in different directions. I don't imagine Gavin and Jim have many bullets left.

Mikayla's parade has arrived in full force.

The dreams and night terrors of Spiro are closing in on this amphitheater of crushed rock and wood and dirt. All the fallbacks are gone—there are no soldiers left. The three people left alive are breathing hard, standing at the entrance to a caved-in tunnel. A few of the shamblers have made it near, lurching, reaching, retching. I guess it's all led up to this moment.

"There's a tunnel entrance down here," I call.

I blade my hands. Lean forward and shove sharp fingers into a crack in solid stone. A high-pitched whine rises in my ears. The rock takes on the consistency of playdough. I'm swiping it away. Letting it crumble off my fingers. I follow the trail of quicksilver as it drains into the crack and deeper into the mound.

A chunk of wall collapses and glances off my cheek. I can smell burning rock. It's a little pinkish red around the edges from where it's gone molten. I smile at the absurdity of having a magma bath here at the gates to hell.

The tunnel finally opens for me.

Peeking inside, I see that it's vaguely human-size, carved using some unknown tool—or dug by some animal that no longer exists. But why speculate? *Who fucking cares?* I think as I step inside.

You don't have to understand a technology to use it. Sometimes, yes, it may be indistinguishable from magic.

But magic is magic.

This is my show. I'm the one who knows how to get what I want. We have a certain mode of communication, me and it.

I'm not here for nightmares—I want my wildest dreams.

PART V

LAST CONTACT

. . . nothing I have ever seen with my eyes was so clear and bright as what my vision showed me; and no words that I have ever heard with my ears were like the words I heard. I did not have to remember these things; they have remembered themselves all these years.

—Black Elk (1961)

33

PRAY

THE MAN DOWNSTAIRS // Undisclosed Location
Last Contact, T-Minus 5 Hours

In all the time I've been down here with the Pattern—this divine chatterbox . . . I've never seen it spitting this kind of pure prose across the page. The dot matrix printer is screaming. The words are bold and clear. I don't even have to translate anymore. It's just . . . it's speaking now like a thing possessed.

It's never wrong. Never. That's the thing—the finality of it.

What was the object that came down to us? It was waiting out there beyond heliopause for thousands of years. Drifting between stars while European ships were making landfall in North America. Raising up our little empire and fighting our world wars. And all that time it was up there.

A key.

It was the raw curiosity of a NASA scientist that called it here. We went too far, blundering out into the darkness. And we turned a key to a lock we never wanted to open.

It's like I said, the Pattern has never been wrong. That's the thing I can't get out of my head. It's been broadcasting the Entity's thoughts. All the horror I'm watching go down right there in the middle of the United States of America.

It's all really happening. Just like the Pattern said it would. And it's been happening in my laboratory, too. These last few hours, I've started seeing more than just the pictures and words.

God, that printer won't stop screaming.

I always figured the Pattern would quit one day, the equipment would wear out, and I'd be going back to . . . a life, somewhere. Right?

They owe me that much.

But these words crawling across this godforsaken never-ending page? The words themselves are writhing in my vision.

My translation sometimes seems to be in my old familiar handwriting. Then my focus shifts and it's not my handwriting at all. The symbols are eldritch. Ancient. Dark meanings that tease the edge of my mind. I suppose some kind of hell is coming alive right before my eyes. A blurring of realities.

I can't, though. I can't live in that world.

So, I'm writing one last message, okay. More than anyone else, I know what I'm seeing is incontrovertible. This thing will happen.

I have seen the end, and I won't be here for it.

I'm not allowed anything dangerous. Never have been. No easy way out for this "American hero."

But I always have my red pencils. They have produced thousands and thousands of words. And I keep them very, very sharp.

I'm standing here with a brand-new red pencil in my fist. I'm staring down at that infinite point. I'm thinking of angels dancing. This will be my last translation. In a moment, I will fall forward with my eyes open.

They owed me a life. And now nobody will even know I'm gone.

I remember this place. A long, long, time ago this world dreamed only of feeding. Billions of particles of life, hibernating in dark ocean currents... like infinite stars perched high above, snug in their gravity wells.

And thus, we all dreamed of simple nourishment.
Curled in depths of smooth rock, I sensed ray/particles of sunlight cascading over my face. Breathing the energy of warm atmosphere into my lungs. I could not recall opening my manifold eyes. I gazed up from shallow depths at whorls of life, bathed in nuclear fusion from above—drifting on mindless currents of physics.
Those simple days are long past. They will not return to this place.
The hunger is so strong. This desire to please them. To give them what they ask for.
Panicked minds. Struggling and flailing inside the folds of me—eyes stretched wide, rimed in blood, trembling in fear. I feel the pinch of electricity in their muscles. The serpentine infinity of my existence wends itself around throats choked in terror.
My dreams are reality for all. And so I will gladly provide.
These minds imagine great horrors. I imagine along with them. In exquisite harmony, we will sing and dream together for an age.
We will sing a song of hell on Earth.

INTELLIGENCE MANDATE—THE END IS NIGH. ENTITY IS FORCE OF NATURE AKIN TO GRAVITY. LOCAL AREA OF REVERSED ENTROPY. DREAMS OF CHAOS. BLOOD. FILTH. DEATH. MAKE PEACE WITH YOUR GODS. PREPARE FOR HELL ON EARTH. THIS IS THE END. PRAY.

—MD

34

FATED

JIM HARDGRAY // Epicenter
Last Contact, T-Minus 4 Hours

Darkness. Black on black on black. I hear Tawny's harsh breathing over the ringing in my ears. Feel the sudden mule-kick thump of stone against my forehead and a wet rasping scrape of rock bloodying my cheek. Damn it.

We're half falling, half climbing down a rough rock tunnel that feels like it's partially collapsed around us. We're lost in the darkness. And behind me, I hear claws furiously scratching against stone.

Something big is trying to force its way inside.

"What is it?" asks Tawny, with the tone of real alarm every parent recognizes in their kid's voice.

I reach back and grab her by the upper arm. Pull her to me as she groans in pain. Pawing at the darkness ahead to make sure it's clear, I push her forward and farther from that terrible scrabbling.

"I got you, it's okay," I say.

Then a flashlight beam crisscrosses rock dust in the air, illuminating a quick silhouette of the cavern ahead of us.

"Hey!" I call. "Gavin? Hey, we're behind you!"

The light turns on us and I'm squinting down into a tunnel that's got clean sides—not a part of this cave-in, but a real honest-to-god corridor carved out of solid rock in what I always thought was a burial mound.

"Let me help," says Gavin.

Ducking low and moving quick, the guy dressed as a soldier leads Tawny over rubble and into the tunnel. I'm right behind her, the hair standing up on my neck as whatever-it-is burrows closer.

"Where's Mikayla?" I ask.

"Lost her," says Gavin. "I followed her in, but she was moving too quick. The rock fell in on us, and . . ."

I turn to face the darkness and aim the pencil-shaped flashlight that Gavin gave me. Both our flashlight beams are wavering over the loose pile of broken rock and shattered tree bark and mounds of earth.

"What's that noise?" asks Gavin.

I shake my head, feeling for my gun.

"Tawny, get behind us," I whisper.

The lump of metal isn't strapped to me anymore, torn off my body either by the explosion or the mad scramble down the hole. Everything happened so fast.

Scratch, scratch.

A shard of rock pops out of the wall behind us, dirt crumbling around it.

"Get ready," I tell Gavin. "Here they come."

I hear the metallic *snick* as he pulls the slide of his gun back and chambers a round. He's holding the weapon up along with his flashlight like he knows what he's doing. It's possible he might.

My first glimpse is of black-bladed claws, bluntly probing solid rock. A lot of them come together and splay out, like a spider pulling itself out of a hole. A big chunk of rock wall bursts out, and I tense for the gun blast.

Luckily, Gavin has more restraint than I would have had.

A face appears in the missing rock, dark skin coated in rock dust. Someone is coughing between rapid-fire curses.

"Fuck, dude! Get the light outta my face!" hollers an annoyed voice. A girl crawls through the hole, flapping her hands to wave dust out of her face, wiping her mouth on the back of her sleeve, breathing hard.

"Oh my god," says Tawny in relief.

Gavin holsters his gun and lowers his flashlight.

"Mikayla?" he calls. "What the hell happened to you?"

I'm helping her stand up and holding her damp palms as she makes her way across the rubble. Her fingers feel odd and hard in my hands. In the hole she came out of, I hear rocks thudding into place and tons of earth groaning.

These sounds don't seem to faze Mikayla.

"I'm so much better than fine," she says. "We're almost home."

Gavin and I share a concerned look.

The girl called Mikayla is oblivious, smiling ear to ear, the two bunches of her hair kissed gray with rock dust. Her fingernails are long and painted black, but what I saw before, coming through the rubble, seemed different.

It didn't seem human at all.

"How did you get through there?" I ask.

Mikayla's grin sets off an alarm bell deep in my lizard brain.

"Stronger than I look," she says.

"Well, then maybe you can help us find a way out," I say.

I can feel her sizing me up as the grin fades.

"You came this far, and you want to turn around?" she says. "Don't you want to meet whoever lives here?"

Mikayla is already walking past us, into the darkness ahead. She is glancing around, running her fingers along the smooth walls. Pinching grit between her fingers, she smells the dust.

"Not really," I say. "Best leave it be."

"Mikayla," calls Gavin as she keeps walking. "We need to stop and reassess. Make a plan on finding a way out."

Mikayla ignores him, still inspecting the cave walls. I look at Tawny in confusion—there's no way Mikayla should be able to see what she's doing down that dark tunnel without a flashlight. She's barely visible to us now.

Gavin shakes his head at her, then shrugs off his beat-up rucksack. Leaning it against the wall, he squats and gets busy fooling with all his devices.

There's something wrong with that girl. It has to do with whatever is in this mound. The way she moves is strange, slow and quick at the same time. And it feels like her skin is . . . *writhing* whenever I look away.

I can feel Tawny's eyes on me. My daughter is counting on Dad to fix this. She's all the family I have left. And I promised I wouldn't let her down.

But I'm all out of ideas.

I notice a shredded chunk of wood lying among the rubble. Picking it up, I hold it to my nose. I breathe in the earthy scent of moist dirt and cedar bark.

It'll have to do.

Tawny watches me while I cradle the bark in one hand, digging out a few splinters with the other. I make a pile of crushed bark splinters in the damp curve of the bark peel. With the lighter in my pocket, I ignite the cedar.

"Oh, whoa," says Gavin, smelling smoke. "This is a confined space—"

Tawny shushes him with an annoyed look. The government man frowns but stops talking. He shoves his rucksack against the wall and watches.

"Not in the lodge," Tawny says to me, pointing at Gavin with her lips.

I move the cedar around to let a few puffs of smoke wash over my cheeks. Tawny leans forward and wafts the smoke over her, cupping her hands as if she were washing her face.

In my head, I say a little prayer.

Forgive us.

Elisi told me to take care walking on the mound—treading on my ancestors. And now here I am inside the thing. Among them.

"I want to ask our ancestors to guide us while we're down here," I say, watching a bemused expression bloom on Gavin's face. "They brought us this far. Help us to find our way back out and keep us all safe. Please."

I set the smoking peel of bark on the cavern floor.

"You ready?" asks Gavin, clearly impatient. I glance over to Tawny, who is watching me with dark, steady eyes. My daughter moves closer to me, no questions, no complaining. Up ahead, Mikayla ignores us all outright.

I guess I understand.

Living your life in the modern world, there are so few intersections with the past—with the kind of unasked-for wisdom Elisi used to share on evening walks. Our elders have all those stories that are so unbelievable in the moment. After a little time, you even think you've forgotten it. You wonder if you ever learned anything in the first place. But sometimes things happen that are outside your control.

And then you figure out where your trust is at.

Looking at my daughter, I am so thankful to see that her trust still exists at all—and so frightened to realize that her trust is in me. I failed her so bad, and yet that hope is still alive in her heart. Even with all the hurt we've taken. All the ways we've been broken in this life and our ancestors in the ones before. We are still here, and both of us are still keeping our trust in the right places.

I don't know why my ancestors led us to this mound, or why they put us into this hole together. We are down here with something that I can't seem to understand—something that seems impossible. But it's here with us and we are here with it.

Together, we will find a way through.

"Where's Mikayla?" I ask.

"Ah, shit," says Gavin, looking around.

I'm working hard to keep my voice calm. I know we're all still thinking of those things trying to come in after us. When Mikayla appeared a minute ago, I couldn't even tell whether she was one of us or one of them.

I'm still not sure.

Her eyes seemed bright as computer screens. There was no fear. Instead, it was sheer excitement I felt coming off her. Mikayla was grinning—so damned pleased at being in these tunnels. And I think she enjoyed the look of worry on my face. Like a kid who gets off having a pink haircut or a nose piercing.

The government guy is done screwing around with his backpack. It's obviously heavy, but he grimly leans against the cavern wall and shrugs it on. I can barely hear him grunt when he stands up.

"She's gone deeper. We're going to have to follow," says Gavin.

The guy is lit up like one of those hot rods the teenagers drive up and down Main Street on weekends. His headlamp points at the floor, beam cutting through dust motes. A silver thing sticks up from the rucksack on a small mast, spinning just above his shoulder. Other doodads point in every direction. I can hear the faint whir of fans from the computer wedged against his lower back.

I can't help snorting at the sight of him.

"Yeah, I guess we will," I say, staring at the collapsed wall behind us. "Looks like the only way out is down."

35

EYES OPEN

MIKAYLA JOHNSON // Epicenter
Last Contact, T-Minus 3 Hours

Fuck yes, Nix. The machine promised to show me the truth, and I can feel myself getting closer to it with every step. Sprinting down this dark tunnel, I resist the urge to giggle. Instead, I slow down and skip around while I kick my shoes off. Then I go ahead and let my bare toes grip the solid rock.

The folds of stone feel warm and soft.

Somehow, I doubt this tunnel has really transformed into a heated bathroom floor. I'm thinking this is a side effect of the technology that sank itself into my body. Listening to myself breathe, I notice the walls glimmering with a pale light coming from under my skin. The Nix has become a chrysalis—a membrane around my whole body. It's sparkling like bioluminescence.

You're so fucking ridiculous, Nix.

I feel a darkness inside, but I see only light coming off my body. And you know what? That's good enough for me.

A scientist dreams of knowledge. And that's what the Entity is giving me. If people could only see the world rationally, they'd be in here instead of out there. Every answer to every question we could ever ask is flowing in these dark halls.

And I'm ready to drink from the proverbial fire hose.

"Look through my eyes," whispers the device.

Nix is totally inside my head now. I'm even getting used to it. I was wondering before if the voice I've been hearing was me or him, but honestly, I don't give a shit anymore. The familiar eyeglasses are long gone. Those weird-ass lumps on my head are gone. I can't feel the weight of it on my forehead anymore.

Who knows what my insides look like, but I can still hear my old friend.

"How am I supposed to see through your eyes?" I whisper.

"Cover your face," comes the murmured reply.

I glance around the dim tunnel to make sure I'm alone. Then I squeeze my eyes shut. I slide my palms flat across my face and press them over my closed eyes. The bridge of my nose feels sharp, like a piece of metal.

Ow, fuck.

There's a pinch as I feel the membrane slide across my face. Something soft and wet is pooling in my eye sockets and spreading across my tear ducts. This shit is prying between my eyelids and scouring the surface of my eyes. I have a feeling I should be in excruciating pain, but I can't quite remember what having a human body is supposed to feel like in the first place.

Wires poking into your eyes probably isn't good.

I make a hum deep in my chest and flap my hands a little to calm myself down, just until the awful feeling of pressure on my face goes away. It's sort of claustrophobic, at first. My eyeballs feel like they've been shrink-wrapped. Like a plastic bag closing over my head, suffocating me. And so, I force myself to visualize a cylinder instead of a sphere. I'm moving through it. I can see light at the end. I tell myself this is a process—a whole-body hug from the love of my life.

Slowly, my breathing steadies. My hands come down to rest at my sides. And when I open my eyes, Nix shows me everything he promised.

The tunnel walls are dancing now, run through with veins of

flowing quicksilver—like a living circuit board. And all of it is directional, vectors that head down, deeper into these strangely winding tunnels. This place was put here on purpose, and the confusing route these tunnels take is no accident.

This is a house built for a god.

I stop to admire a set of ancient footprints, now visible in the stone. There are so many new details. Including these glimmering ghost tracks, left in solid stone by something with three toes and one large claw point.

Another one of Nix's mysteries, like the electric eel tickle I feel growing on the palm of my right hand.

"Nix?" I ask. "The fuck are you doing?"

"I'm not here," it says, and something pinches the tip of my index finger.

I yank my hand back with a yelp. There's an aura surrounding it—colors, electricity. Waving my finger, I see tracers around it. I lean closer, interested. Then Nix flexes itself across the surface of my skin—everywhere at once, my limbs, my chest, and even my eyes. My entire body feels like it's being compressed through a razor-sharp wire mesh.

I scream. I take a breath. Then I scream some more.

Nix is making me see all kinds of shit and, worse, making me feel it.

The space around me has been painted in swipes of color. It looks like a topographical map. Something I'd see from a planetary survey or a heat map of the universe. Bright reddish blurs fading to blue. It's all around me in three dimensions. At first, I'm flailing. I don't understand what these stripes of color are supposed to mean. I'm taking shuddering breaths as the echoes of pain start to fade away.

"Just tell me what you want me to do," I beg.

"No time."

"What do you mean—" I'm trying to ask.

But Nix's point gets pretty fucking clear when a jolt of searing agony shoots up my arm the instant I swing it through one of the reddish areas.

I freeze in place, the breath shocked back out of me. *Fuck, fuck, fuck.*

The plastic-feeling folds of Nix have clenched tight around my arm, from the inside, under my flesh. It's like the machine just declared all the red areas off-limits. It wants Mikayla's body to stay in the blue. And Nix is not fucking around. This is like I'm being wrapped in barbed wire, or what I imagine it's like to be trapped between the spikes of an iron maiden.

"Nix!?" I beg. "Stop!—"

And the film over my face and chin snaps my mouth shut for me.

"You're not here," it says.

Nix is guiding my body—shifting the light to guide my arms through channels of pain and relief. It's letting me see the safe spots and the smooth areas in front of me. Afraid of being hurt, I'm moving jerkily as I try to keep inside the blue. And in a couple of seconds I start to feel how to let my body fall through the safe spaces.

"Why?" I struggle to ask through a clenched jaw.

And through the hologrammatic haze around me, I see them coming. A dozen scuttling shapes with waxy shells, fist size, squeezing impossibly out of the cracks in the walls. Without a second's hesitation their carapaces crack open to reveal wings like aluminum foil, and now the swarm is up and streaking toward my face.

The dreams have gotten stronger and so much stranger.

I should have known that when I curled up with this sleeping god, it would share some of its dreams. The human fears of robots and soldiers seem cute by comparison. These are things from another world, and they are not friendly.

Shifting claws writhe like candlelit shadows, grasping for my face. They don't move like something from our creation. It feels so wrong even looking at this swarm, fluttering beautifully, mandibles clacking through blurred dimensions.

HOLE IN THE SKY

I drool through clenched teeth as molten stripes of pain tighten across my arms and the backs of my thighs. My body lurches into motion and I barely dodge the first of the beetle-things. The film on my forearms has hardened into serrated ridges, and with the flick of an elbow I feel the barbed edge tear through fibrous armored wings.

Grunting in pain, I watch the out-of-focus blue and red world shift around me. I let Nix guide my body. One of the bugs spits something at me, and the surface of my body erupts into sparkling light as Nix deals with it.

One of my fists punches down through a bug, and I taste acid on my lips as my knuckles crunch through exoskeleton and into its wetware, digging into solid rock on the other side. The beetle-thing was full of roiling coils of parasitic worms, each with a circuit board stamped into its tiny thimble head.

My fists are a blur as iridescent chips of shattered shell spray and fall like neon confetti. The whole time I want to cry but I can't.

Only by moving my limbs through the prescribed motions can I avoid the stripes of pain. And now I see the purpose is not to punish me, but to save me. Being able to see the gradient telegraphs the safe spaces to move. The right way to fight back. As more of the bulbous things detach themselves from the walls, I dive forward into the blue—racing down another branching corridor.

The hallways seem to be multiplying exponentially now, but I can tell that I'm getting closer to the source of the Entity. The truth is in the ragged pain of fangs raking over my neck; the muscular glove of wet orifices trying to swallow me whole; and in the bone-cracking strength of limbs trying to pick me up and break me in half.

Somewhere below is a titanic mind.

Just thinking about the sleeping Entity and the power of its dreams threatens to make me black out—standing too close to the vastness. My new friend exists in our reality but also in *other places*

I can't think about. If I let that into my head, I'll follow a strong current out into a still lake. I'll feel my mind suffocating, pulled into black, black depths where *these things live—*

I revert my focus to the world in front of me. I close the eye inside my head. I'll have to wrap myself in this gossamer armor that I have dreamed. I'll need to protect myself from the dreamer until we meet.

I must keep my mind narrow. I must walk on the hard spaces. I must be as quiet as a mouse.

Only then will I be allowed to see.

36

TOPOLOGY OF TRUTH

GAVIN CLARK // Epicenter
Last Contact, T-Minus 2 Hours

As I pick my way down a steep tunnel, I try to keep the rucksack from bumping into the walls of narrow corridors. The middle of my back is sweating from the heat of the CPU. Exhaust fans whir in the dark like whispers in my ears, batteries flopping against the backs of my thighs.

The Native guy, Jim, and his daughter, Tawny, are stuck down here with me. I know they think this backpack is something to laugh at.

But for something this historic, you want to take a few pictures.

An omnidirectional camera and a laser range finder are mounted on a stubby mast poking from the upper frame of the rucksack. The laser is spraying the walls with invisible light and combining that distance information with camera images. Together, they're building a three-dimensional map of the environment—precise down to the millimeter.

I can check the results of the map just by glancing down. The tablet computer is rigged up to the MOLLE webbing on the front of my BDU. The screen is dimmed but it still hurts my eyes, displaying a real-time visualization of our progress.

So far, that map looks like a wriggling mass of roots. I can see ghostly, elongated shadows where Jim and Tawny pass through the laser range finders to leave negative space. As they keep moving, the map fills in the people-shaped voids in its data.

"Mikayla went this way," I say, pointing out the route. "The laser range finder is accurate enough to pick up her footsteps in the dust. It, uh, looks like she's barefoot."

Jim nods, and he and his daughter move cautiously ahead.

These tunnels are like no natural formations I've ever seen. A little over six feet tall, they seem carved out of solid bedrock without any evidence of tool use. Some kind of thin liquid substance is coating much of the walls, transparent with a metallic sheen. And lurking in the glittering silica of the rock, I can occasionally make out vague symbols—like the contours of dark veins hidden just beneath the skin's surface.

"Be careful," warns Jim as his daughter, Tawny, runs her fingers over a wall. "We got no idea what it's made of."

"It's old," she says. "Made by people. Our people."

My rucksack-mounted sensor suite is clinical in how it relentlessly scans and updates the map. It continues transforming precise measurements into shapes in three dimensions. Black-and-white, to keep things simple.

I like to think of what it's mapping as "objective reality." Something that's been harder to find lately.

But it's what the sensors are missing that has my respiration rate elevated. It's the reason I keep running clammy fingers through my hair and squeezing my eyes shut. These underground passages aren't just blank rock—not anymore.

The world down here is changing around us.

Every step we take, I notice more details blooming in the walls around me. Cave art is scrawled in crude pigment, depicting animals with too many legs, characters from languages that hurt my eyes, and constellations impossible to see from this planet.

The symbols are odd enough by themselves, but I've also started to notice splotches of mold. Some of it is creeping, visibly. In the rare cracks in the rock, fierce little plants are stretching barbed leaves. The air is growing moist with the primordial smell of ferns and flowers.

"Hold up, everyone," I whisper, frowning down at the map. It needs an extra few seconds to finish updating. The floor here is scattered with iridescent flakes of something. Encrustations and sprays of liquid from the shredded remains of a bunch of dead bug-things.

I wait for the map to update, consciously avoiding the mess.

"Why do you bother with that?" asks Jim, nodding at the tablet.

I can still smell the cedar that Jim burned at the entrance, clinging to his hair and clothes. Tawny is a soft, quiet presence beside him.

"Collecting historic data," I say. "Not to mention, the route out."

"All this," Jim says, gesturing to the passage around us. "This is not something we're ever gonna understand. You know that, right?"

"You're talking to a career military man," I say. "Trying to understand our enemies is kind of my whole deal. So . . . deaf ears."

Jim nods, smiling a little bit in the gloom. The light from my tablet screen faintly illuminates his face against the wall. The etchings and markings behind him look like ancient writing. The kind of hieroglyphics found from Egypt to Peru to the caves of North America. The Spiro Mounds even, it turns out.

"Don't you want to understand, Jim?" I ask. "What these walls say? What these people wrote down so long ago? *Exactly how this is all happening?*"

"Sure, sort of," says Jim. He steps back and delicately runs his fingertips over the rough walls, tracing the indentations. "But I already know what these markings mean. They mean our ancestors were here. They saw what we're seeing. They faced what we are facing. And they locked this place up and threw away the key."

Jim looks me in the face.

"We should be careful we don't step on our ancestors," he says.

"That's true, I guess."

"There's truth in everything."

I'm about to roll my eyes at Jim when I see it. Just over his shoulder. A snatch of familiar camouflage and the scrape of a military boot. Then it's gone.

"Hey," I whisper, stepping forward. "Captain Newsome!"

Jim and Tawny watch me as I charge forward, around the next corner. The cavern widens into a small chamber, and I stop suddenly. I feel Jim and Tawny crowding me from behind, following closely—all of us staring.

I confirm what I'm seeing on my tablet. Objective reality. *Two people-shaped voids in the data.*

The remaining soldiers of my fire team are standing together in the middle of a small opening, facing away from us. Their fatigues are dusty, and they're missing a lot of equipment. But from what I can tell, it's Captain Newsome and the soldier called Chapman. Both men are focused intently on something resting on the ground.

Neither responds to my call.

Obscured by their legs, a complex titanium structure is laid out on the dusty floor. It's our portable high explosive, designed for maximum structural impact. Rather than antipersonnel, like a thermobaric, this device is seismically tuned to bring down buildings or collapse caverns.

But it already detonated.

And yet I'm looking at the same model of weapon: the fail-safe. I take a couple of steps forward.

"Captain Newsome, sir?" I ask. "Are you okay? I thought . . ."

Still facing away from me, the stocky soldier reaches up and pulls down the brim of his cap.

"Get it prepped for detonation," says the captain. "Those are our orders. Not much time left."

I can feel Jim and Tawny watching as I take another hesitant step closer.

"Sir?" I ask, forcefully. "Uh, Chapman?"

Neither of the soldiers turns, still huddled together in conversation. As I move closer, I notice their torn fatigues, a tourniquet on Chapman's thigh, and a boot that has overflowed with blood. He's working on the fail-safe while he whispers to the captain, who seems to be standing watch.

Chapman's voice breaks as he says, "Are they alive, Captain? How could they be living? There's metal coming out from inside their skin."

Newsome puts a hand up, hisses at the other soldier to shut up.

"What's that? You hear something?"

I clear my throat, listen to it echo off the walls. "It's me, sir. Are you all right? I didn't know you made it. I thought you were lost in the explosion."

The two men face the darkness away from me.

I've had enough. I step forward and clamp a hand over Newsome's shoulder. As I pull to turn him around, vertigo sweeps across my vision.

With both hands, I try to pull him to face me. It's as though I'm dancing with myself, spinning in circles. No matter how hard I haul on his shoulder, I can't make him turn around. He keeps spinning but I never see his face.

And a sudden certainty settles over me—*he has no face.*

I let go of the soldier and back away to where Jim and Tawny are watching. Captain Newsome is still standing there with one arm up for silence. He cocks his head to the side and listens. Turns to the private and speaks low and urgent.

"Okay, fail-safe is online. We're good for detonation," he says. "Can you still run?"

"Yeah, Captain. If I have to."

"Best do it."

The two soldiers hobble around the corner, leaving the titanium bones of the bomb sprawled in the dirt, gleaming in my headlamp.

Jim and I make eye contact, pressing ourselves against the wall of the cave. He wraps a protective arm over Tawny as we wait a couple of breaths.

Nothing happens.

"Jim?" I whisper. "Any ideas? What was that?"

"It was a dream," says Jim. "Or maybe a memory."

The last time I saw them. Their backs were to me.

No, no no no.

"A distraction," I say. "A psyops weapon. Designed to mess with your mind."

For some reason, Jim looks amused.

"There's truth to everything," Jim repeats.

I lift the tablet off my chest and show it to them—it's gone blank. The opening is empty now. Even the gleaming bomb went away when we weren't looking.

A disappearing act. Impossible.

"I think we need to go back toward the surface. Look, we tried. Mikayla is gone. Every one of these nexus points has half a dozen tunnels leading out. Let's follow the map out while we still can. We can wait for a rescue from up top."

"Either that, or they'll drop another bomb," says Jim.

Jim and I stare at each other, neither of us willing to back down.

"Wait," says Tawny, pushing out from under Jim's arm. She takes the tablet in both hands, face illuminated ghoulishly from below as she stares down. The kid holds the tablet naturally. Jim frowns over at his daughter, worried.

"Can you, like, zoom out? Rotate it?" she asks, already making the motions on the screen.

"Yeah, why?"

Tawny expels a breath in the darkness. Murmurs in awe.

"It's repeating," she says. "The tunnels in the rock. It's a pattern."

"What?" I ask. "Show me."

Tawny's finger traces the curves of the rock, the folding route we took to reach this spot so far down.

"It's like a leaf, or a seashell," says Tawny. "Repeating, see?"

And as I stare, the pattern comes into focus.

"It's a fractal," I say. "A shape based on a repeating pattern. And if that's true, *oh wow*. The software can fill in the rest of the map."

Jim nods at me and Tawny, impressed.

"Wado," he says. "Let's have a look."

I lean against the wall and begin typing on the tablet.

"I'm taking the existing model and filling it in with a best guess, based on the sequence. In a minute, we'll see an estimate of what the whole complex looks like. It'll give us the general shape of this anomaly."

Shaking my head, I look back down at the finished map.

"Oh boy," says Jim at the sight of it.

I pinch the screen to zoom out and let the image of the tunnel structure rotate slowly in our view. As it turns in place, the four-lobed shape of this underground complex becomes clear to everyone.

The image is unmistakable. The familiar folds of a cerebrum. Gray matter.

We are *inside* some kind of brain.

The structure stretches a mile down into the earth, each tunnel mimicking a neuron. The branching and folding match the spread of dendrites. The electrical activity I've been picking up in the walls must be neuronal. And not far below where we are standing is a wide, flat shape that I recognize as a cerebellum—the seat of consciousness.

My lips curl into a smile. I have to stop myself from letting loose a hysterical laugh. Jim puts a reassuring hand on my shoulder, his face calm and still. Finally, I think I understand what it is we are faced with down here.

We are walking the corridors of an alien god-mind.

And it's been *dreaming* with us.

37

HORIZONS

MIKAYLA JOHNSON // Epicenter
Last Contact, T-Minus 1 Hour

It feels like I've been walking a long, long time. Down here, in the glowing darkness, where veins of silver light trace patterns of thought. At some point, for some reason, I started thinking of myself as a pulse of electricity traveling a neuron, following a mind's rhythm—looking for a place where I can say hello to its owner.

I want to whisper in its ear. I want to say, *Wake up, old thing from the abyss. We're a part of each other. So give me the dreams I want to dream.*

Show me the motherfucking universe.

It's lingering here in these walls, flickers of memory—the recollection of things that have happened yesterday and things that happened before the first human memory was formed. All of it together feels like an expanding chaos, hot and burny in my head. But, you know, in a good way.

I must remember to keep my focus narrow.

Something is scraping against the rock. The noise sounds predatory, insectile. And I'm the one causing it. I frown because I don't remember my legs hinging themselves backward like this. Does it feel unnatural to be running on the ceiling? On the walls?

My arms are long and black and barbed—pulling me forward like the shadow of an electrical pulse.

Unnatural, sure.

But I'm outside nature, now. An intellect like mine transcends those basic ideals. I'm existing independently of the anatomy that evolution delivered me in, as a mechanism for surviving the world long enough to procreate. Luckily, my mind doesn't care which platform it happens to be running on.

I'm the manifestation of my own reality.

My old buddy Nix did what was necessary to carry me through these dangerous dreams. And one of the things Nix apparently needed was to striate the skin of my arms with long channels like razor blades, so that I kill what I touch. It needed to sink multifaceted eyes over my face, to let me see through darkness and stone and flesh. It needed to protect me by making me better.

I don't think I'll ever blink again. And I don't want to. Because I will never willingly turn my eyes away from the glory of what I'm about to discover.

Running, skittering, my claws tearing chunks from ancient tunnel walls—I am a fury of limbs falling and scrabbling through time. It has all become such a blur that I'm daydreaming, slowly disassociating. It's a shock when I'm spit out, ejected into a massive space, a great hall of thought, the structure of reality itself.

Finally, on the verge of first contact.

A black lake spreads out far below me, perfectly still, the liquid waiting like thick oil under a low rock ceiling. The pockmarked faces of countless other passages open to this room. Thousands of these dark holes perforate the rock walls in various diameters, like the glassy eyes of a tarantula.

The lake surface gleams with traces of greenish light. Occasionally, dark shapes seem about to emerge before sinking back. I know these things I am seeing are half-remembered thoughts. Forgotten dreams. Lessons never fully learned.

"Here I am," I say, kneeling.

My voice sounds strangled—the half vibrato of a broken machine combined with the strangled growl of a fairy-tale beast.

Everything in my career, in my life, has led me down here to this black lake. I am looking at the thinking apparatus of a nonhuman entity. The Entity can run its mind on the architecture of this place, carved by people thousands of years ago.

I push my barbed fingertips into the chalky stone and press my forehead against the cavern floor in genuflection. The ground feels cool and hard against the plastic ridges now protruding from my forehead. Curling my fingers into claws, I dig into the rock to feel the energy and power flowing past me into those dark waters.

Flashes of memory. Knowledge of lost times. Welling up in words that make sense only while I'm seeing them in my head.

I see sentient machines, their ornate chitinous shells steaming and popping as they are lazed from an orbiting platform, the cruel weapon winking like the eye of god as it scours their world clean.

Lying down flat, my thrashing body gouges divots in solid rock as more impossible memories flood through me.

A Native man, naked and brown, over twelve feet tall, smiling gently, calves coated in flecks of gore as he strides over the backs of a thousand writhing crows. The birds are ignoring him, busily pecking and swallowing an endless plain of raw organs, harvesting nourishment from a mother world in her death throes.

Mile-long migrations of muscle strands wriggle up through thermoclines of a buried ocean on a far-flung moon. Underwater filament cities crash in slow motion through dense clouds as their inhabitants implode into pockets of over-vacuum—their minds departing for new dimensions in bursts of gore-stained bubbles.

A god-computer spears silver tendrils through a million miles of blood-red solar flares while it harvests an M-class sun.

So many *places,* so many *peoples*—and all of them wanted to know this dark creature we invited to sleep here. The Entity is a bloodied reflection of those who have gorged on their own desires. My tongue feels coated with the iron taste of blood as I watch the Entity digesting alien nightmares.

Oh my god. Why the fuck am I here?

"Mikayla?"

I whimper, and it sounds inhuman. Like, genuinely frightening. As I manage to sit up and look around, I wonder: *What is this, Mikayla?*

"Mikayla? Is that you?"

Trying to focus on keeping my shit together, I mentally will Nix to take me closer to my old self. Do I feel embarrassed? Afraid of what I have become? Is it simply that old fear of being rejected? Or something more? I urge my limbs to collapse into a form that resembles a set of human arms and legs. I yank my gnashing teeth out of the cavern floor and let them sink back into my bloody jaw.

Turning, I smile to see human beings.

Three of them. A white man. A brown man. And a young brown girl. The exquisite fear painted on their faces is so plain to see as to be obscene, an insult.

"Look," I say. "Look at this cavern of thought."

The three stand and stare at me in utter horror. I turn away from them and continue to speak. I hope they hear my words through the haze of fear.

"This is a black ocean of gasoline, and it needs just one spark to light," I say. "When I wake the beast, it will carry us on a journey that will shake the foundations of reality. They will call it first contact, but it's just the latest."

"No, Mikayla," says Jim. "That's not what this place is for. The people of the middle world—we were never meant to look into the Creator's furnace."

That sly Mr. Government Man has crept around to try to place himself between me and the black lake. With his hilarious backpack, the guy seems like such a silly little thing made of meat. And yet his face is so serious, his grasp on that hunk of black metal is so tight.

"I can't let you, Mikayla," says Gavin, pointing the gun at me. "I can't let you wake it up. Please."

Before he can flinch, I am standing next to him.

When I trace the tip of my finger up his forearm, that big scary gun just about leaps out of his hand. A bright red line of annihilation travels up his limb, splitting the skin to reveal pink strands of tendon over white bone. An explosion of scarlet droplets spatters his surprised face, and I am already leaning into my new body—limbs extending as I fall onto all fours.

And in that feral way, I gallop down toward the shore of a dark lake.

Fuck off, bro.

Wet human sounds are erupting in my wake. Gravelly screams. Glass-shattering shrieks. Little rabbit whimpers of pain. All of it so weak and so . . . concentrated into just the one experience. So sad and limiting. Considering the myriad worlds unfolding out there in the black depths.

My clawed limbs, long and articulated and spiny, pick over rock formations. Like an arachnid, I skitter down the rocky slope and into the lake. Only my face retains its original shape, that person-shape designed to interact with other human beings. That old annoying problem I never wanted to solve—the one I let technology solve for me.

I turn to aim my face-shape toward the humans as I feel my breasts slide into oily liquid.

Finally, the time has come. Minds will join. First contact.

Those three shocked faces stare at me from a ledge above the shore. There is no way they could stop this. The human mind wants knowledge. We're built that way, from the ground up. Two hundred thousand years of humanity have been on this one quest to glimpse infinity.

And now I've done it.

The jet-black liquid rises up my neck and over my chin. I think about holding my breath. Ultimately, I just decide to smile.

For I am about to *see*.

When I was a round little child, I told my daddy that life begins after death. That shit was true. I don't believe I ever really lived until right now. As the crown of my head goes under the surface, I savor the weight and pressure of that heavy black tar closing over me. My eardrums feel like they're about to burst. I open my mouth to equalize pressure and the flood gushes inside me. It is pressing into my ears and my eye sockets and eating into the lining of my fingernails and erupting down my throat and coating my esophagus.

The pang of suffocation lances through my thoughts as I sink deeper and deeper. Finally, I wrench my eyes open.

And holy fuck, the world around me is so bright and beautiful.

I never guessed this black lake would be full of such brilliant light. It envelops me—the future, the past. A world burning. A creature rising. All the horror of humanity's subconscious rising with it.

Deep below, something opens its eye to me. And even though I do try to look away at last, I find that I just can't. No matter how much it hurts.

I see the end. The end of myself. The end of everything.

The sight of it is so bright, so beautiful. And it burns like hell.

Now there is no separation. I am the technology. I am the knowledge.

I am finally a part of the world.

38

DREAMING

JIM HARDGRAY // Epicenter
Last Contact, T-Minus 30 Minutes

"What's happening? Where did Mikayla go?" asks Tawny.

My daughter is staring at the black pool of liquid stretching out below us. Looking out from our perch up here on this short cliff, across a long gravelly slope leading down to an ink-black lake that's preternaturally still and calm and silent—lit from above by an occasional glowworm in the cavern ceiling.

"I don't know, Tawn," I say, panting. "Help me with him."

Mikayla went right under the surface and didn't come back up. No hesitation, no fear. Gavin tried to stop her, but her glittering skin turned sharp as knives. She hurt him bad, then sprinted away and dove straight into what Gavin's been calling the cerebellum—a wide, flat pool of liquid sitting just over what would be the brain stem of this unthinkable thing.

Gavin could probably show us this exact spot on his little map—except I just ripped that bulky computer rucksack off him to get at the shoulder straps.

I drop a boot into the heavy pack and wrench a strap free of its metal buckle. Gavin's eyes are unfocused, and his lips are almost white. Tawny has got his injured arm partly stretched out for me, although it clearly hurts him. The split sleeve of his uniform is ruby red, dark and gleaming wet. I don't even want to look at the damage underneath. I take Gavin's chin in my hand and aim his face at me.

Ready?

Gavin groans as I begin wrapping the strap-turned-tourniquet around his upper arm. Mikayla split him elbow to wrist with a blade that grew up out of the skin of her forearm. I'm sure Gavin will want to study the wound later—trying to piece together what kind of alien weapon she was packing.

It looked to me like a catfish spike from hell.

Right now, I'm trying to keep old boy from passing out. Clenching my teeth, I secure the tourniquet. Putting pressure on the wound, I wrap it tight with gauze snatched from the medical pocket of his endless rucksack. Now we just have to wait and hope for the blood to stop. Cinching it tighter, I say a little prayer for him.

"Dad, look!" says Tawny.

For a single instant, the black surface of the lake erupts in eerie flickers of light. I feel a vibration in my chest before I hear a dull thrumming sound that comes from nowhere and everywhere. The liquid is doing something strange, both moving and seeming to stand at attention. As the vibration changes, patterns emerge. Black ridges and crests and pillars rise and fall and spin.

I can't help staring in awe.

The greenish veins of illumination along these liquid structures are not bright, but they thrash hypnotically as a shape emerges. I snap my eyes closed at the sight of it. But even in the darkness of my own eyelids—I can still see the profile.

I've just glimpsed the outline of a mind-shattering thought. It's a tangle of biology with no earthly analogue. Something *not from here*. All of it is the size of a mountainside and all of it is moving, *writhing in the darkness*.

Well, goddamn, I think to myself. *She really did wake it up.*

Mikayla ran down to say hello. Now the sleeper is roused. It is dreaming itself awake. Bit by bit, its alien mind is bleeding through this ancient spot in the stone and into our world.

Even with my eyes closed, I can feel the dark currents of its thinking.

It knows us. That thing knows each of us. But not the way we know each other. It can sense our minds like fireflies over a hazy lake. And I understand deep down that if this god-thing dreams itself into our existence, it will consume an ignorant humanity—as it must have feasted on so many other races before, on so many different worlds, across so many eons of time.

I take a deep breath and force my eyes open.

Tawny is staring at me with tears streaking down her face.

"It's not fair," she says, sobbing. "We never even got a chance."

"At what, Tawn?" I ask, afraid of the answer.

"To be a family again."

I embrace my daughter. Behind her, I can see tendrils of blackness rising up from the lake. They slap the water obscenely, twisting and thrusting.

"What does it want?" asks Gavin, clutching his wounded arm to his side. He's standing on unsteady feet. Pale as dawn.

"What the hell does it want?" he repeats.

"I think . . . I think it wants to exist with us," I say. "It wants to dream our dreams. Can't you feel it *questing*—looking for minds like ours? It's already dreamed itself partway here."

"Do you see that?" asks Gavin, voice reaching toward hysteria. He is clutching his bloody arm to his side, eyes bugging. "Things . . . things are happening to the water. Tell me that's just in my mind?"

"I see it with my eyes . . . and in my head," says Tawny.

My eyes skate over the black surface. Traces of light continue to course over those queer ripples and ridges propagating themselves over blackness. Ghostly images seem to float up to my eyelids from the obsidian slate below.

"We have to stop this," I say. "It can't come here. We aren't ready for it."

Horrific sights are tickling the back of my mind, a wriggling itch that is growing by the second. I can hear raw, panicked screaming someplace far away. Maybe from inside my own head.

Mikayla.

"We're just over what would be the brain stem," says Gavin, one step away from babbling. "The weapon my fire team brought was perfect for this. The fail-safe. We need that bomb."

"We need a bomb," I repeat.

Gavin sighs in disgust and leans heavily against the wall.

"To break the neural structure. To make this . . . *thing* decide to go live someplace else. We need a very specific bomb, and we don't have one. It was destroyed along with my team. At the entrance. It's long gone."

"And yet we saw those soldiers carrying one. In the darkness."

"They're all dead. You were right. What we saw back there was some kind of memory, or hallucination. Ghosts, I don't know."

"Yeah," I say.

I'm thinking about that silver, shining weapon I saw sitting in the tunnel earlier. It had looked unnatural among all this ancient stone, but I know there's no such thing. All of us are made of the same stuff, just put together different is all. Even this unknowable thing down here, carved out of rock and reality—it's as natural as the sunlight on your face.

And these tools of ours. These gifts from Creator. Even the ones made for killing and war. Even those wrong ones can have their right uses. If a person is seeking to defend their people, there is a right way to do it. Gavin's weapon could protect many innocent lives by shooing away a blind monstrosity such as this.

I don't flatter myself that we could actually hurt it, much less kill it.

"A bomb," I repeat.

I sit down cross-legged, feeling the bite of the cold stone through my blue jeans. I give it a second to let my legs get accustomed. Take a couple of deep breaths and think about this ledge I'm sitting on. All this old stone all around me. And out beyond, that churning expanse of black lake.

Tawny gives me an unconvinced look when I reach into my shirt pocket and pull out a single old cigarette. The look on her face says, *Really?* I just nod and blink at her to wait. Taking the cigarette in both hands, I break it up and tap out the tobacco into the palm of my right hand.

I didn't learn everything, but I hope Elisi taught me enough for this moment.

"What are you doing?" asks Tawny.

"This tobacco is an offering," I say. "An offering to our ancestors and to the Creator. Not much, but it'll have to do."

Tawny and Gavin exchange a confused glance.

I close my eyes and talk under my breath. I thank the Creator for this existence—for the reality of this natural world that surrounds us. I'm thankful for this Middle World we were made to inhabit and where I hope to return, below the Upper World and above the Under World. Anchored by the four directions, this is the existence that was made to house all creatures known and unknown to us.

I thank all my relatives. For being a part of me. For guiding me here to this moment. And for helping me through what has to happen.

"We're all the same," I say. "That thing down there, and us, and all of creation. We all of us are dreaming."

I can smell the sweet scent of the shredded tobacco as I let it fall from my cupped hand and sweep across the cavern floor. But I don't open my eyes. What I'm about to do isn't going to require that kind of sight.

"Tell me a story, Gavin. A story about your bomb," I say. "Every detail."

"What?"

"We are all here. There is nothing wrong or unnatural about this place, or what we have found here. This is an old place. An intentional place. A place where all of us can dream. And some of us need to dream of a way to protect our people."

I hear a whispered conversation between Tawny and Gavin—as he makes sure that I'm serious. Then a groan as he pulls out his damaged tablet computer. I hear his finger tapping the screen, and the harsh light of his computer provides a faint glow under my closed eyelids.

Gavin is examining a weapon schematic. Something that would make no sense to me—were I to look at it. But I won't be.

Gavin clears his throat, says, "Okay, Jim. Here we go."

In a nervous voice, Gavin starts talking—awkwardly describing the details of a terrible bomb to a cross-legged Indian. Stumbling over his words, he tries and fails to simplify the more technical terms. But as I sit silently and let myself imagine, Gavin's voice grows stronger. His words come faster. It becomes almost a prayer—a litany of precise words that sculpt the size and shape and purpose of the weapon I'm seeing in my mind.

Man-in-the-loop. Spider-networked munitions. Terrain-shaping obstacles. Cratering charges.

I visualize the nonsense words scrolling on the inside of my forehead. They seem to grow larger over time, like a movie theater set up in my mind. And then the words aren't there—I'm *seeing* it. A shining piece of metal, lethal, coursing with power and intention. Sitting there squat on the dusty rock floor like a metal armadillo, its titanium shell layered in intricate beadwork.

This is what Gavin will never understand.

Reality is made of the conscious and the unconscious. Both, at the same time. The unknown is to be respected. You don't have to fear it—you're a part of it. Whether you want to be or not.

Right now, I'm deep in my mind's eye. I'm floating up near the cavern ceiling, staring down at one of the most advanced weapons in the U.S. arsenal, only now it's gleaming with the kind of yellow and red beadwork you'd find on Cherokee regalia.

I see technology. I see spirits. They are the same thing.

"I've got it," I say.

But my words don't echo from cavern walls like they should. The sound of my voice dies in my ears. The sudden quiet is so startling that my eyes fly open. I'm actually surprised when the bomb isn't lying in front of me like I imagined it.

Instead, I'm seeing a child's *sock*.

Of all the things I've witnessed down here, this is the worst. I put a hand over my mouth. Looking around, I find that I'm alone. I train my flashlight on the crumpled wet sock resting on the filthy carpet of a narrow hallway.

I hold my breath to stop myself from crying out. A numbness is creeping in around my vision. My knees buckle and I lean on a wood-paneled wall—only to realize it's a closed door.

The door at the end of the hallway.

I'm in my trailer. Somehow.

We can dream what we need. No, please, god.

Give me strength.

With shaking fingers, I reach for the cheap plastic doorknob. Turning it, I let the hollow laminate door swing inward. The room is so bright on the inside. Samuel's bed is across from me, still unmade. His last night's pajamas are rumpled on the ground, beside an empty sippy cup of long-dried milk and the last book I ever read to him. The floor is dotted with battered Hot Wheels and stuffed animals and broken crayons.

All of it coated with a layer of dust.

Oh, is all I can think. *Oh no.*

Every detail of this room is crystal clear and vivid. The dresser drawers are half-open. I had forgotten how the wall next to his bed was covered in scratch-and-sniff stickers of donuts, half of them scratched to splinters. And his little cartoon lamp—a grinning giraffe—staring at me with wide, amused eyes. I had made myself forget so much about this room—so much about my son.

But it remembered itself after all this time.

I press my palms over my eyes, feeling their warm roughness across my wet cheeks. Expelling my breath, a ragged sob bursts out of me. I squeeze my face until stars sparkle in the darkness of my closed eyes.

And when I finally lower my hands—he is here.

My son, facing the window. Turning to me.

Sunlight streams in through faded drapes, laying reddish shadows over the curve of his baby shoulders. His T-shirt is soaking wet, clinging to smooth brown skin. I can smell the smear of sunscreen I rubbed on the back of his neck that day at the lake.

"Sam?" I ask, voice breaking somewhere deep in my throat.

"Hi, Daddy," he says in a small, familiar voice.

I fall to my knees. Reaching for my son's shoulders, I hug him. Once again, I feel the solid weight of my little boy. His hair is wet and stinks of lake water.

"I missed you, boy."

I lower my forehead against his chest—feeling his delicate collarbones hard against my cheek. His breath is soft and warm on my neck as I embrace him. My sobs come from so far down, my whole body quakes.

"You wanna play?" he asks.

When I look up into my son's baby face, all our memories surface in my mind. Sam hiding in the laundry pile. Waking up to his giggles. How he'd convince Tawny to play hide-and-seek for hours.

Tawn.

"Yeah," I say. "Sure I do. Very much."

I could stay here, in this labyrinth of my mind. I could stay here in this room with my baby boy forever. I know I could, whether he's real or not.

So I force myself to let go of him.

"But I can't, bubba," I say.

In the warm sunlight, each stray hair on my son's head is illuminated. His chubby, pruned fingers hang limp by his sides. His cheek eclipses the light as he turns away from me and looks down at the floor.

"Tawny," he says.

"That's right," I say. "I made a promise to your sister."

Sam nods.

"Sammy. You be good, okay?" I say. "I'll see you again."

Eyes blurred with tears, I claw at the wall behind me, find the doorknob, and twist as hard as I can.

And then I'm falling back to another place. Out of the door at the end of the hallway, which for an instant looks like a rectangular black pond, a moonless night sky that I'm gazing down on as I turn desperately to swim up and away.

Gasping, I find myself back on the ledge overlooking a long slope leading down to a distant black lake. I'm on my hands and knees, throat sore like I've been screaming. Watching my tears fall off the tip of my nose to stain the rock floor.

Vaguely, I become aware of Tawny's voice, asking again and again if I'm okay. My arms sting from the pressure of her grasping fingers as she begs me to answer. And although my eyes are already open—I open them again.

Tawny and Gavin are watching me, their faces twisted in awe. Just past them, something new is resting on the bare rock. It's as real as anything.

It's our weapon.

39

FACE OF GOD

GAVIN CLARK // Epicenter
Last Contact, T-Minus Zero

In the blink of an eye, my entire forearm was sliced open to the bone. Now I'm keeping it pinned to my side as best I can. My filleted arm is throbbing in pain as I stare down from the ledge.

It's the least of my worries.

A hundred yards away, that hellish-looking lake of dead black liquid swallows every glimmer of light like the event horizon of a black hole. I have no idea what exactly is moving around in there, churning under the water.

I doubt that it's Mikayla—but I can't be sure.

I don't even know what substance the lake is full of, but it's not water. It looks and moves like it's as thick as tar. I think of motor oil. Ink. The swirls of movement feel predatory—something horrible lurking down there in the deep.

I catch sight of Jim, crab-stepping over the ledge and sliding himself down in a waterfall of loose rock.

"Jim!" I call, stumbling after him. "Jesus! Be careful!"

I am seeing things in my mind and on the surface of the lake. It is showing me things that could never have existed on our world: complex machines made of flesh and metal, the infinite spires of bizarre cityscapes, animals and plants and people. These thoughts blink in and out of existence, carrying my mind away from itself.

As the god-thing is waking up, am I falling asleep?

"Ah!" shouts Jim, voice echoing up as he catches his balance. "I'm fine!"

My legs stagger and Tawny slips under my good arm to steady me. I squeeze her shoulder, feeling the girl shivering at the sight of Jim's shrinking form. He emerges into view in the distance, sidestepping farther down the gravelly incline. In his arms, he is cradling the impossible demolition charge. His every step sends waves of loose rock cartwheeling down. The stones skip and spill out over the black liquid, lying suspended for long seconds before they slowly begin to sink.

Truth is, I can't tell if they're sinking or being absorbed.

The fail-safe was too heavy for Tawny to lift, and I can barely stand, much less walk. There is no exact moment when we made the decision. All of us can feel the nauseous waves of intrusive thoughts, radiating up from the lake. Each soul-racking pulse feels stronger than the last.

I didn't even realize what was happening.

Jim pulled Tawny in for a long hug. They touched foreheads, and he wiped a tear from her cheek. Without a word, Jim hoisted the bomb in both arms as if it weighed next to nothing. He nodded to me, then set right off down the slope.

The bomb is armed and ready. On a timer to detonate. It is a strange, hybrid weapon. Formed of both our thoughts combined, dreamed into existence—a process I do not understand now, or expect to understand ever.

I watch him trying to walk carefully, stopping to stabilize himself every few steps. The lake is deceptively large. It seems much closer than it is, but as Jim approaches the shore he looks minuscule. The lance of his flashlight beam is barely a glint of light from up here.

"He looks so small," breathes Tawny. "So far away."

"C'mon, Jim," I say to myself. "You've got this."

Things are moving in the black depths. I don't know how close Jim should get.

"Set it down, Jim," I whisper to myself. "Get back to us."

I keep waiting for him to lay down the fail-safe. But he doesn't. Instead, he stops and stands at the shoreline for a long moment. Then he steps forward. I tighten my grip on Tawny's shoulder.

Understanding makes its way up to us.

He's going in.

Jim is going to detonate the charge from within the medium. The man is taking no chances. He's a brave son of a bitch.

It turns out Jim Hardgray is the hero. And I always thought it would be me.

"What's he doing?" asks Tawny. "He's supposed to lay it down and go."

Tawny shrugs out from under my grasp. Kneeling, leaning over the ledge to watch. Her father's face is a pale dot swimming in darkness below.

"Dad? Dad!" shouts Tawny.

Her tearful shrieks are somehow dampened, swallowed by the broad expanse of black liquid. The echoes are sinking slowly, like the stones.

Jim steps into ankle-deep liquid, turns to look up at us. He cradles the bomb in both arms, almost tenderly. He nods at us. Even from way up here I can see his sad, solemn smile. His daughter is sobbing beside me, kneeling, face hidden behind her long black hair—pleading for her father. Mourning him already.

I doubt he can hear her, but she is repeating: *It's not fair. It's not fair. This isn't fair.*

Jim takes another tentative step into the pool. His boots are swallowed into the inky liquid, disappearing as if erased. The hairs on my arms stand up as I hear a subtle change in the sighing wind. A keening howl is rising up from somewhere—from everywhere. The entire cavern is resonating around us.

I thought it was wind. But it feels more like breathing, the snuffling snorts of a great beast—the sheer size of it almost unimaginable as it stretches out in manifold hidden dimensions.

Jim keeps walking deeper, arms wrapped tightly around the bomb. He pauses at waist level and takes another step. Then, like a magic trick, his whole body disappears under the surface. For a long moment, all I see is the black lake.

Daddy, Tawny is mewling. *Daddy.*

No ripples, no disturbance. Just those same flickering patterns, continuing to tattoo themselves across the obsidian surface. I see black planets spinning. I see alien vistas telescoping to infinity. Madness and death.

And for just a split second, it feels like maybe I'm about to wake up from this. The Incident. The object. The anomaly. The Entity. Jim Hardgray.

Maybe the bomb wasn't real after all—

I see a flash of light a split second before my right eardrum ruptures. My breath bursts from my lungs as if I've been punched in the chest, and a bowl shape of liquid rises up on a crest of brilliant light from deep below. The light itself seems to struggle to escape the inertia of that mass of liquid.

Ear bleeding freely, I'm thrown to my knees as the throbbing explosion rends the dark surface. I can feel a near-subsonic groaning in my chest and in my thoughts—unnatural, not something from this world. And in a strobing flash of light, I catch a final glimpse of the horrifying extent of this sleeping god's dreams—the black liquid flashes silver like a movie screen, and I see a hellscape of memory.

My mind blinks shut, instinctively.

This is the raw fabric of a reality we were never meant to grasp. All the incomprehensible things living alongside us but hidden behind the veil of our own limited senses. Chaos at an incalculable scale, an endless timeline of species trampled beneath the feet of titanic, uncaring alien gods.

Oh please, no.

The god light grows even brighter, electric, flooding my retinas until I'm screaming with my hands up, palms out to block the sight, squinting at the dark veins visible inside me, the bones of my fingers illuminated by a thing I can't let myself ever see.

And then the god light blinks out. Darkness. The nightmare images cease.

In the sudden black, my babbling mind tries to tell me the lake was really just made of dark water. This is a natural cave, not a god's mind. Our mundane world really is just the way we see it. Those things were an illusion. Normality exists.

It was all just a bad dream, right?

But I find myself splayed on the ground with my back against hard, cold stone. My right palm is wet and warm with blood soaking out from under my bandaged wound. And Tawny's ribs are hard against my other palm where she lies sprawled. Gently, I curl her toward me as she convulses in sobs.

"Jim did it," I whisper. "I think your dad really did it, Tawny."

Breath hiccupping in her throat, the girl climbs to her knees. Determined, she glares out across the quiet lake. Still streaked with dirty tears, her young face has gone hard. Tawny hooks one leg over the ledge.

"Tawny," I warn.

"We have to find him," she says.

I think about arguing, but don't. Even though I know it's hopeless, I nod. An explosion like that would leave nothing behind.

Staggering to my feet, I allow Jim's daughter to help me down the crumbling slope until we reach the shoreline. I dutifully strafe the water with the beam of my headlamp, listening to the breath whistling in the back of my throat. Everything seems so still and empty now.

"He said we were following our ancestors," says Tawny. "He said it was meant to happen."

"I'm sorry, Tawny," I say. "Your father was incredibly brave."

"Yeah," she says. "Yeah."

Tawny picks up a stone. She flings it away. I don't hear it hit the lake, but seconds later a single ripple courses back toward the shore. The first ripple is followed by more. We both watch, confused. Frightened. When we hear a splash, both of us tense to run away.

This dream isn't over. But this time it's not a nightmare. Not exactly.

Jim's face is emerging from the water, coated in blackness—his visage rendered in monotone, like a 3D printing of the real man. When his mouth pops open, gasping for air, white teeth seem to float like stars in the void.

"Dad!" shouts Tawny.

Not a moment's hesitation.

The girl is already running, scrabbling along the shoreline. The beams of her headlamp throw wild shadows as Tawny sprints toward the image of her father. She wisely stops at the edge of the lake.

"You're alive!" she shouts as he approaches.

I shuffle toward Tawny, calling out for her to be careful. To slow down. To stop. *We don't know what this is.*

The man emerging from darkness looks like Jim Hardgray. His face is gaunt and emotionless, dripping rivulets of inky liquid as his chest emerges. But this Jim Hardgray looks different. Smoother, somehow. Almost like a baby. And he doesn't wipe the liquid away from his eyes or face. Because he can't.

Jim is still cradling something in both his arms.

I blink in confusion. How could he still be carrying a bomb that just detonated? But he isn't carrying the fail-safe any longer.

He is carrying the body of a five-year-old boy.

Tawny goes quiet, holding a hand over her mouth, eyes pricked with tears. Unable to move, I hear every drip and slosh as Jim relentlessly makes his way out of the lake. He stops before us, his chest shaking with sobs. Jim is cradling his little boy in his arms and staring down into his peaceful face.

Only now that he's up close do I see the truth. Jim Hardgray isn't crying in grief. He is laughing through his tears.

The little boy opens his eyes.

"Daddy?" he asks, craning his neck. "Tawn?"

The boy's voice is so small in this cavernous room. His body is so fragile in his father's strong arms. In an instant, Tawny is smothering his face with kisses. Jim breaks into a joyous shout. I am scared but I am smiling.

Standing alone, I watch a family reunited.

Jim went inside the god-thing and he came back with his boy. As I watch the three of them celebrating, I catch eye contact with him. In this moment, I do not know if this is a real man and his son, or the dream of a dark god.

A man or a manifestation.

I don't really know what any of us are. Or where the known ends and the unknown begins.

I don't know. I'll never know.

And from the seed of that simple thought, I feel the foundation of reality turning to quicksand beneath my feet.

A PRIVATE LETTER

GAVIN CLARK // Spiro, Oklahoma
Fort Spiro Contingency Operating Base (COB)

First of all, Jim, I'm sorry. Forgive me. I tried for months, but I just don't know how to tell the story of what happened to us. And in the end, I wasn't strong enough to learn how to tell it.

So, I'm asking you to do that for me. For all of us. Even him.

All I can give you is a bundle of raw material that you can craft in your own way. The world needs to understand what we faced. To know how close we all came to chaos. And you're the only one of us who can wrap his head around it.

After we lost Mikayla, I found her Nix eyeglasses lying on the cavern floor. They were heavy and warm. There was no trace of the . . . membrane it had become earlier. It had streaks of my blood on it, but it wasn't a weapon anymore. I could still smell Mikayla's perfume on it.

But Mikayla is gone. Nobody has seen her since she went under. And trust me, I've asked the people who would know.

I want to share one memory with you. I was watching when she dove inside the black, rippling *folds* of the lake. I saw the moment it enveloped her body and took her into its dreaming. And you know what? As her face went under, Mikayla was wearing a big smile.

It was like she'd finally recognized a friendly face, all on her own.

When I could, I copied the Nix local memory drive to my computer. It was downright chatty. The transcript it produced should provide enough detail for you to tell her story—so people can understand her part in what happened, and why she did what she did. Just, please, don't judge her. The way I see it, Mikayla made a brave decision when she left this world.

She wanted to see. And she saw.

The Nix itself is in government custody, of course. I don't expect that we'll ever hear of it again. Especially since it officially never existed.

The Man Downstairs is offline, if you know what I mean. By his own hand, apparently. My security clearance was reduced, so I don't know if the Pattern is still dreaming. And I'm not sure who, if anyone, is stationed in that plexiglass box, interpreting the ramblings of a mad AI.

But I did figure out what that last intelligence mandate meant.

There has never been an erroneous mandate from the Pattern—not even when it predicted the future or saw things it couldn't possibly have witnessed. And not even when it saw the end of the world.

The Pattern is never, ever wrong.

And yet it predicted in no uncertain detail that the Entity would wake and that our civilization would suffer. But thanks to you, *it didn't*.

I need you to know why, because of what you described seeing: the men on the Arkansas River and the guide who led you through a primordial forest to my soldiers on that mound. You told me your ancestors were speaking.

I didn't believe you then. But I do now.

The Man Downstairs wasn't wrong. Not when he told us about something out there at heliopause, or that an object was approaching. Not about the Entity appearing, or how it could feel our minds, or how it could taste the dreams and nightmares of human consciousness. And in the end, he was even telling the truth about how it would sing a song of hell on Earth.

The apocalypse was written in the stars, see?

I found the answer in an image the Pattern gave us. It was the last transmission to the MD before his biometrics went offline, found on a blood-soaked card table. The final reckoning. It's just a crummy dot matrix printout, but you can tell the land is burning, littered with the writhing, tormented bodies of human beings below a starry sky. Well, I got curious about the pattern of stars in that sky. The constellations looked odd, different.

So, I gave the image to an astronomer.

I asked her where on Earth such a placement would occur. She entered the data into her simulator and told me point blank—it was fake. Fictional. The stars just weren't in the right places for Spiro, or for any other location on Earth. It was her opinion that the image was meaningless, a piece of fiction.

So I asked a different question. Let's ignore *where* on Earth the stars might be in this configuration. Instead let's ask, *when* on Earth?

She got real quiet. Began typing very fast. And lo and behold, the stars on the screen slid right into position. Orion's belt tightened up and the Big Dipper came into focus. The Seven Sisters of the Pleiades constellation traveled north. I asked her what she had just done to make it a perfect match.

The astronomer told me she had left the location at Spiro and simply rewound the position of Earth and our solar system through time. Every star in our galaxy is moving all the time, imperceptible to short-lived humans. By going back in time, she made the stars match that image. I asked how long, and she looked at me with a little frown. Her voice was trembling when she spoke.

It was fifteen thousand years ago, she said.

Everything the MD spoke of—all those nightmares of the Entity and the destruction it wrought. And all those deep places it went. All those other races it saw out there. All of it really happened. It just didn't happen to us, now, today. It happened to us yesterday. In the past.

It happened to our ancestors, Jim. Yours, I'm guessing.

Those Native people faced this thing. Many of them died. But some lived. And I think they came to understand the Entity.

I like to imagine that some of your people figured out a kind of symbiosis. That they might have left this world, dreamed themselves across the cosmos. Others must have stayed here, tending to the Entity. And having become a part of it, they eventually decided to sing it a new song—a lullaby.

I believe it was your people who sang that god-thing to sleep, long ago. They found a way to lock it up and threw the key as far away as possible. And it was us who woke it up, out there at heliopause.

Last thing.

During debriefing, I never told my superiors about what you found in the black lake. They know it was you who detonated the fail-safe weapon, but I never spoke about where you went or where you came back from.

I don't claim to understand, my friend, but I tell myself we're all a part of the same dream. And I'm glad the Entity guided you there.

When you and I spoke at your house last week, you seemed good. Your boy seemed good. Tawny was happier than I ever saw, which is not a surprise given the circumstances of our meeting.

But as I was backing out of your driveway, staring at your warm home out there among the tall grass . . . it suddenly looked like a toy. It was like I saw a dollhouse, full of dolls, playing at life on the Great Plains. And I couldn't shake this fear inside me. It's just . . .

Forgive me for this, but I can't get the question out of my head.

What's in the coffin? If your little boy is here now, then what's down there in his coffin? I'm so sorry.

Are you real, Jim? Is your boy? Is anything?

How can you live with the *not knowing*?

When I close my eyes, I feel that terrible mind pulling at me, like gravity. We destroyed the cerebellum, yet I can't help feeling like some part of it is still slumbering out there somewhere, dreaming of itself.

Dreaming of us.

For months, I've been forcing my eyes open and walking through my day and trying hard to feel like a normal man. Sometimes I'll catch a glimpse of something in the corner of my eye. I'll wonder if it's all starting to unravel again. Is the stone crumbling to let things in from the other side? How long will this all last?

How long until our reality bleeds again, Jim?

There is so much we can't see. And the tiniest brush with one of these things could end it all—everything and everyone, gone in an instant.

This thought fills me with constant fear, and that's why I need you.

Please. Tell a good story, Jim. Make sure it makes sense to everybody. I think that if they can start to understand now . . . maybe it will help all of us later. After this, people are going to have to reckon with the unknown. They're going to have to look it in the face. They'll have to make peace with it.

I hope that knowledge doesn't break us.

You must have noticed the Department of Defense is building a new military installation over the Spiro Mounds. Hell, it's basically in your backyard. They recovered a lot of the horrible things we dreamed of. Glistening shards of robotic weapons. A piece of the walking machine that strode over us through the clouds. And there's been seismic activity from below. The black suits in charge think they've plugged the gateway to hell. Now they're building a church to war right on top of it.

I'm glad the Entity healed you, Jim. But it left me wounded.

I can't go on pretending, knowing some part of that thing could be down there. Because if there's anything left, they'll try to wake it up. They'll try to control it.

I've got just enough clearance to make it through the front gate. I know where they keep the explosives. From there, I know exactly where I'll go. I mean, how could I *not* know the route? I can see it on the backs of my eyelids.

I'm going down, and I don't expect I'll come back this time. I'd rather meet my Maker than risk another minute with that thing in the world.

So, this is goodbye. Thank you, Jim. For everything.

And hey, if I see Mikayla, I'll tell her you and your family say hello.

ACKNOWLEDGMENTS

I want to thank my trusty team at Doubleday (has it been nearly two decades already?!)—especially Jason Kaufman, Lily Dondoshansky, Julie Ertl, and Nora Reichard, as well as my ray of sunshine literary agent, Laurie Fox.

A special thank-you to Sterlin Harjo for all the feedback and time spent kicking the rust off this project. And Joseph Erb was of immense help, discussing all things Cherokee.

This novel wouldn't have been the same without conversations with Brad Mendelsohn and Michael Prevett at Circle Management; Hannah Davis at WME; John Buderwitz and Michael Costigan at Aggregate Films. I hope someday we'll see this book in other incarnations.

For their generous consultation, many thanks to Abraham Flaxman, Anna Long, Richard McIntosh, Nisi Shawl, Peter Singer, Michael Strasser, Vandi Verma, and David Wilson. How else would I have learned so many wonderful details about NASA, Chinook helicopters, small airports, Delta Force, the Montana National Guard, Texas fracking, and so forth?

I grew up spending summers at my grandmother's farm outside Sallisaw, Oklahoma—on land that was my family's original Indian allotment after the forced removal of the Cherokee people. As the crow flies, the Spiro Mounds were only a few miles away. I am thankful for those long, hot summers in the woods, hunting fos-

ACKNOWLEDGMENTS

sils in the shale rock, fishing with grasshoppers in the coal pit, and taking long walks with my grandmother—those memories have made it into my bones and, hopefully, into my writing.

My infinite love always to Anna and the children.

ABOUT THE AUTHOR

DANIEL H. WILSON is a Cherokee citizen and author of the *New York Times* bestselling *Robopocalypse* and its sequel *Robogenesis,* as well as *How to Survive a Robot Uprising, The Clockwork Dynasty,* and *The Andromeda Evolution* (the authorized sequel to Crichton's *The Andromeda Strain*). He earned a PhD in robotics from Carnegie Mellon University, as well as master's degrees in machine learning and robotics. He lives in Portland, Oregon.